ALSO BY EMILY MCINTIRE

Be Still My Heart: A Romantic Suspense

THE SUGARLAKE SERIES

Beneath the Stars

Beneath the Stands

Beneath the Hood

Beneath the Surface

THE NEVER AFTER SERIES

Hooked: A Dark, Contemporary Romance

Scarred: A Dark, Royal Romance

Wretched: A Dark Contemporary Romance

WRETCHED

A Never After Novel

EMILY MCINTIRE

Bloom books

Cover design by Cat at TRC Designs
Cover images © AntonMatukha/DepositPhotos, Rastan/DepositPhotos, rehananlisoomro10/DepositPhotos, tanantornaunt/DepositPhotos, Cassandra Madsen/Shutterstock, P Maxwell Photography/Shutterstock

Published by Bloom Books, an imprint of Sourcebooks
P.O. Box 4410, Naperville, Illinois 60567-4410
(630) 961-3900
sourcebooks.com

Originally self-published in 2022 by Emily McIntire.

Cataloging-in-Publication Data is on file with the Library of Congress.

Printed and bound in the United States of America.
KP 19

Playlist

"Natural"—Imagine Dragons

"Teeth"—5 Seconds of Summer

"Genius"—LSD ft. Sia, Diplo, Labrinth

"Ruin My Life"—Zara Larsson

"Fire on Fire"—Sam Smith

"I Don't Wanna Live Forever"—ZAYN, Taylor Swift

"Don't Speak"—No Doubt

"Crying Over You"—The Band CAMINO and Chelsea Cutler

"If I Killed Someone For You"—Alec Benjamin

"Over the Rainbow"—Israel Kamakawiwo'ole

For the misunderstood.

"A heart is not judged by how much you love,
but by how much you are loved by others."
—L. Frank Baum, *The Wonderful Wizard of Oz*

Author's Note

Wretched is a dark contemporary romance.

It is a fractured fairy tale, not fantasy or a retelling.

The main character is a villain. If you're looking for a safe read, you will not find it in these pages.

Wretched contains mature and graphic content not suitable for all audiences. Dark romance is a sliding scale and what is considered pitch-black for some will be light gray for others. **Reader discretion is advised.**

I highly prefer for you to go in blind, but if you would like a detailed trigger warning list, you can find it on EmilyMcIntire .com.

PROLOGUE

Evelina (Ehv-ah-leen-ah)

Seventeen Years Old

GRIEF IS A WEIRD THING.

It's the only emotion in the world people claim to understand yet treat as an inconvenience.

"Time heals all wounds, Evie."

Spare me.

Time heals nothing. Just gives things more space to grow and fester and rot.

I fidget in my seat, the old wooden bench tearing into the skin of my thighs and making me flinch. My sister Dorothy—the one still alive—peers over at me, glaring down as if my movement is going to draw the wrong type of attention. As if every single man in the room isn't *already* looking our way just to get a glimpse of her.

Her brown hair is perfect and bouncy, a high ponytail swinging behind her as she turns back toward the front, listening to the priest drone on about things he knows nothing about. About memories made and life not forgotten. But *my* eyes stay on her. Her and that stupid, bouncy brown hair.

My hands itch with the urge to reach out and wrap the strands around my fists, pulling until it tears from the root. I sit on them instead. No matter how much I want to strangle Dorothy, this isn't about her. Not today.

Today is about Nessa.

And Nessa always told me I was a slave to my impulses, so the least I can do is try to contain them. It's *her* memorial Mass after all.

That weird feeling surges up my throat again.

Grief.

Sometimes it's fluid, like waves of the ocean, and sometimes it's stagnant, like sculptures carved in stone. Right now, it's rock solid and heavy in the center of my chest.

I bite my cheek, trying to hold it together.

My father clears his throat, and I snap my eyes to him sitting on the other side of Dorothy, soaking in the tattoos that line his fingers and disappear up the sleeve of his shirt. Every once in a while, I'll try to get a better look, searching for hidden clues about what they mean, wondering if one of them represents me. More than likely, though, he was just bored rotting away in a six-by-eight prison cell for the last eight years and wanted ink on his skin.

He peers at me from his peripheral, sadness weaving through his weathered light-brown eyes as he wraps his arm around Dorothy, and she rests her head on his shoulder. I'm not sure if the pained look is for the loss of Nessa herself or because of all the years he missed. Maybe it's neither.

Not that it matters, really.

We made a life without him, and now he's back, pretending as though he didn't leave his family with nothing to their name when he made stupid mistakes.

It's hot today, and while the middle of summer in Kinland, Illinois isn't unbearable, right now, it feels like I'm burning alive. My eyes scan the room, taking in the random carved initials and scratches that mar the light wood pews, splays of color beaming through the stained glass windows, reflecting off the gleaming floors. I count the bobbing heads of people who cared to show up, choosing to ignore how they're either nodding off to sleep or whispering to each other like it's somehow appropriate to be gossiping during the memorial Mass of the most important person in my life.

"But above all else," the priest's voice cuts in, echoing off the high arches and soaring ceiling of the cathedral, "Nessa Westerly was a woman of family. Of faith. And who better to speak on her love of both than someone *she* loved more than anything…her sister."

My heart stutters in my chest, fingernails digging into the wood beneath my thighs until they feel like they might split in half. *I didn't know I'd need to speak.* But I'll do it because Nessa was more than just my sister. Ten years older and eons wiser, she raised me from the time I was nine, after our father got caught with ten kilos of coke in the back of a carrier plane and thrown in the slammer. Although truthfully, she was caring for me long before that. My throat swells as I wonder what the hell I'm supposed to do now that she's gone.

A passing thought slips through my brain, curious if our mom will show her slimy face, if she even knows her oldest daughter is dead or that the man she claimed to love—then abandoned—is free. I shake off the notion, deciding to manifest that *she's* dead and rotting instead. It would serve her right for jumping ship after my father was locked up.

I side-eye Dorothy again, narrowing my gaze as she wipes a handkerchief under her eyes. As if she has any right to be sad. She hated Nessa.

To be fair, she hates me too, but with our sister, it was different. More volatile. At first, it was pure jealousy. Nessa was the oldest and the most beautiful, catching the attention of everyone just by simply existing. And Dorothy was...second best. Middle child syndrome at its finest.

When Dad got locked up, his last words for Nessa were to *make him proud*. Not a single word for Dorothy or me. Dorothy changed after that. Her envy hardened into hatred, and her persona went from a bitter kid to the "ideal" woman with deep-rooted daddy issues.

She would have made a wonderful actress with how well she plays the part.

Sucking in a deep breath at the memories, I move to stand, but before I can even straighten my legs, Dorothy rises instead, pushing me back as she slips down the pews and into the aisle. She barely passes me a glance, but my eyes burn as I stare at her making her way up to the dais, that brown *fucking* ponytail fluttering, bright-silver heels clacking on the wood floor.

My teeth clench so tightly my molars ache as I zone in on her feet.

Nessa's shoes.

God, what a bitch.

Yeah...grief is a weird thing.

But so is anger.

And I'm *angry*.
I'm angry at Nessa for getting herself killed.
And I'm angry at Dorothy for killing her.

CHAPTER 1

Nicholas

Seven Years Later

"WHAT'S HER NAME?"

I side-eye Seth, watching as he finger brushes his dark beard.

"You know, it's no wonder you get no pussy when you've got that shit on your face."

He grins at me. "Women love this shit. And you're deflecting."

"*What* women?"

"All the ones your pretty ass leaves behind." Winking, he stands up and grabs his jacket, the tan leather complementing his dark skin, dropping it over the gun holstered on his hip. "You're really not gonna tell me?"

Shrugging, I spin around in my desk chair, the small walls of my cubicle pressing in on me from either side. "I don't remember."

"Typical," Seth scoffs.

Laughter bubbles from my chest. "She knew the deal. We fucked. I didn't ask for her hand in marriage."

He shakes his head. "I don't think anyone's stupid enough to think they're getting more than one night with you, dude."

My chest pulls and I force a grin. He's not wrong. Even if I *wanted* to, there's no room for a relationship in this job. There are risks that come with being a DEA agent. I have a hard enough time keeping my sister safe. Everyone else would be baggage I have no interest in.

"Don't get mad at me for refusing to play into some made-up fairy-tale emotion."

His brow rises. "What the hell does that even mean?"

"Love." I shrug. "It's fake. Just a chemical reaction that people pretend is more."

"Whatever you say, man." Seth chuckles. "You wanna grab a bite?"

I stare down the long aisle of uniform gray desks, accented by grungy blue carpet. "Nah, Cap wants to see me."

Seth's eyes follow my gaze until they hit the closed office door of our Chicago division supervisor, Agent Galen. "What for?"

"Probably babysitting duty again. God knows it's been long enough since he's put me on an actual case."

The side of his mouth lifts. "Well, maybe you shouldn't have fucked his daughter."

Groaning, I run my hands over my face. "That was *one* time, and I didn't know it was his daughter."

Seth laughs and I frown, tossing a random pen from my desk at his head. Honestly, rude of him to get joy from my misfortune.

The door to Cap's office at the front of the room swings open and we both wheel around at the noise. Seth's laughter dies off, his body straightening as he clears his throat. I glance at him and smirk.

Pussy.

He's always been afraid of our boss, no matter how many times I've told him Cap is all bark and no bite. We've both been agents here for almost a decade, and yet he acts like he's fresh out of school and afraid of losing his position. But they don't make just anyone field agents; you have to work for it. It's part of the reason why I love it so much. Nothing is handed to you. And when I go undercover, I can *feel* the difference I make in the world. With every asshole drug dealer we get off the streets, the guilt of how I failed my own family lessens.

"Woodsworth."

Galen's voice is gruff, and I wink at Seth as I stand up and make my way to his office, feeling the burn of Cap's stare with every step. It's no secret he hates me and wants me out of his division and subsequently out of his life. But regardless of his personal emotions, I live and breathe this job, and I'm the best at what I do.

Plopping down in the stiff gray chair opposite his desk, my eyes roam along the framed portraits of his wife and three daughters, my cock twitching when I spot Samantha grinning with her perfect olive skin and skinny arm slung around her younger sister's shoulder.

I lied to Seth. I *did* know it was Cap's daughter. I just didn't give a fuck. Served him right for ripping me out of an active investigation and slapping me on desk duty.

Cap clears his throat as he walks by me, narrowing his eyes and snapping his hand out to flip the picture frame until it's facedown. The side of my lip pulls up, but I smother it, adopting an air of boredom instead.

He points his finger at me. "Don't look at her, you little shit."

Chuckling, I raise my hands in surrender. "My bad, Cap."

He scowls. "I'm your supervisor, not a fucking captain. And your apology means shit."

"Well, you're the captain of my heart, and I'm not happy if you're not happy." I press a hand to my chest, grinning. "Come on. I said I was sorry. What more can I do?"

His dark eyes narrow. "You've already done *more* than enough."

I sit back in my seat. "Nothing she didn't ask for."

A sharp slap rings through the room, Cap's fingers tensing as they press into the top of his desk. "You're fired."

Shrugging, I place my hands on the arms of the chair and push myself up. "All right."

"Sit down. *Fuck.*" He runs his hand over his bald head and blows out a deep breath as he plops behind his desk. "God, I hate your ass," he grumbles.

I quirk a brow. "Are you allowed to say that to a subordinate?"

"I have a job for you."

Now *this* gets my attention, and I sit forward, the amusement dropping from my face.

Finally.

"You ever been to Kinland?" He tosses a manila folder, the smack of its weight hitting the desk's top ringing in my ears, a few black-and-white surveillance photos slinking out of the side.

I reach over, picking them up.

"Yeah, a few times," I say nonchalantly, not wanting to focus on the way my insides wring tight when I think about the two-hour trek from Chicago to Kinland my mom used to take me and my sister on. "I haven't been in a long time though. Not since I was a kid." My voice breaks a little on the last word, discomfort wrapping around my neck. Clearing my throat, I flip through the photos. There's one of people unloading crates off a semi. Then another of an older man with slicked-back gray hair and tattoos from his fingers to his neck, grinning down at the guy by his side. "Who's this?"

"*That* is Farrell Westerly. Ever heard of him?"

I shake my head.

"Pure-blooded Irish American with your run-of-the-mill rap sheet. Spent eight years in Gilyken Penitentiary before being released on parole for good behavior. He's been popping up again the last few years. Seems like the guy's *everywhere*."

I grin. "A reformed convict?"

"Aren't they all?" Cap huffs. "They're running an operation out of Kinland, flooding the streets with that new shit."

My stomach twists. That "new" shit is called Flying Monkey, and it's taking over. Similar to every other type of heroin, only *not*. It's popular as fuck, which means copycats are springing up everywhere, trying to emulate the product and failing. All that ends up happening is more death from overdosing on badly cut drugs.

Squinting my eyes, I look closer at the photo of the two men. "Is that...?"

"It is."

Blowing out a breath, I sit back in the chair, recognizing the bright-auburn hair and large build. "Ezekiel O'Connor."

My stomach sours as I set the photos back on his desk. Ezekiel is well known in our circles. His father, Jack O'Connor, was notorious in Chicago as king of the Irish mob. He was ruthless. But that was before their power was dismantled years ago and Jack was murdered in the pen while serving time for his *numerous* crimes.

"So what then...you want me to do some recon?"

His eyes narrow. "I want you to go in and find their supplier. If we get the big dog, we can drag in the rest. I didn't spend the best years of my career hunting them down just to have the Irish mob sprout back up with new faces in a new location, thinking they can take everything over again."

My brows shoot high. "Undercover?"

"You're surprised?" His head cocks.

My hands shake from the sudden jolt of adrenaline. "It's just been a while."

He grumbles, his thick set of brows bunching together until a crease forms in the middle of his forehead. "You saying you're not up for it?"

My stomach twists and I shoot up straighter. "Are you crazy? No one else can do this like me, and you know it, Cap."

He reaches to the side of his computer and grabs another photo, placing it in front of me. It's of a woman. A *beautiful* woman with shiny brown hair pulled back in a high ponytail, designer clothes dripping from her body. "That's Dorothy Westerly, Farrell's kid. Rumor has it she's his weak spot. Once you're in, try to cozy up to her. She'll crack."

Surprise flickers through my gut. "Why her?"

A slow smile tips up the corners of his lips and he leans back in his chair. "Don't you have a thing for pretty daughters?"

CHAPTER 2

Evelina

THERE'S BLOOD ON MY SHOE.

Damn it.

I squint down at the worn black pleather of my heeled boot, my stomach tensing with irritation that I have to spend the rest of the night in this shitty club with parts of a dead man soaking into my foot.

Hope that doesn't mean he'll come back to haunt me.

"What's up, grump?" my best friend—my only friend—Cody asks, grinning wide as he rests on the bar next to me.

I snap my gaze up, bringing my hand to my chest and raising my brows. "I'm not grumpy."

His blond hair bounces as he throws his head back, a bubbly laugh pouring from his mouth. "You're one hundred percent a pessimist."

I glance at the people crowding in behind him for a drink and shrug. "I'm a realist. There's a difference."

"Well, you're being fucking *boring*." He rolls his eyes. "This is what you dragged me out for? I thought with that fake hair, you'd loosen up a little. Blonds are supposed to have more fun."

I grit my teeth, drumming my almond-shaped nails on the wood bar top, the black manicure I gave myself mirroring my mood. The only reason I'm even here in Chicago is because, like usual when it comes to people who get in my father's way, I've been tasked with the unfortunate duty of tracking down some nobody *idiot* who needs to be taught a lesson. The blond wig glued to my head and colored contacts are just insurance. Not for *fun*.

"Want a shot?" he tries again, wiggling his brows that are half-hidden by his glasses.

"I don't drink."

The words come out harsher than I intended, but I have a headache growing between my eyes and a temper that's been fraying since this morning when some *asshole* interrupted me while I was doing the books to make my family's business seem legitimate, even though it's really anything but.

I peek down at the dried blood again.

He frowns. "Since when?"

Sighing, I run a hand over the thick hair, the bleached-blond strands falling across my shoulder. "Since forever, Cody. I don't know. Christ, are you planning to give me the tenth degree the entire time? I just wanted to help you get out of your mom's house." I shrug. "Live a little instead of spending all your time staring at computer screens."

He blinks at me.

"Fine," he finally breathes out. "I'm gonna go dance. Find me a nice fat dick to suck." My smile cracks for the first time all night, and he winks. "After you're done with whatever you really came here for, you should do the same. Maybe a good fuck will make you lose that giant stick up your ass."

Waving him off, I spin around, my stomach clenching as the bartender walks toward me and smiles. *Just the man I've been sent to see.*

"Want something to drink yet?" he asks.

"I'm not sure *what* I want." I force a sly grin, peering at him through my lashes. It's a lie, of course. I'm here to see if he's selling a rip-off of *our* product.

His blue eyes spark. "No favorites?"

I mimic his movements, making sure the top of my cleavage is pushed up from where I have it pressed against the bar, giving him a good view. "I'm not really into drinking, you know? I think I'd rather... *fly*."

His gaze drops from my eyes to the swell of my chest, and I bite back the disgust at how predictable he is. Honestly, I'm not even that attractive. Not compared to my sister's delicate facial features, but throw a pair of tits in a man's face and all the blood rushes to their dick instead of their brains.

He licks his lips.

"I just like to have a good time." I cock my head, drumming my long nails on the bar top. "Don't you?"

He slings an off-white cloth over his shoulder and places his elbow on the edge of the bar.

"Andrew!" a voice yells. His attention snaps to a server who's standing with an empty tray and an annoyed look on her face. "Dude, can I get my drinks?"

Grimacing, he looks back at me, tapping the bar top with his knuckles. "Don't go anywhere. I've got just the thing for you."

The second his back is turned, I let the facade drop, picking up a coaster and twirling it around in my hand, trying to keep from asking for soda water and a napkin so I can scrub the stain from the toe of my shoe.

It's not noticeable, but it's *bothering* me.

"You're trying too hard."

My head snaps up and I lock my gaze on a strong jawline and bright-green eyes. I quirk a brow. "Excuse me?"

The man grins, dimples framing his pouty lips as he takes a sip of his beer and props himself against the bar.

I scoff, irritated that this guy decided to annoy me and even more irritated that he's attractive enough to make my stomach clench. "Who says I'm trying?"

His throat bobs and he steps closer, sending a whiff of cinnamon into my nose as he runs his hand through his short and slightly curly brown locks. My eyes track the movement, then move farther down his black leather jacket and dark jeans.

"You can practice on me if you want," he continues, nodding toward the bartender. "Before he gets back."

I tilt my head, trying to figure out if he's hitting on me or making fun of me. "Wow, what an offer."

He shrugs. "I'm in a giving mood."

Normally, I wouldn't react well to someone getting in my space. But this guy intrigues me. Plus, he's hot, and quite frankly, I'm horny. It's hard to find someone I can tolerate long enough to let them get me off.

Reaching out my hand, I grab the beer from his fingers, bringing it to my mouth and taking a small sip. I hide the cringe from the taste, running my tongue along my lips as I swallow. It feels weird without the piercing that's usually there, but identifiable things like tongue rings aren't great for maintaining anonymity.

And I wasn't lying earlier. I'm *not* a drinker.

"Well, that's good news." I slide from the stool and move forward until my chest grazes his torso. His breath hitches as I rise up slightly, my lips ghosting across his jaw. "Because I'm a taker."

His eyes flare as I back away and that perfect smile blooms on his face. "You're interesting."

"And you're annoying," I reply.

He chuckles.

My chest tightens and I bite my lip to hide the grin wanting to escape, shaking my head.

"What's your name?" he asks.

I peek at him. "Why?"

"It's only natural. Guy sees an attractive woman at the bar, wants to get to know her better." He sticks his hand out. "I'm Nick."

Crossing my arms, I look down at his palm. "How do I know you're not trying to find out my name so you can stalk me?"

"That's pretty arrogant."

"Is it? I mean, you're here in a club, all alone, hitting on random women and asking their names. Haven't you ever seen *Dateline*, Nicholas?"

He points toward the dance floor. "I'm *not* here alone. And it's Nick."

My eyes follow where he's pointing toward an attractive guy dancing up against a random woman in the middle of the floor.

"That's my friend Seth. I got put on a new job today that's taking me out of town, so we're 'celebrating' one last time."

"I'd probably celebrate too if you were leaving."

Laughing, he takes another sip of his drink, exactly on the

same spot I did earlier, his tongue peeking out and running over his lips, not dropping my stare for a single second. My insides tighten, heat flooding between my legs.

It's obnoxious how much he's affecting me.

"Listen, I don't have time for"—I wave my arm between us—"whatever this is. So either get to the point or go find someone else. I'm sure there are plenty of desperate women willing to give up their personal information so you can peek in their windows."

He sets down his glass and glances past me before stepping forward and bending down, his lips impossibly close to my cheek. I suck in a breath, my heart ramping up in my chest.

"I don't want to stalk you, pretty girl." He tucks a strand of hair behind my ear. "I want to fuck you."

Oh.

Something hot and wicked swirls through my middle. This guy is dangerous. A distraction—one I can't afford. *Although*… I peek over at Andrew, the bartender, realizing there are at least a couple hours before he gets off work. A little bit of fun wouldn't hurt, and why shouldn't I reward myself? Besides, I'm not used to being the center of attention. Usually, I hide in dark corners, trying my best to blend in with the shadows. Makes it easier to watch my sister, Dorothy, and see if her picture-perfect persona slips long enough for me to prove what I've thought for years. That *she* killed Nessa.

This change of pace is kind of nice, in an unexpected way.

"Well…" I tap the bar with my fingertips, feeling the burn of *Nicholas's* stare as it trails down my body. "This has been fun, but I've got to use the ladies. If you know what's good for you, you won't follow me, stalker."

He purses his lips like he's holding back a grin and tips his head.

Honestly, I expect him to follow anyway, but as I make my way through the dance floor and down the narrow halls, pushing past a dozen sticky, sweaty bodies, he's nowhere to be found.

It's better this way.

I pull open the door to the ladies' room and step inside. It's a small bathroom, with black and white subway tiles on the walls and only two toilets. I walk over, peeking underneath both stalls to make sure there's no one else in here before heading to the sink and resting my arms against the edge, blowing out a deep breath.

The door swings open and then shuts, making my heart shoot to my throat and my defenses spike, a lock clicking into place. I spin, excitement squeezing my middle as I meet Nicholas's stare, his eyes dark as he strides toward me. He tilts his head, taking off his black leather jacket and tossing it on the sink's counter. I step back until I'm flush against the grungy tile of the bathroom wall, but he continues until his body is pressed against mine, a thrill racing through my insides.

"I knew you'd follow me." I roll my eyes. "Predictable."

His hand reaches around and threads through the strands of my hair, tightening as he pulls, forcing my eyes to meet his as my neck stretches back.

Jesus.

My heart speeds, hoping like hell the glue I used will keep the wig in place.

"Turns out I don't know what's good for me," he says.

And then he bends down and kisses me.

I moan, my hands flying to the back of his head as his tongue dives into my mouth, tangling with mine. He tastes sweet and spicy, and I let myself get lost in the moment. I'll never see this guy again, but I'm hopeful he lives up to his bravado and can at least give me an orgasm before he disappears.

His hands come down to my thighs, lifting me up, and he presses himself into me until every single inch is nestled between my legs. He thrusts and I whimper into his mouth.

So glad I left my gun in the car. That would be awkward to explain.

Locking my ankles together behind his back, I move my hips, grinding against him.

"Fuck," he curses, breaking away to trail his lips along the column of my neck.

Wetness leaks from me, and I arch my back until my head hits the wall, giving him more room to work.

"You gonna give me your name yet?" he rasps.

"No."

Reaching down, I pop the button on the top of his jeans, slipping my hand inside and grasping his dick, my stomach tensing when I realize just how big he really is.

He drops my legs, backing up slightly and pulling out a condom from his pocket. I snatch it from him, dropping to my knees and grabbing the waistband of his pants, lowering them just enough so I can reach through his boxers and pull his cock out. The head is dripping with his precum, and I lean in, licking up the salty liquid, moaning when it hits my tongue. It tastes *good*, and I decide I need to have more, so I put my mouth over him and slide it down, letting him hit the back of my throat.

"*Jesus Christ*," he groans, his palm slapping against the wall.

I bob my head a few times, sliding my tongue along the thick vein running up his shaft, then letting him slip out of me with a pop, moving back and ripping open the condom package with my teeth. I place it on him, his stare burning into the top of my head as I do.

His hands grip my shoulders, lifting me up aggressively, and before I can even blink, he's got my skirt up and my panties pushed to the side. "I need to be inside you."

He hoists my legs back around him, and with one solid thrust, he's there.

So deep.

He starts a quick and punishing pace, and my eyes roll back in my head because I don't think anyone has ever fucked me like this. Quick and dirty and like he doesn't want anything else but me.

That thought combined with the way he's filling me up makes my orgasm climb quickly, my clit swelling as tension coils tight in my abdomen.

"Oh god," I murmur, my head cracking against the wall. "I love your cock."

He chuckles, pressing into me harder, his grip on my thighs almost bruising with how tight they squeeze. "Show me," he says, sucking my earlobe between his teeth and biting down. "Show me how much you love my cock."

His words are the last thing I need, and I explode, bright lights blinding my vision, my nails digging into his shoulders as he continues to fuck me through the pleasure.

"That's it, pretty girl. Give it to me."

A few more thrusts and he pushes in deep until his hips press against mine, his low groans vibrating through every bone in my body as his dick jerks wildly.

Slowly, I come back down to earth and realize what just happened and where I am.

What I'm supposed to be doing.

He drops my trembling legs, running the pads of his fingers up my thighs and gripping my sides as he presses his forehead to mine. "Tell me your name," he whispers.

I don't, choosing to push him away and turning around, my limbs still shaky from the way he just fucked me.

Definitely the best I've ever had.

Suddenly, the air feels stifling, and I need to leave. Now.

I don't like the way he makes me feel. Because I *want* to give him my name. I want to ask about where he's going and who his friends are, and that isn't how I work.

That isn't how I function.

So instead, I spin back, the walls feeling like they're closing in around me. Walking up to him, I slide my fingers around his neck and rise up on my toes, leaving a soft kiss on his swollen lips.

His eyes darken.

Then I walk out of the restroom, moving as quickly as possible to make sure he won't follow.

He doesn't.

And when I shoot a bullet into the neck of Andrew the bartender three hours later in the back alley, watching his blood douse the cracked pavement while he drops the imitation drug in his hands and falls to his knees...all I can think of is how I wish I could have given Nicholas my name.

CHAPTER 3

Nicholas

MY STOMACH IS IN KNOTS. THE KIND THAT SEND anxiety spinning into your head and bile surging up the back of your throat.

There's not much that gets under my skin and even less that worries me, but every time I look at my sister, Rose, the knots are in the background, nagging at my conscience like a bird pecking at a tree. Knowing this is the last I'll see her for who knows how long makes the sensation stronger.

It isn't the first time I've gone undercover, but it *is* the first time since it's been just the two of us. Since I tracked her down off the backstreets of Chicago and finally—fucking *finally*—got her ass clean and set up in my apartment.

"Hungry?" she asks, lifting a brow at me and plopping a hand on her hips.

"I could eat." I shrug, tapping my fingers on the round wood dining table as I watch her flit around the tiny kitchen. She fidgets as she pours boxed pasta into a pot and runs her bitten nails through her deep-red hair.

"When's the last time you met with your sponsor?"

Her body jolts and she places her hands against the lip of the white stove, dropping her head with a heavy sigh. "Don't start, Nick."

"I'm not starting anything. I'm just asking."

"Well, *stop* asking," she snaps.

My chest pinches and I frown at her, my eyes moving from the freckles on her face, down to her protruding hip bones, although not as prominent as they once were, then to the scars and faded marks scattered between her fingers and up her arms.

She grabs a wooden spoon from the drawer to her right, the other utensils clattering as she shuts it harshly. "I can *feel* you investigating me. Quit it."

The corner of my mouth lifts and I reach up to rub at my jaw, the stubble scratching against the pads of my fingers. "Listen, kid…"

"I'm three years older than you."

I grin. "Semantics."

She laughs, shaking her head as she turns back to the stove and stirs the pasta.

My stomach tightens, my brain trying to push the words from my mouth when I don't want to say them. There's not much I care for other than work, but if there's anything I *do* care for, it's right here in this room, and leaving her all alone for an undetermined amount of time makes nausea churn in my gut.

"I've gotta go away for a while."

Her shoulders drop. "For what?"

My tongue runs over the front of my teeth.

She hesitates. "For work?"

I nod.

Her head bobs, fingers shooting up to her mouth where she nibbles on the ends.

Blowing out a heavy breath, I stand up, the wood chair legs scratching against the ugly parquet floor, and I stride toward her. "That's a disgusting habit."

She stares up at me, her lips twitching into a ghost of a smile. "Yeah, well...I've had worse."

Scowling, I lightly slap her hand from her mouth.

She lets out a soft chuckle, spinning back around to keep stirring the pasta. "Lighten up, Nick. If we can't joke about the past, we'll never move on. Besides, the humor helps me."

"Humor's supposed to be funny."

"Not my problem you've got bad taste."

I move fast, reaching out to grab her and draw her into me, locking her neck beneath my arm and rubbing my fist on the top of her head.

She screeches, bringing the wooden spoon up to smack at my arm. "Let me go, asshole!"

Amusement warms my chest and spreads through my limbs as I release her, smiling as she curses and straightens her hair. Glaring at me, she walks to the small pantry on the left wall and reaches up on her tiptoes to grab a jar before moving back to the pot.

The lighthearted air twists and turns with every second of silence until it starts to press down on my chest.

"Will you be able to come by still?" she asks.

Something lodges in my throat and I swallow around the lump. "I don't know."

She nods her head and turns back to the stove, mixing in the tomato sauce. I stay silent, not knowing what else to say and hoping she'll be okay while I'm gone.

"I want a lawyer."

Ezekiel O'Connor's voice is gruff and low, raspy as he spits the words across the metal table in the small interrogation room. Ezekiel is a large man with broad shoulders and long auburn hair that hits his chest, and if I were anyone else, I'd probably be intimidated. He looks like a mix of rough and jolly, like he'd smash you over the head with his pint before helping you up and buying you another round.

"Sure." I grin, leaning back in my chair until the front two legs tilt off the ground, my eyes scanning the plain gray walls, then flicking over the darkened two-way mirror directly across from me. "But we're just a couple of guys having a conversation, yeah?"

His golden eyes narrow.

"Unless…" I sigh, running a hand through my hair, feeling the slight waves bounce back into place after I do. "Nah, never mind."

His jaw clenches.

"God, don't start that shit, Woodsworth," Seth groans from beside me. "You know I can't stand it when you 'never mind' like a woman."

I point a finger in Seth's direction. "You're a sexist fuck. And I'm just trying not to scare the guy." I toss my hand haphazardly in Ezekiel's direction, noting the way he sits forward slightly in his chair, as if he's listening to our conversation without wanting to admit it. This is my favorite part of interrogating. The mind games. The back-and-forth. We don't directly *tell* people what's in their future should they not comply, but a few subtle hints usually do the trick, and Seth and I have mastered the art.

Ezekiel's leg jitters so fast it shakes the foundation of the table. "I don't wanna be a fuckin' rat, man."

"Well..." I blow out a breath, grabbing my leather jacket off the back of the chair as I stand up. "It's either us or jail."

"Yeah," he grumbles, running his hand over the bright-auburn bun on his head.

"You could always take your chances," Seth pipes in. "I'm sure your dad's got connections, right?"

Ezekiel's eyes grow dark, his fingers tap, tap, tapping against the tabletop.

"Oh." Seth smacks his head. "That's right, I forgot. My bad, man."

"Forgot what?" I ask, even though I already know the answer. Tension wraps around my stomach, because this is a gamble within itself, showing my face to a man involved in the criminal organization I'm being sent to infiltrate. I'm confident in how we run things here, and showing myself lends a sense of trust that needs to be established, but there are always moments of anxiety that pepper through the foundation of the initial setup.

Seth presses his lips together as he glances at Ezekiel before turning his attention to me. "His dad died in prison."

I nod, bringing up my hand to rub at my chin. "That's right." I turn to look at Ezekiel. "What was it? Stabbed forty-*seven* times and found hanging in the showers?"

His chin quivers, his large hands curling into fists.

It's a gamble, using the angle of Ezekiel's father to get him to flip. We're banking on the rumor mill—the whispers that were written in his file from other agents' basic recon work stating how he was terrified to end up like his dad.

I whistle, shrugging my jacket on my arms. "Hope they don't hold a grudge."

"Fine," he spits. "I'm in, but you gotta understand. If this gets out, if this shit goes bad? They'll kill me."

Relief douses my insides like a broken dam.

"Then don't fuck it up." I rest my knuckles on the tabletop and meet Ezekiel's golden gaze. "Now tell me about Dorothy Westerly."

CHAPTER 4

Evelina

"WANT SOME?" EZEKIEL ASKS, DROPPING IN THE kitchen chair across from me, the stench of his fried chicken and gravy swirling across the small round table and into the air. A chef's kitchen the size of a small house, and still, he chooses to sit right next to me. He's been gone all day, but that doesn't mean I want him *near*.

I scrunch my nose, glancing up from my small black notebook, shaking my head.

He laughs. "I forgot you were doing that whole vegan thing."

"It's not a *thing*," I snap.

"Then what is it?" His auburn brow arches as he shovels half the chicken leg into his mouth.

"It's me not wanting to have a hand in the slaughter of animals just for temporary enjoyment. It's selfish."

He chuckles again, smacking his lips dramatically and groaning as he takes his next bite.

Rolling my eyes, I glance back to the paper and focus on the words, tipping my pen in the corner of my mouth and nibbling on the hard plastic. Disgust crawls up my throat as I bring the ink down and draw harsh lines through the letters until my hand stings from the pressure and everything I've written is scratched out and obsolete.

Absolute shit.

"Yum, what smells so good?" Dorothy's voice soars through the air. It's light and airy, and it grates against my ears, the same way it does *every* time she speaks. I look up through my lashes, tracking her as she walks into the kitchen and smiles wide as she steps up next to Ezekiel.

"It's animal flesh." Ezekiel winks at me.

I scoff.

She giggles. "Sounds delicious."

"Does it? Your sister thinks I'm disgusting for eating it."

"I couldn't care less about what you choose to do with your life, Ezekiel." I snap my notebook closed, pulling it up to my chest.

"Well, Evie isn't exactly known for her good taste," Dorothy says, sparing me a small glance. "No offense."

I narrow my eyes, taking in her perfectly pressed baby-blue checked pantsuit and bright-red lips. She's always put together, but today, she looks just a little *extra*, and while not having her in the house is a blessing, I also don't like the idea of her going out on the town and plastering her face everywhere in public.

She either fails to realize that she constantly puts us at risk or she simply doesn't care, and our father loves her too much to rein her in, allowing his guilt over Nessa to bleed into his affection for Dorothy while she slips effortlessly into the role as "Daddy's favorite." But that's perfectly fine with me. I don't want to be anyone's favorite. I just want to be left the hell alone.

I'd have killed Dorothy years ago if it weren't for the fact that it would devastate my dad, and while I don't care much for people in general, family was everything to Nessa, so as a result, it's everything to me. But I wait and I watch, searching for proof that Nessa falling over the railing of a boat was more than just an "accident." One of these days, Dorothy has to slip up. I *know* in my bones that it was her.

"You ready to go?" Ezekiel asks her.

"Yep," she replies. "Dad already gave me the rundown."

My head tilts, curiosity spinning webs through my middle. I've never seen Ezekiel and Dorothy go anywhere together, much less run an errand for our dad. "Where are you going?"

For just a slight second, confusion mars Dorothy's features, brows drawing inward and eyes moving back and forth, like my question unlocked an invisible puzzle for her to piece together. But that's all it lasts for—a moment. As quick as the look came, it vanishes, her eyes clearing as a smile spreads across her face. "There's some guy Ezekiel wants to bring on. Dad asked me to go with, make sure he checks out."

Ezekiel's shoulders stiffen. "I'd *know* if he wasn't good for it. You think I'm lyin'? Fuck outta here with that shit. He's the best thief there is, and your dad wants to expand into the jewelry business. No one knows more about that than this guy."

She laughs. "I don't think anything, Ezekiel. Just saying what Dad said." She cocks her head as she looks at me again. "Didn't he tell you?"

My chest pinches from her words because *no*, he didn't tell me. I knew he was thinking about getting into diamonds but not that we were bringing in outsiders to accomplish that goal, and while I don't need to know everything that goes on, it still stings when he keeps me in the background, blind from omission and bound by blood.

Especially when he tells me in private how important I am.

But I get why he didn't. I wouldn't be on board with bringing on *anyone* new right now. It's taken years for our family to get where we are, and if it weren't for Nessa, we wouldn't even *be* here. She's the one who held us afloat while Dad was in prison, changing us from being a midrange gang to *the* Irish stronghold in the community, and now that she's gone and our dad is here, it's like we're being attacked by an invisible enemy from all sides. The Italians from Chicago are moving into our area, making backroom deals with the mayor—*our* mayor—and the idiot drug pushers we use are skimming off the top and cutting our drugs to pocket the extra money. It's not a good time for a fresh face.

Ezekiel's eyes flick to me. "He didn't tell you 'cause there's nothin' to tell. Not yet anyway."

I nod, my fingers playing with the edges of the notebook paper.

He stands up, cracking his neck. "I'm gonna go start the car. We leave in five minutes."

Dorothy smiles at him, her eyes following as he walks through the arched hallway and disappears before she spins to face me. "He's just trying to make you feel better...you know that, right?"

"Feel better for what?"

She shrugs, lifting one of her hands and picking at her nail beds. "Because Dad's showing me the ropes."

I lift my brows. "Have fun with that."

Her grin drops. "What's that supposed to mean?"

"It means...have *fun* with that," I repeat. "I'm sure I'll get pulled in when it's time to clean up your mess."

Her eyes flicker toward my small notebook. "Whatever, Evie. *You* have fun sitting here being pissed off at the world and writing your stupid little love spells. Maybe if you tried a bit harder to be normal, Dad would pay you some attention instead of hiding you in corners and only bringing you out at night."

I grit my teeth, my fingers tightening around the edges of the paper. "It's *poetry*."

She smirks. "Sure."

"Dorothy, we need to go," Ezekiel says, walking back into the room and glancing at me. "Want me to pick up anything on the way back?"

I smile wide. "A new sister would be nice."

Dorothy scoffs. "Why? You couldn't even keep your old one."

My grin drops, and my fingers move from my notebook to the edge of the table, grief blazing in the center of my gut like acid. Closing my eyes, I count back from ten, letting Nessa's memory coach me into a sense of calm that I don't truly feel. Otherwise, I'll be inclined to act on those pesky impulses again, and that won't do me any favors.

"Dorothy," Ezekiel snaps. "Shut the fuck up and get in the car."

"But I—"

"Now."

She pouts and leaves with one last look over her shoulder.

The silence presses in, feeling heavier with every second, but still, I keep my eyes squeezed so tight my head starts to ache.

Ten. Nine. Eight. Seven...

"She didn't mean it," Ezekiel finally whispers.

I pry my lids apart, peering over at him. "She did. But it's fine."

Closing my notebook, I push to stand, fury pulsing through my veins. Moving out from behind the small table, I press past

Ezekiel, walking so quickly my legs burn. I don't stop until I'm at the front entrance, the black-and-white-checkered marble gleaming beneath the crystal chandelier, a large princess staircase splitting to either side. My feet stomp as I make my way up the steps, and I focus on counting while I head toward my room.

Anything to keep my mind off the simmering *feelings* bubbling beneath the surface of my skin.

Little splashes of muted sunshine splay across the glossy wood floor and I purposely step around them as I walk down the hall. This house feels nothing like when I was a kid and Nessa was here, raising me and Dorothy, filling up every room with personality and love. Now, it feels too big. Too bright, with all the abstract paintings hanging on the walls and the light peeking in through the windowpanes.

Pushing open the door to my room, I rush toward the end table and slip my notebook into the drawer before heading to the vanity and sighing as I look at myself in the mirror.

My face looks drawn. Tired. I reach my fingers up and press them underneath my eyes, the dark circles making the muddy brown of my irises look like pits of black. I push firmly until pressure bleats across my sockets and I drag my nails down my cheeks, the rings that adorn each of my fingers clacking when they touch.

Get it together.

Reaching for the oversize scrunchie on the table, I throw my dyed-black hair into a messy bun and grab a hoodie, heading out of my room and back downstairs to make sure Ezekiel and Dorothy are really gone.

They are.

Ezekiel doesn't *technically* live here, but most of his time is spent at the estate. My father prefers to keep his inner circle as close as possible, which is why it doesn't extend far beyond his actual family and a few of his closest associates. Fortunately, the mansion is over ten thousand square feet, one of the nicest properties in Kinland, and has plenty of room for me to disappear entirely without much fanfare.

Me and people don't really get along.

I walk down the small hallway off the back of the main kitchen and leave the house through a side door, making sure to pull my hoodie tighter and keep to the edges of the premises, out of the line of sight of the numerous security cameras installed.

Eventually, I make it to the trees protecting the property and head into the thick of them, fallen leaves crunching beneath my feet. I've never been much for summer. Something about the cool weather and the smell of autumn brings a type of peace that I sink into, and as the September breeze whips across my face, making my nose tingle and my ears burn, a sense of contentment warms the center of my chest. For the first time since talking to my sister, the anger fades away, focus dropping into its place as I hit the clearing in the trees. I make my way to the small cottage sitting in the center, walking down the faded and chipped yellow brick pathway, half overrun with vegetation and weeds, until I reach the wooden porch. Reaching into my pocket, the metal prongs of a key dig into my fingers and I pull it out, unlocking the front door and moving inside.

There's a tiny living room with a green velvet couch, a small oak coffee table that rarely gets used, and just off to the side is a kitchenette with a white stove and a mini fridge.

It's nothing special. But it's *mine*.

I walk straight by it all, heading to the back bedroom and flinging open the door to the walk-in closet.

With a deep breath, I push apart the racks of clothing and sink to my knees, brushing my hand over the small indent in the drywall. It's faint, made specifically to blend in with the scuffed-up paint. You'd hardly notice it's there unless you knew where to look.

My fingers fit beneath the small notch and pull, allowing the hidden door to unlatch and swing open, revealing the dark room and concrete steps that lead deep underground. My knees crack when I stand, sending a dull throb of pain through my leg, and I wince as I walk into the blackened space, pulling on the string light before spinning around and closing up the secret entrance behind me.

I make my way down the steps and along the narrow concrete hallway. Goose bumps prickle along the back of my neck and scatter across my arms. I quicken my pace, the sounds of each step ricocheting off the walls and bouncing back into my ears.

There's a certain chill that happens when you're beneath sea level and surrounded by concrete. The kind that soaks into your bones and sends a shiver ghosting up your spine, and no matter how many times I make this trek, I never quite get used to it.

Finally, I hit the end of the hall, stopping in front of a large steel door with an illuminated screen to its left. Lifting up my fingers, I press my hand to it, watching as it scans my prints and triggers the lock to unlatch.

I pull the door open, hundreds of metal halide lights shining so brightly they make my eyes flinch. There's a faint click of the lock reengaging behind me, but I'm already allowing my gaze to focus on what's in front of me.

Satisfaction settles deep in my chest as I make my way down the long rows of garden beds, heading toward the center of the room where the digital thermostat sits, then leaning over to look at the numbers.

Seventy-five degrees Fahrenheit. Perfect.

I note the time. Two hours until it adjusts to thirty degrees, just after the sun drops beneath the horizon.

These plants are a temperamental breed.

This isn't the only thermostat I'll need to check. This underground area spans across two acres and is separated into smaller rooms for easier containment. Smiling to myself, I imagine what Nessa would think about the enhancements our father made to the cottage she gifted me.

Warmth spreads through my limbs and I shrug out of my hoodie before placing my hands on my hips and soaking in the sight. Out of all the places I've been in my life, right here is where I truly feel at home. Maybe it's because this is the only time I'm not constantly looking over my shoulder as I sink into my favorite pastime.

Solitude.

And botany, of course, although that isn't really a passion as much as it's a means to an end.

My eyes flicker to the thousands of pods growing beautifully, almost ready for lancing.

Another day...maybe two.

See, what Dorothy doesn't realize—what nobody else knows—is while our father may be the face of the family business, he's not the brains.

He needs me for that.

So she may have his attention and get showered in his love, but she doesn't *truly* have his favor.

I do.

And it starts right here, in my greenhouse full of poppies.

CHAPTER 5

Nicholas

I'VE NEVER SPENT SO MUCH TIME LOOKING AT shiny rocks.

The past month has been spent in isolation, distancing myself from Nick Woodsworth and becoming Brayden Walsh, thief extraordinaire, while subsequently learning the ins and outs of rare jewels. I've been hiding away in my new apartment smack-dab in the center of Kinland, courtesy of the DEA. The only people I've talked to are Cap, Seth, and Desmond Dillam, the top jeweler in the tristate area. I've been living and breathing cuts, clarity, colors, and everything in between until my eyes bleed and I dream of sparkles. Farrell Westerly wants to dip his toes into the diamond trade, and I need to be the man he trusts.

When I'm not learning that, I'm drowning in all I can about Farrell Westerly and his influence, although there isn't *too* much I can find out. While Farrell clearly runs the streets of Kinland, the city itself is tight-lipped, and the inner workings of their operation are locked up better than Fort Knox. All I have to go on are grainy surveillance photos that prove nothing and a hunch.

Add to the fact that Farrell is apparently a modern-day Robin Hood who shares his wealth with the community, and it makes gaining insight like ripping out a tooth with no novocaine.

He has two living daughters, but it's clear his older one, Dorothy, likes to live in the spotlight. My files have dozens of photos of her walking around town, going to brunches with friends, sitting in the cart with her father while they play rounds of golf with his "business associates."

His other daughter, Evelina, seems to be more reclusive. There are a few photos but always taken from a distance. I know she's incredibly intelligent, graduating early as valedictorian of Kinland High at the tender age of sixteen, but the clearest photo we have on file is old. Light-brown hair, dark-brown eyes, and a face that hadn't lost the roundness that comes with youth. The newer photos are all surveillance.

I tense my fingers while Seth blabbers in my ear. He's my point of contact—the one I'm assigned to check in with every week. Other than that, there will be no outside interaction with my real life.

"Shame we didn't go out one last time," Seth sighs.

"We *did*," I reply, closing the old and weathered book in my hand.

It's a book of poems, the only thing I have left of my mother, and while I can't stand to so much as think about her these days, for some reason, even when I'm pretending to be someone else, I hold on to it. Maybe because it reminds me of why I do what I do. Some of the only sober moments we had were when she'd lain down in my bed and read these poems until I fell asleep.

"That hardly counts, bro. You didn't even spend it with me,

you prick. Disappeared to get your dick wet instead. What kind of a friend does that?"

Flashes of the feisty blond and the way she lit my body up from a single look race through my mind. My cock jerks and I shake my head, grinning as I stare down at the high-end chestnut-colored coffee table in my temporary living room.

I should have gotten her number. Or her name.

"Miss me already, buddy?" I ask, trying to clear my brain of things that don't matter.

He chuckles. "Please. You know how much easier it is to get a woman when I don't have to compete with your pick-me smile?"

"That's not very nice." I stand up and walk over to the wall of windows leading to the deck overlooking downtown. It's a beautiful city, about half the size of Chicago but far more grand in appearance. Silhouettes of skyscrapers kiss the stars, thousands of green-tinted windows sparkling even in the moon.

And maybe if I was a sentimental man, I could find the beauty. Instead, I just feel hollow.

"Hey," I interrupt as Seth continues to ramble. "You'll check on Rose for me, yeah? While I'm gone?"

The line goes quiet for a few seconds. "Of course. I've been going over every couple of days. I'll keep her safe."

Nodding, I bite the inside of my cheek. "Good." The knots in my stomach tighten. "Well, that means there's only one thing left."

"What's that?" Seth asks.

"Tell me you miss my smile."

He groans. "Fuck off, Nick."

"Don't," I retort, the name ringing in my ears. "Don't call me that. I don't want to get confused."

He hesitates, the silence buzzing in my ear. "You ready for this, man?"

Pressing my knuckles against the glass, I gaze out over the city that's my new home for the foreseeable future. "Yeah. I'm ready. Let's take these fucks down."

Two nights later and I'm lounging in the booth at Winkies, the Westerly-owned bar on the eastern side of Kinland. I've never been a fan of whiskey, but it's what I'm swirling as I take in the scene. It's a nice place, as far as dive bars go, busy enough to pass as legit but not in an affluent enough part of town to attract too much attention.

They say Farrell opened it up to help the community prosper, but more than likely, he uses it as an easy way to launder money in a protected area untouched by both the feds and, more importantly, the Italians.

The Cantanellis are the stronghold syndicate in Chicago, and they've been trying to sink their claws into Kinland territory for the past ten years.

Right now, at three o'clock on a Wednesday, Winkies sits mostly empty, with TVs in the corners blaring the stats of the upcoming football season and forest-green vinyl-covered booths that house a spattering of heavy drinkers or people taking advantage of an early happy hour.

My back is facing the wall in one of the tables that sits in the far-right corner, and while I won't show it on my face, my insides wring tight, anxiety causing pops of apprehension to stab at my middle.

These first few moments of undercover work are always the

most nerve-racking. Make or break. You either set yourself up for success or you fail before you have a chance to fall.

But I've never faltered under pressure; I thrive.

Not everyone is meant for this work. Not everyone *gets* it. Some people are too ingrained in their morals, in their egos, to do what it takes to act the part. You have to live and breathe the job. *Become* it. Otherwise, you end up with concrete shoes and a bullet in your head.

Or pulled from the middle of an investigation and deemed unfit.

My jaw clenches as I remember my last gig and how it ended. The way I was ripped from the streets, forced to watch as they let the case turn cold.

A little bell jingles from the front door, and I tap my fingers against the rim of my glass, watching as Ezekiel O'Connor and Dorothy Westerly make their way inside and straight toward me.

My stomach twists.

Showtime.

Ezekiel's under firm instructions to get me in and then act like I don't exist outside of "working" together with the Westerlys. If I need him, I'll let him know. He shows his anxiety plain as day, that was apparent when we first met, and I can't take the risk of him acting unusual every time we come back from a conversation regarding all the ways he's flipping on the people he cares about.

"Brayden," he says when they reach the table. He doesn't offer his hand, so I don't either, choosing to sit back and bring the tumbler of whiskey to my mouth, my eyes skimming over his giant frame before moving to his companion.

Farrell's daughter.

My gaze lingers on hers just a little too long to be considered appropriate.

She's an attractive woman, and in any other situation, she'd be my type.

But she's a job. A way to glean information and funnel it back to camp.

"*You're* the guy we're meeting?" She licks her bright-red lips.

"That's right," I say, placing the glass down before bringing up my hand to rub at my jaw. "Problem with that?"

She tilts her head, making her dark-brown ponytail swing to the side and dip down the front of her shoulder. "You're just…not what I expected."

My smirk grows and I lean in until the edge of the table digs into my sternum. "I'm rarely what people expect."

Ezekiel chuckles, pointing a thick finger at me. "Don't fuckin' hit on her."

"Why, you got a boyfriend?" I wink and her cheeks blush a bright shade of crimson.

"Maybe," she replies, smiling as she sits across from me. She reaches out, tapping her red nails on the table. My eyes flick to the small shamrock tattooed on her inner wrist, hidden beneath thin rose-gold bracelets.

Ezekiel sits next to her, crossing a leg over the opposite knee as he watches me. I don't take my gaze off Dorothy, but I feel his stare and a sliver of unease worms its way down my sides, wondering if maybe he didn't flip after all. If this is a setup.

It was stupid to let him see my face before now.

"So are we doing something here?" I finally say. "Or did you call me just to waste my time?"

Ezekiel grins, running a palm over his beard. "You should be honored we want to talk to you at all. Skip doesn't meet with just anyone."

Skip is short for Skipper, which is what they call Farrell.

I turn my head to the left and then the right before looking back at him and shrugging. "Yet he's not here, is he?"

Ezekiel's golden eyes darken and he shoots forward in his seat, his fist pressing into the table. "You think this is a game, Brayden? I'm vouchin' for you as a favor. You want in? You want a piece? This is your chance. I won't give you one again. So quit bein' a fuckin' smart-ass and show some respect."

Licking my lips, I grab my glass and tip back the last of the whiskey, allowing the burn to sear my throat and warm my chest. When I set it down on the table, I run my finger around the rim and nod. "We go back, Ezekiel, and I appreciate you reaching out. I do." I lower my voice. "But don't think you can speak to me like one of your bitches. You guys don't want to do business with me? That's fine. There's plenty of other fish in the sea. *Bigger* fish. Ones that come from Sicily and know opportunity when they see it."

Ezekiel moves back in his seat, his brows hitting his hairline.

"You feel me?" I finish.

He's silent as he stares down his nose at me, and I wait, my insides thrumming as blood rushes through my veins.

Finally, a grin breaks across his face. "Yeah, you lousy fuck. I feel you."

Satisfaction drips through my insides. He played his part well.

Dorothy clears her throat. "Here." She unclasps her necklace, placing it on the table in front of me. "Tell me about this."

I look down at the large green emerald. My nerves tighten,

making my muscles twitch; this is going exactly how I want. But I make sure to keep my facial features mundane and level.

Sighing, I reach up and scratch the corner of my ear before locking eyes with her again. "What about it?"

She gestures toward the piece of jewelry. "You tell me. That's what you're good at, right?"

I pick it up, the thin rose-gold chain feeling cool against my fingers as I inspect the jewel.

"You get this from that boyfriend?" I glance up at her, the left side of my mouth lifting.

She smiles. "From my daddy."

"That what they're calling it these days?"

Her eyes narrow. "My father, you fucking pervert."

Chuckling, I look down at the necklace again before setting it back on the table. "Well, tell your *daddy* he should get a refund."

Her face drops, and Ezekiel sits forward.

"Excuse me?" she sputters, her hand wrapping around the chain and bringing it to her chest.

I shrug. "It's a nice rock, but it's not real."

"Then what is it?" she asks, staring down at the jewel like it's poison.

"Synthetic? Fuck if I know."

She scoffs. "I think I'd be able to tell."

"Just because you think something doesn't make it true." I reach out and grasp her hand in mine, hearing her sharp inhale of breath when I do. Drawing my finger across the surface of the jewel, I bring our palms up so it reflects off the light. "Look. See the way the stone is? It's got yellow undertones." I move our hands, allowing the "emerald" to shine. "Real emeralds have pure green or bluish hues. Never yellow."

"But it looks flawless." She tilts her head.

"And real emeralds have flaws, sweetheart. Just like the rest of us."

Ezekiel coughs. "How do we know you're tellin' the truth?"

Peering over at him, I deliberately run my thumb over the back of Dorothy's hand before dropping it to the table. "You don't."

CHAPTER 6

Evelina

TWENTY-FOUR FEELS DIFFERENT.

I stopped acknowledging my birthday a long time ago. After Nessa died, there wasn't anyone left to force me to celebrate, no one who cared enough to even remember.

But *technically* today is the day.

It's funny looking back on when I was just a kid. I'd spend my entire birthday trying to imagine what it was like when I was born, how my mother reacted when she brought me into the world.

Did she cry?

Did she pull me to her chest and feel our hearts sync up?

Was my father there holding her hand?

"How much longer?"

My dad's gruff voice hits my ears and my shoulders tense at the intrusion. I don't turn toward him, keeping my eyes locked on the flower pod in my hand. I turn it back and forth, inspecting the small crown at the top and making sure the ends aren't curving downward before taking my straightedge blade and slicing a shallow incision into the side.

"Hello, anyone home?" he barks. "I asked you a question."

He's in my peripheral vision, lounging against the wall of my greenhouse with his tattooed hands in his pockets and his silver hair slicked back.

"I heard you," I mutter, cutting another small line.

"And?"

I release the poppy and tighten my fist around the handle of my straightedge as I turn to face him. "And?" I repeat. "Is that the only reason why you're here? To check on my progress?"

An amused grin sneaks onto his face, and I hate the way my heart skips when it does.

"Of course not, Bug."

The nickname scrapes across my skin.

"I need you at Winkies tonight."

And just like that, the sliver of hope shatters into a thousand broken pieces, searing through my stomach as they fall. Sighing, I turn back to my poppies and count down from ten in my head.

"Evelina. Don't ign—"

"About half of them are ready," I interrupt. "But it will be a week before I'm ready to start the chemical process."

"A *week*?"

Another slice, this time on a new bud. "Maybe more."

"That's too long."

"It is what it is." I shrug, irritated that he's coming into *my* space on *my* birthday and acting like I'm not doing enough. "And I'm not going to Winkies."

He straightens. "You are."

"No," I say. "I'm not." My knuckles whiten as I grip the straightedge so tight it cuts off circulation.

He sighs, running a hand over his face and groaning. "Listen, Bug. I'm bringing on a new guy."

I don't say a word, instead just continuing the job of lancing the pods, slowly working my way down the row.

"Did you hear what I said?" he asks.

Slice.

"I heard you."

Honestly, he's really fucking stupid if he thinks I didn't already know. I know everything that goes on. How else does he think our business stays afloat?

"I need you there tonight to represent me. Make sure he's someone we can trust."

"And if he isn't?" I ask.

He shrugs. "Then he isn't."

What he's really saying is he wants me to do the dirty work. Again.

I twist my head, glancing at him from the corner of my eye. "Didn't you already have Dorothy meet him? What'd she think?"

He clears his throat, his face souring. "Dorothy is...smitten. I can't trust she's not letting that cloud her judgment."

My brows lift, because this *does* surprise me. Dorothy loves being the center of attention, but normally she uses and abuses the men in her life, never settling for more than a weekend fling. Whether that's because she doesn't want to be tied down or because she's a sociopath, I'm not sure.

I find it hard to care, to be completely honest.

"Bug, I need you here. Your *family* needs you."

My stomach tightens at his words, the way it does every time he says that, and Nessa's voice whispers in the back of my mind.

"There's no one like family, Evie, and there's no place like home. We have to stick together."

"Fine."

"I didn't know you were coming."

Dorothy appears next to where I'm sitting at the bar, her ruby-red lips pinched.

I look over at her, dipping my fingers into the small bowl of green olives I stole from the garnish tray and smiling wide. "Surprise."

She opens her mouth, but before she can get a word out, Ezekiel walks up behind her, a grin on his face as his gaze moves from her to me.

"She lives!" He slaps a hand to his chest. "I've been tryin' to get a hold of you all day."

Out of everyone who works for my dad, Ezekiel is undoubtedly my favorite. He's one of the only people I can tolerate, and over the years, he's worn me down enough to actually enjoy his company.

"Been busy." I pop another olive into my mouth.

"With what?" Dorothy scoffs. "You've been hanging out with that loser from your high school again?"

I grind my teeth, trying to rein back my irritation at her constant nagging. She's talking about Cody, of course. She's convinced that we're lovers, and I allow her imagination to run wild because what she thinks of me is none of my business.

The truth is far from that, however. Cody is a computer geek, and I realized when he sat next to me in chem class that befriending him would work out for me in the long haul. So I kept him close and tolerated his company, knowing that he'd be in my corner whenever I need. And good thing I did, considering he's now one of the top hackers in the world. Of course, nobody knows that other than me, and most people agree with Dorothy, thinking he's nothing but a loser who failed in Silicon Valley and moved back to live in his mom's basement.

Over time, I suppose you could say I've come to care about him more than almost anyone else in my life, but I don't trust him enough to let him know the deepest, darkest parts of what I do. What I truly am. He gets surface Evelina, just enough for me to utilize him when I need him.

Ezekiel places his hand on Dorothy's shoulder and nods toward the front door behind me. "There he is."

His eyes sharpen and he stands just a bit straighter. My eyes flick to Dorothy, watching as she sticks her chest out, her pupils dilating.

"You're late," Ezekiel says.

"I like making an entrance," a silky voice replies.

A sick feeling drops into my stomach because *I know that voice*. I've had it whispering in my memory ever since it moaned into my ear.

"Brayden," Dorothy coos. "Hi."

The coil unravels just a bit. *Maybe he just sounds the same.*

I spin around on my stool and my breath whooshes from my lungs like a sucker punch to the gut because it's him. Nicholas.

And he looks…shocked.

Did he lie to me about his name?

He's got that same black leather jacket he was wearing the night he fucked me against a bathroom wall and a silver chain slightly peeking out of the neckline of a white shirt.

When our eyes meet, heat floods through my veins, and I'm not sure if it's because I'm remembering how good he felt inside me or because I'm furious he's here now.

He takes his time perusing down the length of my body and then back up before locking on my eyes again. And then he smirks.

Irritation simmers deep in my chest.

"Brayden," Dorothy says again.

The name snaps me out of this weird staring contest we're in, and I let the corner of my mouth tilt up in a sardonic smile.

Brayden. He *did* lie to me about his name.

He settles back into himself, shaking whatever momentary emotion flitted over his face and replacing it with a confident aura that screams laid-back and in control. "Ezekiel. Dorothy," he murmurs, his focus never leaving me. "And who do we have here?"

I glare and that stupid smirk grows.

Popping another olive in my mouth, I chew, then swallow.

His gaze drops to my lips.

"That's really none of your business, *Brayden*," I say.

"Evie!" Dorothy snaps.

Satisfaction sparks in his irises and he tilts his head. "For some reason, I pictured you blonder, Evie."

"It's Evelina."

His face softens. "Now *that's* a beautiful name."

My insides tighten.

Dorothy laughs and steps forward until she's angled herself in front of me, reaching her hand out and running it down the sleeve of his arm. "Come on. Let's get a table in the back."

Finally—*finally*—he stops staring at me and puts his attention on my sister, his entire demeanor shifting in an instant. He nods, placing his hand on her back, allowing her to lead him away, and my shoulders sag from tension I wasn't even aware I was holding.

Ezekiel hums, rubbing his hand over his beard as he takes me in.

"What?" I drop my eyes to the bar, grabbing my phone and standing.

He shakes his head. "Nothin'. You got somethin' you need to say to me?"

My muscles pull tight. "What would you like me to say, Ezekiel? I'm here because dear ol' *Daddy* doesn't trust your judgment. Or Dorothy's, apparently."

My eyes flicker to where she's scooting in next to Brayden in the booth.

Ezekiel nods, puffing out his cheeks. "I've known Brayden since back in the day. Haven't seen him in a long time, but he's good people. And he's lookin' for work."

Tapping my fingers on the bar top, disappointment wraps around my middle. "I fail to see how that's our problem."

He smiles, throwing an arm around my shoulder and pulling me into his side as we walk to the table in the back. "You and your bleedin' heart."

I laugh at his sarcasm and let him lead me to the booth, ignoring the way my *bleeding* heart speeds when I look up and meet a pair of jade-green eyes.

CHAPTER 7

Nicholas

THAT LITTLE FUCKING LIAR.

Technically, I suppose, she never told me her name.

But she's a Westerly. And I…I *did* tell her my name. And that I was starting a new job.

Fuck.

I've been an agent for eight years, since I was twenty-four, and not a single time have I questioned myself. But right now, seeing the girl who won't leave my memories standing right in front of me while I'm in an active undercover investigation? The odds are definitely not in my favor. And to be completely honest, I've already dropped the ball, because if I was doing my job, I would have recognized who she was when I studied her photos in our files. Maybe if I had looked a little closer, I would have noticed the resemblance, but *my* pretty girl is not this black-haired chick with piercings that cover the length of her ears and brown eyes that stare so deep they char my skin.

"I know," Dorothy snaps me out of my daze.

I quirk a brow. "Know what?"

She scoots closer to my side. "You're staring at my sister. She's different. A lot of people call her off-putting. She doesn't get out much."

"Oh?"

"It's not her fault though. Our mom, she…she didn't treat Evie too nice, you know? Caused a lot of issues." She taps her head. "Up here."

The urge to keep asking questions, to learn everything about Evelina Westerly, is strong, but I bite back the notion, unsure if I want to know because of the case or because she's under my skin; the energy wafting off her, even now, is heavy enough to make me teeter on the edge of sanity.

There's never been anyone who's affected me like this. It's the reason I approached her at the club, and it's *definitely* the reason why I fucked her against the dirty bathroom tile while she screamed into my mouth.

My eyes track Evelina and Ezekiel as they walk to the table, his arm slung around her shoulders and a slight smirk lining the corners of her lips. Annoyance flits through me as I take in their compatibility. She's at ease with him. She trusts him.

Are they dating? He's way too old for her.

The second they reach us, our gazes lock, my jaw clenching as she slides into the booth first, sandwiching herself between the wood paneling and Ezekiel, who sits next to her.

A hand touches my arm and jolts me out of my staring problem, and I look over to Dorothy, remembering where I am and, most importantly, what I'm supposed to be doing.

You're Brayden now.

"You hungry?" Dorothy asks, a grin spreading across her face.

She looks so innocent and sweet, it's hard to believe she's

involved in any criminal activity. But I learned a long time ago to never judge a book by its cover. The best criminals are the ones who you'd never suspect. They're the ones you make jokes with, the ones you learn to trust, the ones who become your best friend while they stab you in the back and steal everything out from under you.

My gaze drifts down the front of Dorothy's pale-yellow dress and then back up to her face, her cheeks flushing crimson from my perusal. "I could eat."

"I've already got them cookin' up somethin' in the back for us," Ezekiel cuts in.

My eyes shoot to Ezekiel and then flick toward Evelina, unable to keep myself from engaging with her. "How about you?" I jerk my chin in her direction. "You going to eat?"

Dorothy laughs beside me, covering her mouth and shaking her head to stifle the noise. "*Please*, Evie never eats here."

Evelina's gaze burns through mine until I feel it in my toes.

"Why's that?" I prod. "You too good for bar food, sweetheart?"

She straightens, but she doesn't say a word, just keeps watching me with those lethal fucking eyes of hers.

"They're good for a quick indulgence every once in a while," she finally replies. "But other than that, there's nothing really special about them. Hardly remember they were ever in my mouth once I'm done."

Dorothy makes a face. "Gross, Evie. Why'd you say it that way?"

"That sounds pretty pretentious," I cut in, annoyed that she's hinting at our night together as forgettable. I stretch my arm across the back of the booth, settling deeper into Dorothy's side.

Evelina gives a small grin, a fake one. The type that shows no teeth and barely tips up in the corners. But it's enough to light a spark in my stomach, knowing I'm getting a rise out of her.

Does she remember the name I gave her?

Maybe she hooks up a lot, and I'm just one in a long line. The thought causes a twinge of discomfort to squeeze my middle.

It's weird she isn't calling me out about it, and I can't decide whether I want her to remember or if I'd rather she forget. The latter would be the easiest. But deep down, I know the truth, as much as I wish I didn't have to acknowledge it. I *want* her to remember every second of our time, the same way it's been burned into my brain ever since it happened.

And now she's watching me.

In fact, she hasn't stopped watching me since the moment I walked in, like she's peeling back my layers one by one and rearranging them to fit in her head.

I feel vulnerable, exposed, almost at her mercy. Which means she's a *huge* liability.

My throat closes, nerves racing underneath my skin.

Fuck, fuck, fuck.

"Excuse me," I say, my hand reaching out to press against Dorothy's shoulder, suddenly needing to have a few minutes to gather myself.

Her brows draw in, bottom lip puffing out the slightest bit. "You okay?"

Forcing a grin, I nod. "Yeah, I'll be right back."

She moves, sliding out of the booth and standing, and I'm right behind her, slipping past as I head toward the dark hallway that leads to the restrooms.

But it isn't her gaze I feel searing into my back.

My legs burn as I hustle to the small bathroom, throwing

open the door and closing it quickly behind me, then rushing to the sink and turning it on, cupping the cold water in my hands and splashing it on my face. The icy sensation shocks my nerves back into a steady state and my knuckles tighten around the edge of the counter, water droplets dripping off my nose and into the sink's basin.

Get it together. This isn't a problem. She isn't a problem.

Cracking my neck, I twist to the paper towel dispenser, grabbing a handful. I wipe off my face before blowing out a deep breath and talking myself into a fake confidence I don't truly feel as I walk out of the bathroom and back into the dark hall.

My footsteps stutter when I run into Evelina, resting against the wall, where she's clearly waiting for me.

Her eyes are downcast as she inspects her nails, her black hair pulled back, showcasing the flawless expanse of her neck. My gaze trails along her figure, drinking her in like she's water in the desert. She's so different from who she was the night at that club, with her ripped oversize band tee, black skirt, knee-high stiletto boots, and silver rings, but this suits her more; the deep purple on her lips is somehow even sexier than the bubblegum pink she was wearing the night we met.

"Nicholas." Finally she glances up, straightening off the wall and tilting her head. "Or should I say Brayden?"

She takes a step closer, and as much as I try not to, flashes of her small frame in my hands fly through my mind. How she molded perfectly to every inch of my body. How pliable and warm she was when I wrapped her around my waist and split her with my cock.

I clear my throat, running a hand through my hair.

"Yeah," I wince. "Sorry about that."

Her eyes narrow and she takes another step. "About what?"

"What?" I repeat.

"What are you sorry about, exactly?"

For *everything*. I'm sorry I met her then. I'm sorry I know her now. And I'm sorry she isn't anywhere near the person I imagined her to be. But I don't say any of that. Instead, I stuff Nick Woodsworth away, deep down inside where I won't be able to find him, and I let Brayden Walsh take center stage.

I shrug, adopting a crooked grin on my face.

Her eyes flash, lips pursing the smallest bit. She takes another step closer. "There's two options, *Brayden*. You either lied to me about your name then…or you're lying now."

"It's not that deep, sweetheart." I laugh. "I've met your type a thousand times. Lonely girl at the bar, playing hard to get but desperate to get fucked. All the classic signs of a clinger."

My stare dips along the expanse of her neck as she throws her head back and laughs. "*Please*. I'm not the one who was begging for a name and following me into private spaces just to get a taste."

Now it's me who steps forward, my breath blowing softly on the top of her head.

Goddamn, she's short.

She cranes her neck to meet my gaze, and I suck in a deep breath when she does.

I thought at first that I missed the striking blue of her eyes from the night we met, but this close, the dark browns swirl with yellow and a dash of green, creating a kaleidoscope of color so deep and fucking beautiful they suck me in and drag me under like quicksand.

My cock hardens.

No. I'd give anything to go back to those basic blues.

"And what a delicious taste it was," I rasp.

She sneers. "You're a pig."

Leaning down, my mouth grazes against her ear. "I've never claimed to be a gentleman, and I won't apologize for lying when it ended with you shaking around my cock."

"Did I?" She tilts her head. "I don't remember."

I grin. "Now who's lying?"

She hums, bringing up her fingers and smoothing them down the opening of my jacket. I stare at the movement, my hands clenching into fists to keep from reaching out and dragging her into me. To remind her just how much she *loved* how I made her feel.

"And this is the new job you're starting?" she murmurs, keeping her attention on every place she touches. "Working with my dad?"

"Just a new venture," I murmur. "Broadening my horizons. I didn't know he was your dad."

Her head tilts, as though she's taking in what I say and letting it sink into her brain, slotting it away to use against me later.

I've never met anyone quite like her.

She's unnerving in a type of way that makes your skin crawl. She'd be a fantastic interrogator.

Her fingers wrap around my jacket and she rises up on her tiptoes, dragging me down until her lips skate across my jaw. "Nicholas. *Brayden.* Whatever the fuck your name is…stay the hell away from me and stay the hell away from my family. You aren't welcome here."

She drops her hold and pushes me roughly before turning around and walking away.

CHAPTER 8

Evelina

OSCAR NORMAN, THE MAYOR OF KINLAND, IS A flashy man who spends more time worried about lining his pockets than he does about his morals. I first met him when I was ten years old and Nessa had him over for steak dinner and a "chat."

I, being the kid I was at the time, thought he was her boyfriend. But I should have known better because Nessa never did anything without just cause, and soon enough the Westerly name was bankrolling Oscar's political science degree. Over the years, I would watch with rapt attention while she pulled his strings like a marionette, funneling him down the narrow avenues she wanted him to take until one day, he became a household name.

Exactly like she wanted him to be.

I assumed his loyalty to Nessa was just as strong as mine. They seemed to have a bond, and she's the reason he's worth a damn at all. But I soon realized what a foolish notion that was after she died on *his* boat and he didn't even show up to her funeral.

Cut off all ties with us and hasn't come back around since.

Oscar Norman is a fraud, hiding behind a curtain of debauchery while portraying the image of a morally upstanding family man. And as I watch him being bent over his desk while the city commissioner rams a cock up his ass, that's never been more obvious.

"Can you turn that shit down?" Cody scrunches his nose, reaching beside his triple monitor computer and grabbing his noise-canceling headphones. "Not all of us want to hear the men running our city moaning like stuck pigs."

We're perched in the corner of his basement, and I smirk, tossing a piece of popcorn into my mouth as I keep my eyes on the screen. "Please. They wouldn't know how to run this city if their lives depended on it."

He chuckles, running a hand through his dirty-blond locks. "You've got a point."

"Hey," I say, never taking my eyes from the screen. "Can you do me a favor?"

"You mean another one?" he asks, spinning in his desk chair to face me. "You know, rigging a hidden camera in a government official's office isn't exactly *easy*. A thanks would be nice."

I nod. "Thank you. I need you to look into someone."

He pushes up his wire-framed glasses as he sits forward in his seat, placing his elbows on his knees. "Color me interested. Who?"

My insides twist, and the fact that my body reacts so viscerally to even the thought of Brayden Walsh pisses me off. I crack my neck, trying to alleviate the tension.

A slow smile creeps along Cody's face. "Someone's got you fucked up."

I narrow my eyes. "Someone's annoyed me, if that's what you mean, and I'm trying to decide whether or not to kill him."

His grin grows larger, and with it, so does my irritation until it's a living, breathing, snarling thing inside me.

"Do me a favor?" I snap. "Stop psychoanalyzing and stick to what you know."

Cody's face drops. "God, you're *such* a bitch."

Grinning, I pop another piece of popcorn in my mouth and shrug.

"You have serious issues, babe," he says just as a long groan sounds from the computer in front of me.

Both of us divert our attention back to the screen, watching as our dear mayor stands up from his precarious position, semen dripping out of his ass and down his thigh.

Cody makes a gagging noise. "I could have gone my whole life..."

I move forward, the roller of the mouse pressing into the tip of my finger as I press Save and download the recording onto a USB drive.

"It's just sex." I glance at Cody. "I bet the commissioner would fuck you too if he knew you were the mysterious Oz. He'd probably come just from the thought of being able to use you himself."

He grins, his cheeks tingeing pink. "Yeah, well, unfortunately for him, I like to fuck, not *get* fucked."

"Semantics." I smirk.

The computer pings, letting me know the download is complete, and I reach forward, snatching the USB. Satisfaction settles in the center of my stomach and spreads outward as I slip the drive in my cleavage, tucked into the underwire of my bra.

"For your personal spank bank?" Cody wiggles his brows.

"For insurance," I correct.

"So who is it?" Cody asks.

"What?" Standing up, I stretch my arms above my head, the ripples and pops of my tight muscles making a relieved sigh. I walk over to the red couch against the far wall and grab my jacket off the back cushions.

"Whoever it is you're debating on murdering."

My stomach tightens as a flash of green eyes and leather flits through my memory. "Brayden Walsh."

Cody hums. "Never heard of him. What do you need to know?"

"Everything." I slip my arms through the sleeves of my jacket and untuck my hair from the collar, spinning around to face him.

"Babe, you'll need to be more specific."

I grit my teeth, wishing he'd stop asking so many questions and just do what I need, but I stifle the strong urge to snap, because if I don't play nice, I won't get what I want. Moving across the room, I stop directly in front of him. "I *am* being specific."

His eyes flick down to my chest, and if I didn't know he was gay, I'd bend over and give him a little show to ensure he gave me what I wanted. But unfortunately, Cody isn't seducible, so instead I have to be *friendly*.

"I want to know where he sleeps, who his family is, whether he got gold stars on his fucking elementary workbooks. Everything."

Cody's brows rise and he lifts his hands up in front of him, palms facing out. "Sure. Sure. Give me a couple weeks." He pauses. "You know, if you want some more help with things, I'm here."

I stand up straight, the edge of the USB digging into the skin of my breast.

"You've got two days."

"Don't tell me what to do!" he hollers playfully as I spin and walk out the door.

It's an hour later when I finally make it back to the estate, waving at the security guards posted outside the gated entrance and driving my blacked-out Range Rover down the winding path that's lined with perfectly manicured shrubs.

Running the ball of my tongue ring against the back of my lip, I park my car in the garage and walk toward the door, my leg muscles burning from how quickly I rush inside. The USB is searing a hole against my chest, and I have to physically stop myself from continually grabbing at it just to make sure it's still there.

The door from the garage opens straight into the kitchen, and while I know I'm safe from prying eyes—nobody who lives here notices me until they need something—anxiety still creeps along my spine and wraps around my throat, urging me to move fast until I can get the drive to a safe spot.

Loud laughter rings from down the hall and my heart stutters against my chest, causing my footsteps to falter. It sounds like it's coming from the dining room, and even though it makes no sense for me to change direction and head toward the noise, it's what I do anyway.

I slip off my jacket and shoes, walking as lightly as possible, trying to ensure my footsteps aren't heard on the hardwood floors, and when I hit the dining room off the front entrance, anger floods my system so strongly it immobilizes me.

He's in the house.

In our lives for less than a week and already Brayden Walsh is in our fucking house.

My family is full of idiots. My heart slams against my ribs and my fingers curl into fists, nails cutting into my palms.

Ten. Nine. Eight…

The control slips back into place as I count down to one, and I turn, walking down the hall quickly, making a quick pit stop in the kitchen to grab a water.

It's when I'm bent down in the fridge, my fingers grazing against the side of the bottle, that I hear him again.

"Hi, sweetheart."

His voice skates over my skin like a thousand knives, and the way he uses *sweetheart* makes me want to scream.

I fucking *hate* that word.

"Ignoring me already?"

Groaning, I stand up straight and close the fridge door. "It's Evelina, stalker."

He smirks and it makes me want to punch him in the face. "*Evelina*."

"What do you want?" I ask, trying to move around him. He steps to the side when I do so that I'm boxed in. Tension stretches around my shoulders.

"You're quite the little creeper, peering around walls and into rooms," he notes, tilting his head. "Didn't want to say hi?"

I scoff. "I *live* here, genius. And I was trying to avoid you."

"Why?" he presses.

"Because if I don't, then I'm going to murder you."

His eyes flash, and his grin grows.

Does he think I'm joking?

He steps into me and I lose my breath at how quickly the air changes.

Whether I want to admit it or not, physically, this man affects me more than anyone else ever has, and that causes panic to percolate through every nerve, because the last thing I need is someone I don't trust coming around and making me feel out of control.

I throw my hands up and press them against his chest. "You're in my bubble."

He lifts a brow. "Your bubble?"

Waving my hand between us, I attempt to push him back. "This is my bubble, *dog*. And you're in it."

"Maybe I like your bubble." He leans into me, my palms the only thing separating his body from brushing against mine. "It's cozy. *Tight*."

"Great," I say dryly. "Can you move now?"

He hums and presses into me again, this time pushing until my back is flush against the fridge. When he lifts his hand, my fingers dig into his shirt, my heart pounding in my ears, and he brushes a strand of hair from my forehead before cupping my jaw.

His green eyes flicker from my face down to my lips.

Heat explodes in my stomach.

"Let go of me," I manage to rasp.

"No."

"It wasn't a question," I hiss. "And I want you to leave my family alone. I'm not fucking kidding."

He pushes his hips against me and bends down, his breath ghosting across my neck, causing shivers to trickle down my spine.

"I'm not quite sure who you think I am," he whispers. "But clearly you've mistaken me for someone who gives a fuck about what you want."

I grit my teeth, anger bleeding into my vision until it darkens around the edges.

"So if I want to eat dinner in your home," he continues. "If I want to do business with your dad…if I want to fuck your naive older sister, then that's what I'll do."

My chest tightens, nostrils flaring as I turn my face to the side, trying to rein in my temper. The *one* time I don't have my gun.

"You got me, pretty girl?"

Letting out a low laugh, I nod my head, dipping the tip of my tongue out and running it along the edge of my bottom lip.

His eyes track the movement, the same way they did the night we met at the club.

I rise up on my tiptoes until our noses graze, the smell of cinnamon and pine swimming through my senses. "Go fuck yourself."

Smiling, I shove his chest as forcefully as I can. He doesn't budge much, but it's enough for me to spin out of his hold and slip underneath his arm, and I walk away as fast as possible, my heart slamming against my ribs with every step.

CHAPTER 9

Nicholas

"WHERE ARE WE?" I ASK, LOOKING AROUND THE parking lot.

I already know, of course. We're at the Yellow Brick, which is a strip club in the heart of Kinland, owned by none other than Farrell Westerly himself.

Liam, one of Farrell's associates who's been tasked with babysitting me, grins as he slicks back his greasy red strands in the rearview mirror of his car.

"Let's not play games, okay, rook?" he says, turning toward me and lighting the end of a cigarette. "We both know that *you* know where we are."

My heart shoots into my throat. *Is this a trap? Have I been made?* "What the fuck is that supposed to mean?"

He frowns. "You expect me to believe you don't know what a strip club is?"

Relief floods my system and my muscles relax. He's just being a prick. I lean back in my car seat and smirk.

He purses his lips. "Must be nice to get in so quick with the Skip."

I shrug, not bothering to reply. To be completely honest, I'm just as shocked as anyone else Farrell granted me access to his person that easily, that he allowed me into his home and to meet with him face-to-face. That he doesn't seem to care if his "pride and joy" wants to fuck me six ways from Sunday and that—at least in everyone else's eyes—I'm entertaining the thought.

And that tells me one of two things. Either Farrell Westerly is the dumbest motherfucker to ever run an organized crime ring, or he's gotten overly confident and sloppy.

Either way, it begs the question of how the hell he built such an empire in such a short amount of time if these are the types of decisions he makes.

Liam grunts before opening his car door and slamming it behind him, throwing his half-burned cigarette on the ground. I follow suit, the cool nighttime air whipping across my face when I leave the vehicle and walk toward the front door. The loose gravel of the club's parking lot crunches beneath my shoes as we make our way to the front entrance, and I sink into my role as Brayden, my hand running along the chain on my neck, pulling it to rest on top of my shirt instead of underneath it. The minuscule wire inside wouldn't capture much video if it was hidden beneath fabric.

The inside is exactly what you'd expect from the name. The floor is almost black, and it's accented with muted yellow brick walls. Couches line the perimeter with VIP areas hidden along the back. The dim lighting and the music pumping through the speakers set up a club atmosphere, but instead of being overwhelming and in your face, it's relaxed. There's a bar along the far right that spans the entire length of the building, and in the center of the room, there's a large stage with a pole. Smaller circular stages are scattered throughout, all of them with women in various stages of undress.

I know the layout of this place inside and out, having looked at the architectural blueprints until my eyes bled. But seeing it in person is different.

Liam's hand slaps down on my shoulder, squeezing. "Look at all the tits you want later. Let's go."

I move behind him as he waltzes by the main stage and past the bar, barely sparing anyone a second glance as he heads to the back where the VIP areas are. I spin around as we walk, trying to get a visual of as much of the room as possible. There's a long hall with blank doors, and he moves past the first two before throwing open the third one aggressively, the sound of it slamming against the wall harsh against my ears.

A man sits in the center of a U-shaped booth with a cigar in his mouth and a bottle of Dom in the center of the table. He snaps his head up. The girl in his lap ignores the fact that we're here entirely and continues to rub her naked pussy on top of him.

"Liam, buddy." He peers around her shoulder. "To what do I owe the pleasure?"

"Tony." Liam cracks his knuckles, then puts his hand in his pocket and pulls out an emerald necklace.

My stomach tightens when I realize it's the one I said was a fake.

Liam brings his arm back and then flings it. It hits the woman in the back and she yelps, stuttering in her movement.

Tony's face drops, the laid-back ease that was present morphing into something more sinister. He puts his hands on the hips of the dancer, stopping her. He squeezes her ass roughly and groans like he can't stand the thought of letting it go before tapping her with his palm. "Give me a few minutes, doll."

She rises from him and skims her eyes over Liam and me before leaving the room entirely.

Tony adjusts the waist of his pants before pointing a gold-ringed finger at Liam. "You better have a good fucking reason for doing what you just did."

Liam lifts his chin. "You selling Skip fakes now?"

My chest tightens, my eyes going back and forth between them.

Fucking great.

"Please." Tony laughs. "The fuck outta here with that."

Liam lifts his brows, tossing a thumb in my direction. "This guy says you are."

"Bullshit," Tony spits, his eyes narrowing on me. "You saying I gave a fugazi?"

I clench my jaw, wanting to be anywhere other than in this room. Because no, he *didn't* in all actuality. "Come on, buddy. Let's not play games."

"And now you're calling me a liar?" He sits up straight, looking over to Liam. "Who the fuck is this guy? You come in here and accuse me of shit? I don't gotta answer to no one. Not even your fucking boss."

Liam shakes his head. "He wants his money, Tony."

Tony sits back, crossing his leg over his other knee and grinning. "Tell him to bill me."

There's a moment where I consider what I'm about to do, but it's only that, a moment. I need to gain Farrell's trust enough to make it into the inner circle, and regardless of the repercussions, word will get to him.

I chuckle before snapping forward and gripping Tony by the back of his neck, slamming his head forward into the glass table.

The sound of it smashing is loud, and a searing pain shoots up the side of my arm, a steady trickle of liquid seeping from a cut on my wrist.

"Aye, aye," Liam snaps, pulling me back as Tony struggles and yells in the background. "For fuck's sake, rook, get ahold of yourself. For the love of God."

I scoff, throwing my arm toward him. "You're gonna let some nobody fuck disrespect you, disrespect Skip like that? Here? On your turf?" I shake my head. "Nah, not with me. Not like that."

"*Vattela a pigliare in culo*," Antonio spits.

"The fuck you say?" I reply, turning to go at him again. The fake outbursts of violence make me feel like shit, but everything about my persona has to fit the mold. The lazy speech, the short temper and flares of violence. That's Brayden, so in effect, that's me.

Liam's eyes narrow, his nostrils flaring, and he grabs the front of my shirt, dragging me into him. "Tony is with the Cantanellis. The Italians…you picking up what I'm saying? You don't get to bash in the heads of people with more importance than you. *I can*, but you can't. Got it?"

I shrug out of his hold, my heart slamming against my chest from the adrenaline. "Whatever."

"Go clean yourself up." He glares down at my hand. "Christ."

Sighing, I shake out my wrist and make a beeline toward the restrooms, hoping like hell I didn't make a mistake by fucking with an Italian. I'm assuming if he was hanging out in Westerly territory, he's no one high in the food chain, possibly could even get himself eighty-sixed if people found out, but when it comes to the inner workings of the underworld, you can never be too sure.

I turn the corner and slam into a body, my hands shooting out quickly and gripping slender shoulders, hauling them into me to keep us both steady.

My wrist throbs.

Glancing down, I meet angry brown eyes lined in black.

Evelina. *What the hell is she doing here?*

"Why am I not surprised to see you?" she says, lifting one of her perfectly arched brows. "What are you doing back here?"

My eyes soak her in, taking in the soft lines of her face and her black lace tank top covered by a hoodie that's unzipped in the front, leaving her cleavage on full display.

Should have paid them more attention when I had the chance.

"Got lost."

She narrows her gaze before sucking in a quick and shallow breath, her hand reaching out to grab my wrist. "What happened?"

I lift a brow, surprised by her tender touch, so at odds with the wall she erects anytime she's near me. "Didn't realize you cared so much, sweetheart."

She turns, pulling me toward the nearest door and opening it so we can walk into a large office with mahogany wood and burgundy furniture.

"Just need to make sure you won't bleed out on Westerly property," she mutters as she pushes me into one of the couches against the wall. "It's bad for business."

I fall back willingly, the buttery soft fabric so comfortable I sink into the cushions.

"Stay." She points at me as she walks across the room and into the door of the en suite.

I don't stay, of course, hopping up immediately and walking over to the desk, my eyes flicking to the open door of the private restroom and then back as I hunch over to allow the camera a good view of the desk's top. I don't touch anything, and more than likely there's nothing of importance out, but you never know.

"What are you *doing*?" Evelina's voice breaks through the fog, making my stomach jump into my throat.

Stepping back, I run a hand through my hair. "Snooping, obviously."

Her brows draw in. "I told you to stay put."

I step into her until her ass is pressed against the edge of the desk and my hips are wedged against hers. "And I'm not a dog you can bark demands at, sweetheart."

She smirks. "I beg to differ."

My cock jerks, arousal warring with my brain, warning me to keep my distance. My brain loses, the way it seems to *always* lose with her.

"You're right," I agree, taking my uninjured hand and reaching around to grip her hip and pull her into me. "Tell me to sit and eat like a good boy, and I swear to fucking god I'll do it."

My mouth waters at even the thought of what she tastes like.

Her lips part, and I have the most delicious visual of my dick slipping between them, her big brown eyes staring up at me, and that tongue ring she didn't have the night we met running along the shaft.

"This desk is worth more than your life," she whispers. "And you're bleeding all over it."

I snap out of my thoughts, realizing that my fingers are digging into the meat of her ass, and I step back, letting go like she set me on fire before looking down to where there's a small puddle of red pooling on the wood.

Jesus, what the hell is wrong with me?

A loud sigh pours from Evelina's mouth and then she's pulling me by the hand again, back to the couch, tossing me like a rag doll into it. She sits next to me, dragging my bleeding arm into her lap. Then she grabs the first aid kit and gets to work, pouring hydrogen peroxide over the wound.

The sting permeates through my skin and makes me hiss. "Ouch. *Fuck*."

"Oops." She looks at me with wide eyes. "Did that hurt?"

It gets quiet as she takes out the antiseptic and gauze, cleaning the wound and dabbing at it, her eyes laser-focused on the task at hand.

My stomach tightens and I take the moment to look at her, *really* look at her, wondering again what she's doing here and how she feels about her family's chosen profession. Sadness whirls through my center as I think of everything she could be. What anyone who chooses this life could be, if only they made better decisions.

Maybe it's not too late. Maybe I can get her out.

"Why did you lie to me about your name?" she asks without looking up from where she's bandaging the wound.

My chest twists. "The same reason you didn't give me yours."

She swallows audibly and peers at me through her lashes, her eyes moving back and forth quickly, as if she's trying to see past the facade and drag out my soul. Her lips part and my abs tense, the air growing thick and filling the space between us until it feels like I might snap in half.

Her face is an inch from mine, and when she breathes out, I breathe in, trying like hell to remember that she's the enemy. That I'm here to take her and everyone she cares about down.

That none of this is real.

It can't be real.

Suddenly, the door swings open and slams against the wall, causing us both to jump apart. Liam walks in, barreling straight to us and shoving his thick finger in my face.

"Fuck up like that again, and I'll put a bullet in your fucking mouth. You understand me?"

Evelina's brows jump and she stands, moving across the room to perch behind the desk.

I lean back against the couch cushions. "Remind me when I started to work for you, Liam?"

His cheeks grow red, his body tensing, hands rolling into fists like he's about to try and hit me. Dude's got anger problems, for sure.

"When you two are done measuring dicks, feel free to tell me what's going on," Evelina interrupts.

He spins around to face her, strands of his red hair falling onto his forehead. "Don't worry about what the big boys are doing, sweetheart. Just sit there, look pretty, and run the numbers like your daddy asks."

So she's doing the books. Shit.

Him calling her sweetheart burns deep in my gut, because calling her that is *my* way of pissing her off, not his. Every time I say it, my cock jerks from the angry flush that pinks her skin. When the endearment falls from *his* lips, I want to stand up and shove his face into glass the way I did Tony a few minutes ago. The quick change in temper throws me off guard, because this time, it's unprovoked. Not a calculated move from the character I play but a genuine raw emotion, the kind I haven't felt in years. I'm not really sure what to do with that.

Evelina's entire persona shifts in an instant. She tilts her head to the side and smiles. "Come again?"

"Why don't you give us a minute?" Liam continues.

Clearly, Liam doesn't see the change.

Evelina places her dainty hands on top of the large mahogany desk, dropping her head and shaking it back and forth as she closes her eyes, mouthing what look like numbers.

"Come on, Evie. You don't need to listen to all this," he tries again, winking at her this time. "I know you like to play boss when Skip's not around, but this is guy stuff, okay?"

Her eyes crack open and sharpen like a blade as she grabs a couple of envelopes from the corner of the desk and a silver letter opener before walking toward the door. "Sure, my bad."

My brows rise, surprised she withered so quickly, but I should have known better. She reaches Liam and shoves him forcefully into the wall, using her entire body to pin him, the letter opener pressing into his crotch and the skinny heel of those boots she's always wearing stabbing into his foot.

He pushes back against her, his hands at her shoulders, and I move to jump between them but quickly realize there's no need. She subdues him easily.

It's actually quite a comical sight, a short girl not even clearing five two with a tall man well over six feet at her mercy.

I sit back, half in disgust at what she's capable of and the other half in awe of the power she's suddenly exuding. Part of me wonders if there's more than what meets the eye with her, if maybe keeping the books isn't the only thing she does when it comes to her family. But I brush off the thought, not willing to acknowledge that my first impression of her all those months ago was *that* far off base.

"You know," she starts, "I've always wondered what it would feel like to cut off a man's testicles."

He jerks again, but she shifts her weight, her pointy heel digging into his foot until he groans from the pain. His hands tense at his sides, but even he isn't stupid enough to try anything while she has a sharp blade against his dick.

She tilts her head. "Should I try it on you?"

"Evie, come on. Don't lose it right now." His voice is strained. "Your dad will kill me if I have to hurt you."

"Lose it? I'm not *losing* anything," she says, glancing over at me. "People seem to think I have problems with impulse control. Can you believe that?"

She laughs, and I'm frozen, stuck halfway in my seat and halfway to standing, the burning in my thighs nothing close to the panic swirling through my middle and surging to my throat.

Liam's eyes flick to me, and I…I don't know what the fuck to do. I should stop whatever this is—the *right* thing to do is to stop it—but the other part of me, perhaps the more vindictive part, wants to let it play out. Stepping in is a risk. One that I can't afford to take.

"Oh no," she coos to Liam. "Brayden can't help you. He's assured me that he's incredibly adept at following directions." Her hand presses the letter opener farther into Liam's crotch. "Isn't that right, pup?"

He whimpers.

"Apologize," she demands.

"I'm sorry," he rasps.

She tsks. "Just like a man. Giving the bare minimum and expecting us to be satisfied. Say it like you mean it, Liam, and maybe you won't leave this room a eunuch."

He gulps. "I'm sor-sorry, Evie. I was wrong. I won't disrespect you again."

She reaches up and pats his cheek twice. "Good boy."

When she lets him go, she spins around and moves away quickly, not bothering to keep her eyes on him, like she's completely confident he won't seek retribution at her back.

My eyes, however, don't leave him for a second. Just to make sure.

He doesn't. He just clears his throat and adjusts his rumpled clothing as he straightens from the wall.

Walking back toward the desk, she flips the letter opener through her fingers, flashing me a grin. Liam and I are stone silent, and it doesn't take long for her to notice.

She cackles and I swear no other sound has ever sent a chill through me quite like it.

"Oh, calm down. I was only kidding. It's like you said, Liam. I'm only here to do Dad's books. I'll leave the 'business' up to you big, strong men." Her eyes flick to my bandaged wrist. "You clearly handle it so well."

She grins again, that same thin smile with no teeth and blazing eyes that she always gives, and I realize then that Evelina Westerly is *not* one of the good guys.

And she absolutely cannot be saved.

CHAPTER 10

Evelina

I'VE BEEN THINKING CONSTANTLY ABOUT HOW I snapped on Liam—in front of Brayden—two nights ago. It was stupid of me, and now Brayden looks at me differently.

Where before he was quick to follow, irritating me with his smirk and his stupid questions, now he keeps his distance.

Considering I don't like him anyway, it doesn't bother me.

What *bothers* me is the fact that he's practically moved in and become another extension of the Westerly family. I thought he was supposed to be some jewelry expert, but now he's just always around, hanging out with Ezekiel or whispering things into my sister's ear, and when he isn't with either of them, he's doing runs for my dad, collecting dues from businesses or helping keep our low-level dealers in line. It's like he went from being someone to consult with to just another henchman.

My father seems to have zero issues trusting him, which, quite frankly, blows my fucking mind, because my dad is notoriously paranoid. He always has been, and that increased tenfold when he got out of the pen and realized Nessa had changed the landscape of our name where he failed the first time around. He's hesitant to bring on new people or partners and even more protective of who gets direct access to him. And to Dorothy.

Which is why I end up doing everything that involves more than a simple thought process.

So there's something off-putting about the way he's allowed a complete stranger into his fold. I know Ezekiel vouched for him, and it's not that I don't trust Ezekiel's word, but I don't trust others, and Brayden could be lying to Ezekiel just as easily as the rest of us.

I'm in the back room of the greenhouse, protective gear on, my goggles over my eyes and a KN95 mask over my face, when my phone rings.

I almost don't answer, but at the last second, for some reason, I rip off the yellow glove on my hand and snatch it up.

"I'm busy," I hiss into the phone, setting it on speaker and placing it on the table. I stare at the fifty-five-gallon oil drum across the room sitting on a steel platform with a burner underneath.

"Okay, but I've got that info you wanted," Cody says. "Guess I'll call back later."

"Wait."

He chuckles. "Shit, you're eager. What are you doing anyway?"

I sigh, walking over to the oil drum, pressing a button to start the fire underneath, and then I move back toward the table and cross my arms. "I'm making sure he's trustworthy since no one else in my family seems to give a shit."

"Well, he checks out."

My brows rise. "He does?"

Bending over, I pick up the fifteen kilograms of raw opium I bled from the seed pods, my muscles aching as I carry it toward the drum and drop it in the heating water.

"Yep. Brayden Walsh. Born thirty-two years ago in Chicago to a single mom who died from cancer when he was eighteen. No other relatives."

"Interesting," I murmur, although I'm sure Cody can't hear me.

"Probably for the best. Not many families would be proud of the rap sheet he's racked up. It's honestly kind of impressive."

Smirking, I walk back toward my phone and move the mask down to my neck. "Or embarrassing to be caught so many times."

"True. But he either keeps his crimes petty or he's not bad enough to get caught for the big ones. He's never spent more than a few months behind bars."

I run my tongue ring against the back of my lip. "So that's it? Nothing seemed…off or weird?"

"Nope. You know, Evie, not everyone is out to get you. One day maybe you'll realize that."

My chest pulls.

Honestly, I thought I'd feel relieved that Brayden is who he says he is. After all, it means that he isn't lying to my family. But on the other hand, it makes me irrationally angry he lied to me when we first met. Like *I* was the desperate one.

He doesn't have much, but he does have the fucking audacity.

"Hmm."

"What's that mean?" Cody asks.

"That means 'hmm,' Cody. It doesn't always have to mean something."

"Why do you sound so muffled?" he continues. "I don't know where you always are that has your phone breaking up like this, but honest to god, your cell service sucks."

My muscles tighten, annoyed that I answered the phone in the first place. It's times like these where I wish we hadn't wired the greenhouse with technology, because I'd give *anything* to be out of contact completely while I'm here. He's always prying. Asking questions that I don't want to give him answers for. My greenhouse and what I do in it is my biggest secret, and it's not one I'm willing to share, even with him.

"I told you, I'm busy."

Reaching over, I press End Call before he can say anything else and slide my fingers back into the yellow glove, letting the rubber snap against my skin. I move back to the oil drum, grabbing the stick I use to stir and drop it in the boiling water, swirling it around.

Out of all the things I do for my dad, this is my favorite. It takes skill and precision to create heroin, and even more so when you've crafted a flawless process that yields a drug so pure no one else can match it.

I mastered the art when I was just a kid, back when Nessa was in charge, tired of watching her get shitty deals from shitty men who treated her differently because she had a vagina. And while Nessa was a lot of things, my mentor and my best friend, she was too soft-spoken when it mattered. She didn't make people *fear* her enough, and as a result, she got manhandled.

But when she failed, I learned.

And when our dad got out of the pen, he realized he had a gold mine at his fingertips. Spent three years building this underground greenhouse for me and we've never looked back. Well, *he's* never looked back.

A thick knot surges into my throat, the grief rising like a tidal wave and threatening to capsize my control. My gloved fingers grip the rod until they feel like they'll shatter. I close my eyes and count back.

Ten. Nine. Eight…

Blowing out a slow breath, I peel open my lids, ignoring the sharp burn behind my nose as I swallow down the pain. Slowly but surely, it dies down, allowing me to shove it in the dark where I can keep it hidden, even from myself.

CHAPTER 11

Nicholas

FARRELL SITS DOWN IN HIS HOME OFFICE, HIS woodsy aftershave so strong it wafts across his desk and settles in my nose without even breathing.

His silver hair is slicked back, longer on the top and cropped short on the sides, and he's staring at me with dark, calculating eyes, his tattooed fingers running along the bottom of his jaw. He's swiveling back and forth in his chair just slightly. Over and over again, he repeats the motion, a creaking sound imitating the clicking of a clock.

This is a common tactic. The silence. The staring. The contemplation while I sit in the hot seat and wait for whatever it is he called me in here to say. It's all meant to intimidate, but none of it's worth a damn. You need to fear someone for their tactics to work, and while it's undeniable that Farrell Westerly is a dangerous person, I'm not scared of him.

He should fear *me*.

So if he wants to sit here in silence, I'm game. He won't respect someone who cowers before him, and if I'm to gain his trust, I need his respect.

I cross my leg over the opposite knee and tap my fingers on the arm of the chair, waiting patiently until he's had enough.

Finally, he speaks.

"I heard about what you did to Antonio Cantanelli." He steeples his fingers beneath his chin. "You got anything to say to me about that?"

"Yeah, I should have hit him harder." I shrug.

Farrell's lips twitch. "You know, he's the little cousin of one of the capos for the Cantanellis. You could cause me a lotta shit by running around and making them bleed."

"All due respect, Skip…you walk around letting people, regardless of who they are, sell you fake rocks and disrespect you in your own club? That don't sit right with me."

"No?" he asks.

"No. Fuck that guy. He should be kissing your feet for not putting a bullet in his dome the second you realized what he did. And I'm not an idiot, regardless of what your goon Liam may think." Leaning forward, I rest my elbows on my knees, maintaining our eye contact so he knows how serious I am. "I weigh the options of everything I do. Antonio Cantanelli, an Italian, in *your* club?" I shake my head. "He ain't no problem. His cousin would kill him first for stepping foot in Kinland."

His brows rise and a grin cracks across his face. "You gotta lotta brass, kid. I like it."

He stands up, walking around the desk and resting against the lip, his hands sliding into the pockets of his gray suit pants. He pulls out a Black & Mild and slips it into his mouth, grabbing a matchbox from the corner of his desk and lighting the end. The smell permeates the room immediately, making my stomach turn.

I fucking *hate* that smell. It reminds me of my mom's

boyfriend and all the shitty memories that come with him. The man never went anywhere without a Black & Mild dangling from his pockmarked mouth.

"You remember Evie?" he asks, staring down at the lit match.

My heart jolts, the nausea growing stronger. *Wish I never did.*

"Briefly. Not really a social bird, is she?" I grin.

He chuckles, blowing out a cloud of smoke. "She's a different breed, that's for sure. Nothing like my Dorothy. But when it comes down to it…no one else I'd rather have by my side than her."

My brows lift, and my muscles tighten, anticipation making my nerves sing. I'm not sure what he's about to say, but whatever it is feels important.

"That good of a daughter, huh?" I joke.

His tongue runs over his teeth as he stares at the cigar. "I don't know if those are the words I'd use." He taps his temple, ash dropping to the floor. "She's smart as hell. The most stubborn woman you'll ever meet, but those brains she's got? As good as gold."

I sit forward. "You got her running shit around here?"

His gaze sharpens and he snaps his head up to me.

My stomach flips. *Stupid question. Too nosy.*

"She does whatever the fuck I tell her to do." He points at me. "And so do you. You work for me now, understand? No more of this petty theft bullshit. I can give you money. *Real* money…but you gotta do business my way. That means I say jump, you ask how high."

I nod, swallowing. This is exactly what I need.

"And calm down on the fucking questions. Jesus, you're like my mother, may she rest in peace."

I smile. "My bad, Skip. I've got an inquisitive personality."

He grunts, puffing on his cigar again, then moving to scratch his bushy eyebrow. "Evie's doing rounds the next few weeks for me, taking over some errands while my usual guy is out."

My insides jump in genuine surprise. *He's having Evelina doing runs?*

He purses his lips. "You'll go with her. Be her muscle, have her back, and continue learning the ropes at the same time. Got it?"

Dread sinks into my stomach, even though this is exactly what we've been waiting for.

It's just ever since she snapped on Liam, I've done my best to avoid her. I have no room for a distraction like her, and she fucks with my head. Physically, I've never wanted to throw someone down and fill them with my cock more, but mentally, she fills *me* with disgust.

I will never understand how someone can be so embroiled with putting drugs on the streets and sleep peacefully at night.

Fucking filthy street rats, all of them.

But going out on errands is exactly what I need to be doing to gather information. So while originally we thought Dorothy was my in, maybe it's Evelina instead. And I'll have to do whatever it takes to come to terms with that.

"Get in and shut up," Evelina says as she walks by me, her flowy black skirt swishing at her knees and those same knee-high boots on her feet.

"How can you even drive in those?" I ask, sliding into the passenger side of her Range Rover.

She sighs, running a hand down her face. "Shutting up usually includes less speaking and more silence."

I reach over, clicking the seat belt across my chest. "I have the right to ask questions. You're in charge of my life right now."

She scoffs.

"I'm serious. What if we crash because your tiny feet in those ridiculous eighteen-inch heels can't feel the pedals?"

"They're six inches." Her eyes drift to my lap as she starts the car. "But I'm not surprised you'd exaggerate."

"I think we both know I don't need to stretch the truth, sweetheart."

She laughs. "Sure."

"What's that mean?" I frown.

She stays silent, her eyes on the road as she pulls out of the long drive, ignoring the security guards at the gate, and turns onto the main road.

Irritation sticks my insides like mosquitoes.

Who the fuck has she been with that's bigger than me?

"Don't think too hard. You'll hurt yourself," she quips.

"Where are we going anyway?" I change the subject, resting my arm against the car door.

"None of your business."

"Your dad seems to think it's my business."

She side-eyes me. "Yeah, well, my dad isn't known for his decision-making skills."

I lean in. "Then what *is* he known for?"

"Fishing for information again, stalker? What are you, a cop?"

The words wrap around my neck like a noose and I slam back in my seat. "I'm just making conversation, *Christ*."

"Well, stop."

I don't respond, taking some time to watch her as she drives, my eyes soaking in her features, the dark eyeliner and long lashes doing nothing but highlighting the almost perfect bone structure of her cheeks. Her hair is thrown in a messy bun and her black tank top stretches tight against her breasts. *Goddamn, she's beautiful.*

"You do this often for your dad?"

She peeks at me. "I do it enough."

I nod toward her outfit. "Why the skirt? Not really the best attire for dealing with drug dealers and coercing money from shops."

Her jaw clenches. "Worry about yourself."

Chuckling, I shake my head. "You're so uptight. I think you need to get fucked again. How long has it been?"

She doesn't respond, but I don't miss the way her knuckles whiten around the steering wheel.

Satisfaction teases my middle and I quirk a brow. "Was it *me*?"

She snorts. "Don't flatter yourself."

"I'm just asking." I throw my hands up, palms facing her.

"It's painfully predictable that you'd expect my emotions to be tied to whether I have a dick inside me."

I shrug, grinning. "Just working off experience, sweetheart."

"Quit calling me that. I am *not* your sweetheart." She tightens her grip on the wheel.

"Ever heard of manifestation?" I retort. "You gotta speak things into existence. Maybe if I say it enough, you'll stop being such a bitch."

The car rolls to a stop and she turns to look at me, those brown eyes sucking me in like a vortex. "So that's it then?" She licks her lips. "You think I should find another man who can throw me up against a bathroom wall and fuck me until I scream?"

My abdomen clenches and my mouth dries. "Couldn't hurt," I somehow manage to rasp.

Her gaze flicks down. "No, I agree. Definitely couldn't *hurt*."

My eyes narrow, but I don't speak again, not wanting to give her more ammunition to hurt my pride. I can't tell if she's just being catty or if she's trying to tell me something, and either way, I don't feel like playing her games anymore.

The car gets quiet, nothing but the simmering irritation lingering in the air between us. It allows me time to get lost in my thoughts, watching the streets zoom by as we drive, memorizing the layout in case it's somewhere I'll need to know for later.

Before long, we pull up to a small group of buildings in the main strip of Kinland, parking directly in front of Anderson's, a sub shop.

"You strapped?" she asks.

My stomach tightens, and I glance at her, lifting a brow along with the hem of my shirt. Her eyes drop to where a sliver of my stomach shows and continues her trek down until she sees the gun holstered at the waistband of my pants. I hate how good it feels to have her eyes on me.

She swallows and turns off the car, her arm barely brushing against my chest as she reaches over the console and opens the glove compartment.

A whiff of something floral and earthy hits my nose, and my cock jerks. I grit my teeth, disgusted at my body's reaction. *Get it the fuck together.*

She pulls out a rose-gold Desert Eagle, and my eyes widen as I watch her caress it lovingly.

"Big gun for such a little girl."

"You know, you really have an obsession with size." She pulls back the slide to chamber a round. "Wonder why that is?"

She grabs the bottom of her black skirt, sliding it up her flawless skin. My veins heat and my stomach cramps as she exposes her leg inch by torturous inch. I want to look away, know I *should* look away, but I'm transfixed as she continues to lift until a thigh holster appears.

I swallow a groan. *Fucking hell.*

She slips her gun into its place before dropping the skirt back down and smoothing her hands over the fabric. "To answer your earlier question, skirts allow easy access." She looks up at me. "But you know that already, remember?"

Flashes of me pushing her skirt up around her hips and sinking into her race through me, and I bite the inside of my cheek, my cock now so hard it aches.

Before I can even formulate a thought, she opens the door and hops out.

"Come on, stalker. Let's go get our dues."

CHAPTER 12

Evelina

BENNY ANDERSON IS A SHORT MAN WITH AN attitude. He thinks because he's lived in Kinland for the majority of his life, that means he runs the place and everyone in it. Out of all the people we deal with on the streets, he's by far the worst. But he *does* have connections and he *is* one of our middlemen, the guy all our low-level drug dealers grab their inventory from and pay their dues to.

The fewer people who have direct contact with us, the better.

Normally, I'm not the one even doing these pickups. But when there's a need, here I am, and the fact that Benny's last drop was short fifteen grand creates the *need* for a special visit.

My gut pinches as we walk inside Anderson's sub shop, the weight of my Desert Eagle heavy where it sits against my thigh. I glance over at Brayden, irritation twitching beneath the surface of my skin at just the sight of him. I really, *really* don't want him here.

In all honesty, I wanted this to be a solo gig. I don't need muscle to back me up, and if there's going to be some, I'd rather have Ezekiel at my side. I'm not fully convinced Brayden wouldn't use me as a shield to protect himself instead.

Brayden whips by me as we walk, cutting in front of me to grab the door first. He grips the handle and yanks it open, the bell above the door jingling. For just a moment, I think he's showing chivalry, holding it open for me to walk through, but when I step forward, he lets go, slamming the door in my face.

Asshole.

I fling my foot out, wedging it in the crack before it shuts completely, and grab the knob, stepping inside. Brayden's already in the center of the room, ignoring me completely.

The smell of deli meat is strong and it makes my stomach churn. As I walk through the room, I meet the eyes of patrons scattered throughout the various small white circular tables, not missing the way they all avert their stares, taking small glimpses when they think I'm not paying attention.

Holding my head high, I push my shoulders back and step up to the front register, next to where Brayden's already lounging against the counter.

He crosses his arms, staring out at the room, the muscle in his jaw pulsing. "Why are they looking at you like that?"

I glance behind me, ignoring the way my palms start to sweat when I wonder what they're thinking. Nothing good, I'm sure. "What other people think of me is none of my business."

He makes a face, twisting toward me and lifting a brow. "That sounds like something someone says when they care *too* much." He moves closer to me. "You don't care what I think about you?"

"I'd rather you didn't think of me at all."

He grins, that stupid boyish smile that lights up his eyes and shows the obnoxiously perfect dimples in his cheeks. "So you *do* care."

"Do you ever shut up?" I snap, slamming my hand on the little bell.

"Do you ever stop being such a bitch?" he hits back.

I grind my teeth as I stare up at the blackboard menu written in dark-green chalk.

"What can I get you?" a spritely voice asks.

I look back down, seeing the fresh face of a young girl, her eyes flicking from me to the gnat at my side, cheeks flushing slightly when they linger on Brayden.

Something pinches in my chest.

"Where's Benny?" I ask.

"Oh," she says, her blond brows scrunching. "I'm not, uh, I'm not sure if he's available."

"I didn't ask if he was available. I asked where he was."

Her customer service grin drops and my stomach tightens, knowing she's about to piss me off. She opens her mouth, but before she speaks, Brayden cuts in, resting an elbow on the table and leaning toward her. "What's your name?"

Her smile reblooms like a flower in the sun. "Amanda."

"Really?" He tilts his head, his gaze obviously scanning the length of her body. "Suits you."

Her grin widens, and my chest burns.

"And blond too?" His eyes flick to me as he places a palm over his heart. "My weakness."

I narrow my gaze.

"Listen, I'm sure you can tell that *this one*"—he points his thumb in my direction—"isn't the most pleasant person to be around. And the faster we see Benny, the quicker I can get rid of her."

My brows shoot to my hairline and I cross my arms.

"So if you could just go find him and let him know Evelina Westerly is here, you'd really be helping me out." He winks. "Free me up faster for better things."

The blush staining her cheeks is painful and disgustingly predictable.

"Su-sure," she stutters. "Let me go find him."

"Chop-chop." I clap my hands, watching her spin around and disappear down the deli line into the back rooms. My mood is souring considerably with every second we're here. "Hey, stalker, do me a favor?"

He steps closer and licks his lips, his gaze dropping to my cleavage. "Depends on the favor."

Grinding my teeth, I step into him, placing my foot between the two of his. "Don't *ever* speak for me again."

He smirks and bends slightly until our eyes lock. "Maybe if you were better at getting things done, I wouldn't have to."

Fire ignites in the center of my chest and pummels outward, burning everything in its path. My fists clench, a sharp sting radiating through my palms from the way my nails press into them. "I will fucking kill you."

He laughs. "Oh, *sweetheart*. I'd love to see you try."

A throat clears, and we both jump back, my insides feeling like burned remnants and blazing embers. And it's only then I realize how close we were and how *everyone* in the shop is staring our way.

"Um," the girl starts. "Benny's in the back office."

I blow out a deep breath, pasting a smile on my face.

"I can sho—"

"I know the way," I cut her off. "Come on," I say to Brayden as I walk away.

When we make it to the back office, I kick open the ajar door with my foot, relishing in the jump Benny makes from behind his old scratched-up desk. There're papers stacked up to his elbows and grease stains coating his off-white shirt.

"Hiya, Benny." I smile. "Weren't avoiding me, were you?"

"Nope." He shakes his head. "I'd never do that, Evelina." He focuses behind me, his Adam's apple bobbing with his harsh swallow. "Who's the new guy?"

"Don't look at him." I move toward him, slipping my right hand beneath my skirt to unholster my gun. I lay it on the desk, my fingers locked around it. "Look at me."

His eyes grow round, small beads of sweat percolating on his hairline.

"Benny," I coo. "You know what it means when my father sends me, right?"

He swallows again. "Listen, I don't know what you're here for. I dropped the bands last night with Liam."

I click my tongue, sighing. "You really want things to be this way?"

Straightening, I walk around the desk, keeping my eyes on him the entire time. I don't stop until I'm standing directly next to him. He swivels in his chair until he's facing me.

I bring up my gun and press it against his temple. "Where's the rest of it, Benny?"

He wipes his forehead with the back of his hand and grunts. "Listen, Evelina. I just know what the guys gave me—"

Groaning, I move my hand, bringing it back before striking it down across his face.

"*Fuck!*" he cries, blood spattering on his scattered papers.

"Jesus, Evelina," Brayden says.

I peer at him when I realize he's moving toward us, and whatever he sees makes him pause midstep. Does he have a weak stomach for violence? Not that it matters. If he wants to annoy me by being around, then he can watch while I handle things. Maybe he'll learn something. I wouldn't say I enjoy doing things like this, but I don't feel particularly strong one way or another, and I can't stand disrespect. And right now, Benny is disrespecting me.

I look back down at Benny, pushing the barrel of my Eagle against his head again. "I don't want to have to hurt you, Benny. But I *really* don't enjoy people questioning my intelligence. So here's what we'll do. Either give me the money, or I'll give you five seconds to visualize your wife and kids before I blow your fucking brains out all over their family picture."

Benny's breathing is ragged, and the sound of that combined with the drops of his blood pooling beneath his mouth and on the desk is enough to make me twitch.

I tap the toe of my boot against the tile. "I wouldn't look past my generosity. Not many others in my position would be so kind."

I'm bluffing. It would be stupid for me to kill him right now when there are so many witnesses around the shop. But he doesn't need to know that.

"Fine. *Fine*, fuck!" He sits up straight, glaring over at me.

I smile, pulling back my gun but keeping it aimed at his face.

"Look, I don't know where the money is, okay? I gave you what I got from the idiots peddling your shit on the streets. But I've got some here to make up the difference."

He reaches down and starts to key in a code for the small safe under his desk, but I lift my leg quickly, pressing the heel of my boot into the crotch of his pants, my gun once again pressed to his temple. "Give *him* the numbers." I nod toward Brayden.

He does.

Brayden stares between the two of us, and he walks over, crouching down while he enters the code to unlock the door.

There are stacks of cash filling up the entire safe and a few manila folders.

Brayden looks up at me, grabbing the black bag that's folded up and tucked into the side. "How much are we taking?"

I smile wide. "All of it."

"Evelina, *please*," Benny pleads. "I got kids. Mouths to feed."

Nodding, I move my gun until the side slides down his cheek like a cold caress. "I know." Pulling back my hand again, I bring it forward, smashing my Eagle into his cheek one last time. "I just don't fucking care."

CHAPTER 13

Nicholas

IT'S JUST EVELINA AND ME IN THE BASEMENT OF the Yellow Brick. We're sitting at a long, heavy oak table with a pile of dirty cash on one side, bundled cash on the other, and a money counter right in the middle.

Evelina is currently taking handfuls of the unbound money and funneling them through the machine. The flipping of the dollars creates a buzzing noise similar to a fan in a quiet room, and despite what I witnessed just a few hours earlier, I feel calm.

And so does she. She seems normal. Completely in control. Which is so different from how she was a few hours ago with Benny.

How can someone so fucking beautiful be so goddamn bad?

"Stop staring at me."

I push my chair off the ground with my heels, balancing on the back two legs. "I'm just surprised, that's all."

She glances up at me. "About what?"

"This." I wave my arm around the room.

She laughs. "You, the jewel thief, are surprised by piles of cash?"

"No," I say, shaking my head. "I'm surprised you're so involved. And so *violent*. You should probably see someone about that."

Her brows draw down as the counter spits out another stack. She bands it, then places it to the side. "Surprised because I'm a woman?"

"No, because you're *you*."

I don't even know what I mean by that statement, which isn't wholly shocking considering I can't figure out how the hell I feel. I fucked this woman. I'm insanely attracted to her despite her being unhinged, but I can't correlate the woman I pictured her as when we first met with who she is now. Because *now*, she's who I'm fighting against. She's part of the problem I'm trying to fix.

She pauses, placing a handful of cash back in the unbound pile. Her tongue flicks out, the metal barbell skimming across her lower lip as she stares.

My stomach jolts.

"Well, this *is* me."

"Unfortunately," I mutter.

"What's that supposed to mean?" She tilts her head.

I shrug, knowing I shouldn't prod her but not being able to stop myself. "Just means maybe your sister was right."

Her jaw clenches. "My sister knows *nothing* about me."

"At least she knows how to treat people."

"Great. Go bother her then."

I grin. "Am I annoying you, sweetheart?"

She slams her hands on the table, making everything shake, and she shoves back her chair to stand. She leans in, her breasts spilling from the top of her shirt, and my gaze drops, because I can't *not* take advantage of the view when she's so willing to offer it up.

A flush creeps along her collarbone and scores up her neck, the way it always does when I make her angry.

My cock pulses.

"I am not your fucking sweetheart," she says through clenched teeth. "And for the record, *everything* about you annoys me. The way you walk. The way you constantly show up any place I am. The way you ask question after question yet never seem to have a single answer."

My lips tilt up.

She points a finger. "Those stupid fucking dimples on your cheeks."

The smile grows. I drop the front legs of my chair back down and rest my elbows on the table, propping my chin in my hand. "Give it to me, baby. What else?"

"I hate the way you stare at me," she continues.

I'm half paying attention, my mind too busy wondering how far the blush on her chest goes and what else I could do to make her flush so pink.

"And—" She raises her voice. "You're a liar."

The amusement washes away at her words and now it's me pushing into a stand, my fists pressing against the table. "I am *not* a liar."

"Please," she scoffs. "All you've ever done is lie to me."

I groan, pinching the bridge of my nose. "Here we fucking go. Is this because of the name thing?"

"It's because of your general existence."

"Sweetheart," I sigh. "I didn't think it mattered."

She slaps her hands against the wood again. "I told you not to call me that."

I chuckle, imagining how satisfying it would be to reach out and strangle her, just to shut her the fuck up. For some reason, whenever she's around, the violence I always force to come out when I'm Brayden happens naturally. She *inspires* the anger. "And I told *you* that I'm not your bitch."

The blaze in her eyes is so intense I swear it soars across the air and sinks into my skin until I'm burning from the inside out.

She smirks. "Debatable."

One second I'm thinking about how much I want to choke the brat out of her, and the next I am, my hand shooting across the table and wrapping around her neck.

She sucks in a sharp breath but doesn't fight me, the man she claims to hate so much.

The man who's *supposed* to hate her.

And that pisses me off even more, because I do hate her. I can't fucking *stand* who this girl is. I would give anything to reach inside her and pull out the woman I met that night at the club.

She's the one I'm interested in, the one I'm dying to see.

And when Evelina moves in close, elongating her neck as if she wants me to mark her with my prints, I think maybe I've found her.

But then she purses her lips and spits.

Wet saliva sprays across my cheek and drips down my face, severing the last thread of my sanity. I snap forward, my free arm swiping across the table, the sound of cash and the money counter crashing to the floor muted from the pounding in my ears. I wrap my hand around her waist, dragging her roughly onto the table-top and slamming my mouth to hers.

I don't think about how this is inappropriate. How she stands for everything I'm against. How I'm the villain of her story as surely as she is mine.

And I definitely don't consider the wire hidden around my neck, catching everything as it happens.

My tongue dives into her mouth, searching for the hint of metal, and when I find it, the small ball of her piercing massaging against me, a shock wave rolls through my body.

My hand tightens around her throat, her pulse beating against my skin.

She moans, her talon-like nails digging into the back of my neck, and my cock throbs, pressing against the front of my jeans.

I move my lips across her jaw and down her neck, using my thumb to tilt her head back and give myself more room. She scoots forward, her knees sliding on the few loose hundred-dollar bills that are beneath her, and she reaches out, popping the button on my pants and slipping her warm hand inside. She grips me tight, and I jolt in her palm when she strokes me from the base all the way to the tip. Precum oozes from the head and she swipes her fingertips over it, using it to lubricate her motions on the way back down.

"Fuck," I rasp against her.

"Shut up," she snips, bringing her mouth close to kiss me again.

My chest heats at how she's always fucking *disrespecting* me, and I grip her throat tighter, slamming her down on the table until she's flat against it. Cash flies from the edges and flutters to the ground, the sudden movement making her grip slacken from where it's wrapped around my cock.

She yelps, her eyes flaring, but before she can say another word, I'm on her, my hand moving from her neck up to her jaw. "You and that fucking mouth."

I press a kiss to her swollen lips, my other hand sliding along her chest until her tit is in my hand. My thumb runs over the hardened peak, hiding beneath the fabric. She tries to speak, but I press my fingers against her cheeks until I feel the indent of her teeth. "I'm getting real tired of you walking all over me. *Spitting* on me. Pretending like I hurt you when we both know you don't really care. And I'm done playing nice."

Her lips part, and I take the opportunity, collecting saliva on my tongue and letting it drip down into her open mouth.

I expect her to rage. In fact, my grip on her strengthens, anticipation lighting up my insides at how she'll react.

But she only grins and swallows.

My balls tighten, blood rushing to my dick until it's throbbing so stiff I'm worried I might come.

She moves her hand up the length again, moaning. "That gets you off, doesn't it? I can feel you getting harder."

"Yeah?" I bite my lip. "You gonna do something about it, pretty girl?"

She pushes up on her elbow, her messy bun halfway falling out so it's lopsided on her head, and squeezes me one more time before she removes her touch completely. Leaning in, she presses a kiss to my lips. "I want you to get down on your knees and lick my pussy like a good pup."

My insides flare at the command, but I don't argue, the overwhelming need to have her overriding any sense of authority she may be stripping me of. My hands coast down her body until they reach the hem of her skirt and slip underneath, gliding back up her supple skin until they hit the holsters on both sides of her legs. An image of her naked with nothing but her gun strapped to her flashes through my mind, and I groan at the vision.

Pressing my fingers into her skin, I move my face back to

hers, pressing kisses along her cheek until I reach her ear. "Don't tell me what to do."

And then I move, gripping the meat of her thighs and pulling, her body sliding down the table harshly, sending more cash fluttering to the ground.

Her skirt is bunched at her hips and she's wearing white cotton panties that have a damp spot in the center. The air leaves my lungs in a whoosh at the sight. It's such a dichotomy: simple white underwear hidden beneath layers of black and gallons of bitch.

"Don't just stare at it." Her hands press on the back of my head.

Pressing my thumb into the wet spot, I undo my jeans the rest of the way to free my cock enough so I can grip it in my palm. "Goddamn, you're wet. Soaking through your panties all for me?"

I stroke my shaft, pinpricks of pleasure skittering along my spine at the sensation, and then I grab the fabric of her underwear and pull, ripping them off her in one fluid motion.

She moans and I dive in immediately, because if I don't get to taste her *right now*, I might fucking die.

My tongue swipes up the length of her slit, collecting the wetness seeping from her core, and I groan at the musky taste. *Perfect.* My hand slips up her body until it's pressing against her stomach to hold her in place, and I start to feast, swirling around her hole and up to her sensitive bundle of nerves. Her clit throbs against the flat of my tongue, and the thought of me turning her on turns *me* on, so I suck it into my mouth, bringing up my hand and dipping a finger inside her at the same time.

She's so wet, I slide in easily, and I start a repetitive motion, fucking her with my fingers and gorging on her pussy until she's gasping beneath me.

"Oh god," she whispers, her elbows dropping until she's flat on her back again.

Her thighs tense around my head, her back arching off the table. I release her clit and look up at her, my cock dripping from the sight of her heaving chest and eyes blissed out in pleasure—pleasure that *I* caused.

"Give it to me, pretty girl. Show me how fucking filthy you are coming around the fingers of the man you claim to hate."

She does, immediately. Spectacularly.

Her legs shake and she lets out a loud moan, her pussy pulsing as she rides out her orgasm. I lap her up like milk, so fucking ready to sink my cock inside her and break her from the inside out.

I continue to work her through her comedown and she laughs when I suck her into my mouth one more time, her hands pushing at my shoulders. "Stop, it's sensitive."

Smiling, something warm tumbles around in my chest, and I work my way back up her body, pressing kisses to her thighs, over her covered stomach until I hit her chest. My cock presses between her legs, nudging at her entrance.

Her legs wrap around my hips, pulling me in closer. My head slips through her slick cunt and sends a tendril of pleasure spiking through my dick and into my balls. Gripping the base of my shaft, I slide myself through her folds, tapping the tip of my cock on her needy clit, reveling in the way her body jolts from the touch.

"Fuck me," she whispers.

I allow the tip of my cock to slide in, just the tiniest bit. "Tell me what I want to hear."

She quirks a brow.

I lick the shell of her ear, a shiver coasting down her body.

"Tell me I'm the biggest cock you've ever had."

"Oh my *god*, did that really—"

Grinning, I slam inside her midsentence, her words cutting off with the heavy breath that escapes her lungs. I close my eyes, the sensation of her pussy gripping me so perfectly making my balls draw up and heat collect at the base of my spine.

Starting a steady rhythm, I get lost in the feeling of being inside her again. She threads her fingers through my hair and starts to move her hips from underneath me, causing her clit to grind against my pelvis. I press in harder, wanting—needing—to feel her come around my cock.

"Fuck, you feel good."

Her eyes flare and she tightens her legs, removing her fingers from my hair and pushing at my chest. I ease up, allowing my dick to leave her as she flips us, my head landing on the pile of money at the top of the table.

She straddles me, her knee-high boots suddenly the sexiest thing I've ever fucking seen as she slides back down my shaft, every inch of her cunt swallowing me perfectly until we're flush together.

"*Christ*," I murmur, my hands gripping her hips so tight, I'm sure they'll bruise.

The material of her thigh holsters rubs against my skin, creating a friction burn as she works me fast and hard. She moves herself back and forth, then bounces up and down. My eyes drink up the vision of her above me, her hair mussed, skin flushed, and eyes glazed. Suddenly, I can't stand the thought of not touching her *everywhere*, and my fingers run up her stomach until I'm cupping her breasts, rolling her nipples beneath my fingers. Her movements stutter and I pinch them. *Hard.*

A gush of wetness soaks my lap and she throws her head

back, her fingers creating crescent-shaped marks in my abdomen as she rides me.

Her hand disappears under her skirt and I'm about to protest until I feel the warmth of her fingers caressing my balls while she grinds down on my lap. My entire body shivers.

I tweak her nipples again, then move one hand up, gripping the bun that's only half left on her head and wrenching it back, tugging on the strands harshly.

She moans, her pussy walls spasming around me, making my eyes roll back.

"Come for me again, pretty girl. I want to feel you drench my cock."

Her other hand lifts her skirt, giving me the exceptional view of my dick disappearing inside her, and she starts rubbing at her swollen clit, her mouth parting.

That plus the steady motion of her caressing my balls is my point of no return. The tension snaps just as her walls contract around me, and I shatter into a thousand pieces, shooting deep inside her. One pulse, two, three…she rides me through every single spurt until my limbs go numb and my vision goes white.

Finally she slows before moving off me completely, my cum and her wetness mixing together and dripping down my slick and sated cock.

It takes a few moments for me to catch my breath, and I turn my face to watch her—to say *something*—although I have no clue what.

But her eyes are already hardened into stone.

My chest twists, but I brush it off, not knowing what it means. I smile softly, the echo of whatever just happened pinging off the hollow chambers of my heart. "That quick, huh?"

"Obviously, this was a mistake," she replies.

Nodding, I move to a sitting position, my pulse still racing. "Yeah, whatever you say, sweetheart."

I slide from the table and reach down to grab my jeans, pulling them on and fastening them.

"You know..." I start, looking back up.

But it's no use, because she's already gone.

CHAPTER 14

Evelina

QUADS CEMETERY IS ABOUT A FORTY-FIVE-MINUTE drive from the estate, and every Sunday after Mass, I go there without fail. No one ever bothers to come along, and while part of me is content because I don't need to share my time, the other part is disgusted that nobody seems to care.

The second Nessa was gone, everyone moved on as if she wasn't there in the first place. A used-up toy that gets thrown in the garbage and forgotten. Dorothy was happier than ever, of course, always prancing around and putting on a sad face to play the part of a grieving sister. But her life improved exponentially with Nessa out of the way. She became the oldest and, with Dad out of prison, the apple of his eye. She's always been jealous and bitter.

Normally, I sit through service, then dip out before Sunday dinner at the house, but today, with Brayden sitting two aisles away, I needed an escape.

Needed a reminder of my goals and *why* I have them in the first place. He has this way about him of always distracting me.

Making me lose sight of what I need to do. It happened that night at the club when he fucked me up against the bathroom wall and then again last night.

A sharp stab of arousal smarts between my legs from the memory.

Fallen leaves crunch beneath my shoes as I walk through the graveyard, a mix of headstones lining the way. I stop in front of Nessa's, the gray marble dulled from thin layers of grime, and I place the small bouquet of red roses I picked up from a street vendor at its base.

"Hey, Ness," I murmur.

I reach forward, running my fingers along the engraved letters of her name, *Vanessa Esther Westerly*, wishing I could wipe away the dirt along with it. There's no actual body here; it was never recovered after the "accident" that killed her, but I come here anyway, the memorial to her life somehow making me feel closer to her than anywhere else.

My stomach churns.

"I miss you," I whisper, glancing to either side of me before sitting down. The grass is cold, but I make myself as comfortable as possible, wrapping my arms around my bent knees as I stare at her tombstone.

A ball of sadness forms in my throat, making it difficult to swallow around the pain.

"What are you supposed to be?" Nessa laughs, flicking the top of my pointed hat.

I grin at her, the green paint on my skin still tacky as I throw my hands out to my sides. "A witch, duh."

She smiles, her eyes taking in my costume. I know it's not much, but I made it all by myself and I'm pretty proud of it. It took days.

She places her hands on her hips. "Are you a good witch or a bad witch?"

I tilt my head to the side, not understanding the question. "What do you mean?"

"Well…you either cast wicked spells against your enemies, or you use your powers for good. You know, to help people." She looks me up and down again. "Good witches normally wear white though. At least that's what they say."

I chew on the inside of my lip, my brows furrowing as I take in her words. I hadn't thought about what kind of witch I wanted to be. Honestly, I didn't know there were choices. Embarrassment swirls through me, wondering if people will judge me if I pick wrong.

Dorothy cackles, walking in from the foyer, followed closely by our mother. "No way she's a good one. Look at her."

Nessa's eyes narrow, and my chest twists when I see Mom fawning over Dorothy—as usual—and completely ignoring me.

I twist my fingers together, shifting on my feet, suddenly feeling like my homemade costume is stupid. Especially next to Dorothy, who's dressed in a sparkly pink ball gown, complete with an elaborate silver crown on her head and a magic wand with a star on top.

"Wow. Who are you supposed to be?" I ask, marveling at her costume.

Dorothy's grin widens and she twirls around in a circle, the dress shimmering as she does. "I'm a fairy princess, right, Mama?"

Our mother glances down at her, running her hand through the ends of Dorothy's perfectly curled hair. "That's right, baby girl." She looks over at us. "Doesn't she look great? We had the outfit specially made."

My fingers twist so hard they ache.

Nessa scoffs. "Jesus, Mom."

"Glinda!" Dad's voice pours in from down the hall. "Get your ass in here. Now."

Mom's smile drops and she whips her head behind her before looking back to Dorothy. "I'll be back later. You have fun trick-or-treating, okay? Remember what I told you."

Dorothy nods, smiling, and our mom bends to kiss her on the forehead before spinning around and rushing away.

Nessa blows out a breath, pasting on a smile and clapping her hands together. "Okay, let's go now before everyone steals all the good candy."

"Don't tell me what to do," Dorothy snaps, the sugar-sweet smile dropping off her face.

Nessa grinds her teeth. "Keep being a brat and I won't take you at all."

Dorothy's face turns pink and she stomps her foot on the ground. "Mama will make you."

Nessa grins. "Not if I tell Dad."

"Nice costume, Dorothy," I whisper, trying to interrupt their fight before it gets worse. Once Nessa uses our dad to get Dorothy to do something, all bets are off, and I get the fallout from Dorothy's bad mood. Like always.

I step up beside her, grabbing the black cauldron-shaped bucket sitting on the kitchen counter.

She scrunches her nose, looking past me to Nessa. "I'll be out front. It stinks back here."

My chest aches and I stare at the floor. I don't know what happened to make Dorothy so spiteful and cruel, but it's there no matter how much I try to bridge the gap.

A hand clamps down on my shoulder, Nessa's face coming into view. "You know? I definitely think you're a good witch."

I nod, trying to hold back the sob that wants to break free. I swallow it down, glancing at the empty hallway where Dorothy disappeared. She's so stupid. She thinks just because she's eight and Mom's favorite that she's better than everyone.

Something dark and heavy twists in my middle, heating up my body as it spreads. Good witches help people, but I don't really feel like helping her. Or anyone, for that matter.

"No," I say, stiffening my spine and glaring at the empty space. "I'm the bad one."

That was the last Halloween I saw my mother. Before Dad went away and she decided she was too good to raise kids on her own. What kind of a person leaves their barely adult daughter alone to raise her sisters? Maybe if she had stayed, things wouldn't have gotten so much worse between Nessa and Dorothy, and Nessa would still be here.

Footsteps crunch behind me, and my spine stiffens, jolting me out of the memory.

I've been coming here every single Sunday for the past seven years, and no one has *ever* followed me. No one even cared I went missing in the first place. They never do.

Ezekiel appears at my side and sits down next to me, crossing his legs.

I blow out a sigh, grabbing a fallen leaf and twirling it through my fingers.

"What, no hello?" he asks after a minute of silence.

I shrug, keeping my eyes trained on the browns and golds spinning in my hand.

"That's why you're my favorite," he sighs, leaning back on his elbows and stretching his legs out in front of him. "No bullshit." He slips a cigarette from behind his ear and takes a lighter from his pocket, sparking the end and blowing a ring of smoke into the sky. "This where you come when you disappear?"

"Sometimes."

"Hmm," he hums.

He stays quiet after that, only the sound of the wind caressing the trees and the burning paper of his cigarette keeping it from being complete silence.

"You know," he finally says, "I met Nessa a few times, when she'd go out on that ridiculous yacht with Oscar."

Nausea surges through my stomach and into my throat at the thought of that stupid boat. I went on it one time and ended up having a panic attack from being on the water, so I never went again. Maybe if I had, she'd still be here.

"She had a way about her, didn't she?" He grins. "Every guy was half in love with her back then. Hell, most of the girls were too."

He chuckles, but I can't find the humor as he reminds me of how much darker the world is without her in it.

"Your father—"

"I don't want to talk about him here." I bite the inside of my lip so hard I taste the hint of copper.

He nods, sucking in another drag of his cigarette and lying back until he's completely flat on the ground. "Well, this is important, and I don't know if I'll get a chance to say it again, so just..."

Everything in me wants to tell him to shut the fuck up and leave. I want to snap my teeth and yell how *dare* he bring him up. Him—the man who can't be bothered to even show up. He doesn't deserve to be acknowledged. Not here.

But it's Ezekiel, and he...well, he's one of the only people in my life who doesn't treat me like I'm different. Less than. So instead, I lie back with him, my head pressing against the hard ground, the smell of flowers left by other mourning souls assaulting my senses.

"Your father's been good to me, and he's good as hell at what he does," he tries again. "But a man can be successful and still fail where it matters."

My chest squeezes tight.

"I watch you, Evie, you know? You and that bleedin' heart." He turns his face to stare at me. "Your dad loves you...and he loves her too." He points toward Nessa's headstone. "He just doesn't know how to show it."

My nose burns and I shove my tongue to the roof of my mouth, trying to stem the ache that's sprouting with every word he says.

Sounds nice, but it's all bullshit at the end of the day. Ezekiel can pretend he knows our family dynamic as much as he likes, but it doesn't change how it *feels*. I watch him from my peripheral instead of meeting his gaze. "As much as I love the sentimental bonding, can we be done?"

He chuckles, ash from his cigarette falling on top of his scarred-up knuckles. "I'm sorry you lost your sister, Evie. I don't think I've ever told you that."

I swallow. "It was a long time ago."

There's a type of unspoken bond between people who share the grief of loss, and while I was too young to understand it all those years ago when Ezekiel's father was murdered in the pen, I *do* understand it now. When he came around to work with my father, there was an instant comradery that bloomed in the space between us. A silent understanding. I find peace in his friendship, in the way he doesn't push. Because if anyone knows what it's like to lose the one who raised them and not be able to seek vengeance from the ones they know stole them away, it's Ezekiel.

I turn to face him, taking in the way his eyes are half-lidded, his mane of hair tamed in a bun. "Do you think about your dad at all, Ezekiel?"

His features morph into something heavier. "All the time."

"Did you love him?"

"Thought we were done with the sentimental shit," he grunts.

I lift a shoulder. "Changed my mind."

He brings the cigarette up to his lips, inhaling before blowing out another ring of smoke. "He was a prick."

"So no?"

"Yeah, I loved him." He sighs. "I'd do anything not to end up like him though."

"Well..." I pause, placing my hands on top of my stomach. "I'd do anything to be even a little bit like Nessa."

"That's a shame." He sits up then, looking down on me. "If you were like her, then there wouldn't be a *you*."

I suck in a breath from his words, tendrils of despair breaking through the ground and wrapping around my chest, squeezing until my heart feels like it might explode from the constraint.

Ezekiel stands, dusting off his pants. "See ya around, Evie."

He walks away then, and I stay lying on the ground, basking in the silence.

But for the first time in years, the solitude feels a little less like comfort and a little more empty.

CHAPTER 15

Nicholas

THE MOTEL ON THE OUTSKIRTS OF KINLAND IS A shithole, but it's the most inconspicuous place for Seth to set up shop without me having to travel two hours out of town.

The only source of light in the dark parking lot is from a flickering streetlight and the dim yellow bulbs illuminating the walkways. Parking my car, I glance around to make sure no one else is here before getting out and making my way to the last door on the left, knocking twice.

There's a faint smell of garbage from the large dumpster a few feet away that makes my nose scrunch, and an owl hoots from a tree in the distance. Other than that and the steady hum of cars on the street, there's silence, but it doesn't stop my stomach from flipping as I whip my gaze behind me one more time, just to make sure I haven't been followed.

The door creaks open, Seth's tired and worn face greeting me. He's a welcome sight and he steps to the side for me to enter before closing the door again behind me. The room itself is nothing special, a full bed in the center, a small dark-maroon couch on the other, and tables set up throughout with computer monitors and recording equipment, enough to let me know that he hasn't been doing surveillance here alone.

There are empty coffee cups strewn across the countertops and white to-go containers filling the room with the smell of Chinese takeout.

While I've been spying, they've been receiving.

"Anyone else here?" I ask, looking around before moving to the couch and sitting down.

Seth shakes his head, running a hand over his beard, but he doesn't speak, and his stature catches me off guard, sending anxiety prickling through my insides. I brush it off, figuring he's just tired, the same way I am.

"There's a drop happening tomorrow night."

Seth grabs his mug off the end of the table and moves to sit on the other side of the couch, quirking a brow. "Of what?"

I shrug. "No clue. They didn't say what it was, just that we should be there to pick it up."

He nods, taking a sip from his cup. "You didn't think to ask?"

His tone is accusing, and it soars across the small space between us and hits me in the center of my chest. My hackles rise. "I'm not really in a position to ask a lot of questions, Seth. I may be in, but I'm still a fucking nobody, you know? Questions get people killed."

He bobs his head again, his eyes searing into mine. "Sure."

Irritation lights up my insides. "Everything okay?"

"You tell me." He lifts a shoulder.

I throw my hands up. "Okay, well, I don't have time for this. If you listen to the audio from yesterday, you'll hear about the drop for yourself."

Slapping my hands on my knees, I start to stand but pause when he speaks again.

"Oh, I heard the audio. Too bad it's gone now."

The breath whooshes from my lungs. "What the fuck do you *mean*, it's gone?"

Chuckling, he places his mug down on the coffee table, jabbing two fingers into his temple. "Think for a second, Nick. What could possibly have happened that made me feel like it was necessary to lose evidence?"

"I told you not to call me that," I snap.

Immediately after saying it, a pang hits my chest, realizing how much I sound like Evelina.

Groaning, I run my hands over my face. "This what we do now, Seth? We talk in riddles?"

He frowns. "Bro. I know you're not stupid."

"What?" I repeat, getting irritated.

"Let me lay some shit out for you," he says. "This morning I came here and looked over everything transmitted from your wire last night." He points to the silver chain around my neck. "And there was some good shit, man. The best we've gotten so far. Evelina Westerly? She's fucking scum."

My stomach twists.

"And then I had to fucking delete half of it because you can't keep your dick in your pants."

Every muscle in my body freezes, embarrassment surging through my insides, because how could I be so stupid? The heat of the moment made me forget that I'm here to do a job. That *everything* is recorded.

Seth runs his hand over his mouth and down his short beard. "So after I ran through all the situations in my head, I decided there's no chance Galen will see that and *not* think you're in too deep. So I wiped it. For you. To cover *your* fuckup."

I breathe deeply, trying to stem the nausea that's brewing in my gut. "Listen, Seth..."

He shakes his head. "I need you to tell me honestly that you know what you're doing."

My brows shoot to my hairline and a wall of defense slams down inside me, because regardless of whether I'm fucking Evelina or not, I damn sure don't need him questioning my abilities. "You saying I'm not doing my job, Seth?"

"I'm saying that you fucking the daughter of Farrell Westerly on top of a pile of dirty money isn't exactly making me have confidence you know what the hell you're doing, yeah."

I clear my throat, my mind racing on how to fix this. "When have you ever known me to hold back on a case?" I ask.

"Never, but—"

I hold up a hand, cutting him off. "Right, never. And now suddenly, you think I'm losing it within a few weeks? Give me some fucking credit, dude."

"You're putting both of us on the line with this shit. You know how much trouble I'd be in if they knew I wiped evidence?"

"I didn't ask you to do that," I reply carefully. "She's *involved*, clearly, as you can see. And we got the information we needed, did we not? We have coercion and money laundering cases stacking up quicker than we can blink."

Seth purses his lips. "We both know that's not the goal here. It's not enough. We want the supplier."

I move forward, placing my hand on his shoulder and meeting his eyes. "She's our in, Seth. It's her who can get us the information. And if I have to fuck her so she trusts me, then that's what I'll do."

He's quiet, and with every second he is, guilt spreads through my chest, layer upon layer until it's heavy and thick.

Finally, he cracks a grin. "You're a heartless bastard, man."

I shrug, forcing a weak smile.

That wasn't why I fucked her. But I'm not lying now. At the end of the day, Evelina is the enemy.

Not my friend.

Not my lover.

Not my *anything*.

CHAPTER 16

Nicholas

THERE'S AN ABANDONED WAREHOUSE IN THE middle of Kinland. At least to the wandering eye, it *seems* as though it's abandoned. Being here now, it's clear that isn't the case.

Liam, Ezekiel, and Farrell are all here, along with a few other lower-level associates I've seen in passing but haven't gotten to know yet. One of them isn't even in our files, and I make a note to try and find out more about him later. But right now, it doesn't matter.

What matters are the crates of weapons staring me in the face and making my heart beat out of my chest.

Holy shit.

It's dark out here, the stars and the beams of the headlights from our cars the only source of light, and Ezekiel grins, popping open the back of the SUV. "Come on, boys. It's not gonna move itself."

I lean in toward Liam. "We're in the gun business now?"

He side-eyes me but doesn't respond. Clearly, he still isn't over the other week.

"We need to check 'em, Skip?" he asks, lifting up the top of one of the long wooden crates and peering inside.

Farrell laughs, perching against the bumper of his car, puffing on a Black & Mild. "They're good."

Ezekiel smiles. "Let's load 'em up."

I glance around, the burner phone in my pocket sending anxiety racing through me. My guys know we're here tonight, but we were under the assumption this was going to be a drug pickup. Not *guns*. We passed on the info to the local PD, hoping a quick bust would ruffle some feathers, maybe get some mouths to talk without letting them know they've got the DEA's attention. But with every second the PD doesn't show, my anxiety winds tighter.

A phone pings and Farrell drags his cell out, a cloud of smoke swirling around him while he looks down at whatever's on the screen. His face changes, and his head snaps up, his eyes bouncing from one guy to the next.

My stomach twists.

"Hurry up," he snaps. "We've got company. Ten minutes out."

My heart stalls, dropping to the ground. *Is there…does he have a connection in the PD?*

Of fucking course he does.

I grip one of the crates, my muscles burning as I carry it to the back of the SUV and load it in the trunk, my eyes scanning the area every few seconds, willing the cops to appear. The guns are heavy as fuck and clunky as hell, but it gives me something to do besides focus on the fact that somehow Farrell knows people are on their way.

"Company?" I ask, swiping my hand through my hair.

Farrell walks over to me, resting a hand on my shoulder, his eyes penetrating as they stare directly into mine. "You and those questions." He puffs on his cigar before letting the smoke blow in my face. "Just like my ma, yeah? Always *so* many fucking questions."

Blood races through my veins, my fingers twitching as I debate whether I need to pull my gun. I swallow, shrugging my shoulders. "Just trying to be the best at what I do, Skip."

"Hmm." His grip tightens. "Knowledge is power and all that?"

"Exactly." I grin.

He brings the Black & Mild up to his mouth again and grins around it, his teeth chomping into the filtered tip. "Good man. Now shut the fuck up and load my shit." Spinning away from me, he gestures toward his car. "Ezekiel, let's go. Now."

My muscles are frozen in place, my heart slamming against my ribs.

Jesus Christ.

Ezekiel looks back toward us, one leg already in the driver's side of Farrell's car. "If you fucks get pulled in, I'll kill you myself."

His eyes meet mine and hold for just a second too long. I jerk my chin, hoping it gives him a sense of safety, one that I definitely don't feel. We've been careful, not speaking to each other outside what Farrell demands, but the truth is, while I wish I could guarantee Ezekiel's safety, I can't. Not when I can't even guarantee my own.

I watch as red taillights disappear into the distance, going over a hill until they vanish entirely.

"What the fuck are you doing?" Liam yells. "Get over here and help. For the love of God, it's like you've got no sense in your fuckin' head."

My heart hammers in my chest and I spin around, realizing there are still a dozen crates in the warehouse, but the boys have stopped loading. One of them slams the trunk down and runs to the driver's side door.

Liam has a gas can that he's rushing toward the warehouse with.

Where the hell did that come from?

He starts pouring the gasoline along the perimeter, dousing the grassy areas. I stand still, my mind racing as I try to figure out how I can keep this from happening.

I glance behind me, hoping like hell that I see cars coming around the bend, but I don't.

Liam waltzes up to me, wiping his sweaty forehead with the sleeve of his arm. Then he tosses me a box of matches. "Light it up for me, yeah?"

I look down to the matches and over to the warehouse before meeting Liam's eyes. "But there're still crates."

"Cost of doing business with rats, huh?" He shrugs.

Fuck.

If the warehouse burns down, it burns all the evidence with it. But if I don't… I meet Liam's eyes.

"What's wrong, rook?" He smirks, his eyes calculating as they take me in. "Nervous?"

I pull out the match and jog over to the building, striking it against the box and flicking it onto the grass that lines the perimeter.

Immediately, it goes up in flames.

Turning away, I rush back, the SUV already peeling out of the lot, gravel flying from beneath its tires. Liam's in his car, revving the engine. My lungs burn as I run to the passenger side and slide in right as he starts to pull away.

Flames and smoke rise from behind us and we're gone before there's even a hint of my guys on the scene.

But I already know what they'll find.

Absolutely nothing.

Two hours later and we're in the basement of the Yellow Brick, the silence heavy as it presses in on everything around us. Everyone is on edge, including me, but I can't help letting my mind wander. Farrell is sitting at the head of the exact table I fucked his daughter on two nights ago. And I haven't seen her since.

"I want to know," Farrell starts, his voice low and lethal, "who the *fuck* tipped off the cops? Who's stupid enough to not realize I've got eyes and ears everywhere?"

Nobody says a word.

Farrell shoots up from his seat, slamming his fist on the wood. "No one's got shit to say?"

Liam glares at me from across the room, and anxiety winds its way around my chest and squeezes, making my heart beat double time.

The basement door swings open, the sound of heels clacking on the stairs, but even if I couldn't hear her footsteps, I'd know Evelina was here. As stupid as it sounds, I swear to god I can feel her.

She walks past me and heads straight toward her dad, not even sparing me a glance.

"What happened?" Her voice is sharp.

"A fucking *rat* is what happened," Farrell spits.

Her brows rise and she peers around the room, her gaze lingering on mine, and *fuck* my stomach for flipping the way it does.

Suddenly, there's cold metal pressed against my forehead, making my temperature spike and my muscles tense.

I look up at Liam, his gun pushing into my skin. "Get your fucking gun out of my face."

He chuckles. "No chance, rook. Not until you prove it ain't you."

Leaning back in my chair, I smirk, although bile teases the back of my throat. "I don't have to prove *shit* to you."

Farrell sits forward, his eyes sharp when they land on me, and I already know from our earlier interaction at the warehouse he won't be any help.

Evelina crosses her arms, looking lazily at the scene, as if she couldn't care less that someone is ten seconds away from shoving a bullet through my brain. Most likely, she's wishing it could be her that does it.

"You expect us to believe that you show up and suddenly we've got a leak?" Liam spits, pressing his gun against me harder.

My head tilts to the side from the force and I grimace. "Pretty defensive for someone who's got nothing to hide, Liam. How do we know it isn't *you*?"

My eyes meet Ezekiel's across the room where he leans against the wall with his arms crossed and his jaw tensed, not saying a word.

He's nervous.

"It's not him." Evelina's voice is sharp and strong.

"Of course it's not me," Liam says.

"Not *you*, moron." Evelina's eyes narrow and she waves a hand toward me. "It's not *him*."

Liam's nostrils flare.

"How do you know, Bug?" Farrell asks.

She walks up to me, her stare holding mine, and even in this fucked-up situation, my stomach flips as she catches my gaze.

She cocks her head as she stands next to Liam, whose gun is *still* pressed against my head.

I smile at her.

She frowns in response. "I already ran a check on him. He is who he says he is. Besides, I've had him tailed for weeks."

My chest twists, surprise washing over me. *What the fuck?*

No way she's been following me. If she has, then she'd know I was at that motel, and if she knows that, why would she be saying I'm *not* the rat?

"Liam," she continues. "I know he hurt your ego the other night when you guys played 'whose dick is bigger,' but you don't get to kill one of our guys just because you don't like him."

He adjusts his hold on the gun, the metal clinking beneath his grip. "He's the rat, Evie. I'm telling you."

I see her slip her hand up her thigh before anyone else does, and in a few seconds flat, she has her Desert Eagle pressed beneath his chin.

"He's not," she says calmly.

His eyes flick down to her. "Really, Evie? All these years you've known me and you stand up for this guy?"

She grins, flipping off the safety.

"Liam," Farrell interjects. "Round up every motherfucker who knew what was happening tonight and bring them to me." He looks to Evelina. "You got that fancy thing your mystery friend made, yeah? The one that scans for wires? Bring it."

My insides go wild, anxiety eating through every tendon. A thing that scans for wires? How the fuck? I decide right then that the second I leave, I'm ditching the wire. For good. They'll just have to take me at my word, because I won't take the risk.

Liam's jaw clenches, his arm trembling as he keeps his gun

aimed at my head. I hold eye contact, even though everything in me wants to look over to Evelina. To see how fucking sexy she looks while she defends my honor in the face of a man she's known for years.

My stomach rolls, knowing I don't deserve it.

Finally, he drops the weapon and Evelina steps back, spinning toward her dad. A maniacal gleam enters her eyes, and just like that, I'm reminded that she isn't on my side at all.

CHAPTER 17

Evelina

"EVELINA."

Brayden's voice scrapes against my skin, and I speed up to try and outrun it. I'm almost to my car, and if I can just make it a couple more steps, I'm home free.

It's the middle of the night, so no one else is here besides the boys in the basement, but I don't want to hang around until they need me. I'm already at my limit for "peopling," and I'm desperate for some solitude after the past few days of doing nothing except being around others.

"Wait up, Evelina," Brayden says again.

Of course he's following me. When is he *not* following me? And what the hell was I thinking standing up for him that way? On top of that, I lied. Without a second thought, I said I'd been tailing him, which isn't true. But it was either that or raise more questions about how I know, and I'll never put Cody in their grubby, greedy hands. He's done too much for me in the past three years since he's been back, has done anything I've asked of him without a question of *why* I'm asking. All because he trusts me. The least I can do is make sure no one else in the family finds out that he's my secret weapon.

I can't say my morals are upstanding, but I *am* loyal to a fault if you deserve it. It's just that most people don't.

As I stomp through the doors and into the parking lot, my mind races. The rat isn't Brayden. He's been thoroughly vetted and checked by Cody and myself, but if it isn't him, then who is it? I mentally flip through the people in our inner circle, and the only one I keep circling back to is Liam.

But then a second thought enters my head, unbidden and uncontrolled. Dorothy's been knowing an awful lot about our operations recently, even sometimes before *I* know. Suspicion curdles through my mind, wondering how loyal she really is to our father. After all, if she could shove Nessa overboard and let her drown and fool everyone about her innocence, then who's to say she wouldn't flip and make sure our entire family is gone and she's the only one left standing in the end?

My fingers reach the driver's side door of my car when Brayden's hand grips my arm, spinning me around.

Great.

"What?" I hiss, shoving him in the chest.

He releases me, but he doesn't retreat, choosing to stay in place and cage me in. "Just wanted to say thanks."

I move my face to the side, needing to break away from the intensity of his stare. I'm not sure if it's more potent tonight than normal or if it's the aftereffects of being intimately acquainted with his dick, but either way, looking him in the eyes stirs up emotions I'd rather stay buried.

"Thank you *not* accepted. Can I go now?"

He presses in closer until his hips pin me entirely to the door. My stomach tenses, heat flaring between my legs.

"Did you really run a check on me?" he asks.

When he's this close, it's impossible to not smell the cinnamon and pine, and with every inhale, arousal digs its dirty claws into me further. It's unwanted and does nothing except piss me off that I'm feeling it in the first place.

I lift a brow. "What do you think?"

His tongue swipes across his bottom lip. I track the movement, my pussy throbbing at the simple motion, remembering the way it felt when he was licking my clit.

"And you're following me?" His brow lifts at this, like he doesn't believe it.

"Can you really blame me?" I push my hands against his chest again.

He reaches up and grabs my wrists, pulling them so they're locked in his grip and moving them until they're pinned above my head. He leans in, skimming his nose up the side of my neck, making goose bumps spread down the length of my spine.

My eyes flutter closed.

"Now who's the stalker?" he whispers.

"I hate you," I rasp.

"Back at you, sweetheart. But clearly my dick doesn't, because no matter how much of a bitch you are or how many times I tell myself to stay the fuck away, this is always where I end up."

He thrusts into me, and I bite my lip to keep from moaning at the feel of his thick cock pressing against me.

"Someone will see." I twist my wrists in his hands, trying again to escape. The friction causes a burn to spread across my skin, and his hold tightens.

"And?" He assaults my neck, his tongue running along the expanse of my throat. My clit pulses, desperate for him to do it on my pussy instead of torturing me. "I bet you'd let me flip up your little skirt and pull down your panties right here, wouldn't you?"

My legs tremble. "No."

He licks my ear. "I could bend you over the hood of your car and slide my cock deep inside you, right where everyone could see."

My head snaps back when he bites down just beneath my jaw, my skull cracking against the window.

"You'd be so ready for me, wouldn't you, pretty girl? Your sweet pussy would suck me in and milk me dry, regardless of who might walk by." One of his hands releases my wrists and moves to cup my throat, squeezing the smallest bit. "Would you still hate me then?" he continues. "When I'm filling up your needy little cunt with my cum and you're seeing stars from the pleasure?"

My breath hitches, my stomach somersaulting at his filthy words. At the images he creates in my head. It would feel *so* good having him pump inside me, making me clench around his dick while he groaned in my ear, not caring that we're in the middle of a very public parking lot.

But regardless of what he does to me physically, it doesn't mean I enjoy having him around. Or that it's a good idea to indulge in what he offers.

I turn my head the tiniest bit and whisper, "I'd still hate you if you were the last person on earth. And I wouldn't fuck you again even if you had a knife to my throat. I'd choose death. Every time."

His body freezes, his ministrations stopping.

"Now get the fuck off me," I force out.

I push against his hold again, and this time he does let me go, his eyes void of any emotion at all.

He shakes his head. "Fine, you win. It's not worth it. *You're* not worth it."

My chest cramps, but I let him walk away, because I don't want him to stay.

Bricks are meant for paths,
Yet somehow we're always still.
If there's nothing for us in the now,
Then I know there never will.
You belong up here in the light,
and me in poppies down below.
Maybe one day we'll meet again,
On the other side of a rainbow.

Laughter flows from the hallway and I snap my notebook closed on the kitchen island just as Dorothy waltzes in with a bright smile pasted across her face.

Brayden follows close behind.

She doesn't notice me, jabbering about something inconsequential, but Brayden's eyes find mine immediately, as if we're two ends of a magnet, drawn together by force.

The air grows thick and I grip the edge of the counter.

Dorothy stops speaking midsentence when she follows his gaze.

"Evie," she says, smiling thinly.

"Where have you been?" I ask, tilting my head.

She's never been heavily involved in the darker side of our

dealings, our dad making sure she stays out of harm's way, but she *is* usually around more than she has been lately.

"Busy," she snips. "Some of us have things to do other than sit around all day and daydream in notebooks. Why? Suddenly starting to care?"

I shrug. "Just curious."

But I do care, because *someone* is tipping off the local PD, and with her disappearing act lately, it makes me wonder just what she's getting up to. I make a mental note to keep closer tabs on her. I'd love to find a reason beyond my original suspicions to kill her.

Brayden chuckles and I narrow my gaze at him. "Something funny, stalker?"

He runs a hand over his mouth, stifling his grin. "Just the thought of you caring about anything."

I tilt my head, irritation surging up my throat and sitting heavy on my tongue. "I'd worry more about your proclivity for jumping from one toy to the next and less about how much *I* care about my things."

The second the words pass my lips, I know they're a mistake, but it's too late. I've let my emotions bleed into the moment.

Stupid.

His eyes darken.

"Wow. You two have really gotten more comfortable with each other since I've been gone," Dorothy says, a hint of jealousy tingeing the edges of her voice.

"Don't worry." I smile. "He can still be your little lapdog, Dorothy. I'm not interested in training new bitches."

He smirks, resting his elbows against the counter.

Dorothy lifts a perfectly manicured brow. "You need training, Brayden?"

"That depends," he fires back. "If I make you a mess, will you rub my nose in it?"

She blushes so fiercely I'm amazed she doesn't faint, and I roll my eyes, hating the way my chest tightens. "You're disgusting."

He laughs. "Yeah, sweetheart, it's pretty clear you hate me. We get it."

I pick up my notebook, holding it against my chest, and his eyes drop to it.

"What's that?" he asks.

"Evie writes *love* spells. Isn't that cute?" Dorothy giggles, covering her mouth with her hand.

His brows rise. "Oh? Looking for love, pretty girl?"

My heart stutters at his term of endearment—the one he only calls me when we're alone—and Dorothy's grin drops immediately, the energy in the room shifting into something more sinister.

I ignore the change.

"Maybe I'm looking for someone to curse instead. You volunteering?"

He hooks his thumbs in the pockets of his leather jacket and rocks back on his heels. "Maybe."

"Ugh," Dorothy groans loudly. "I'm bored. This is boring." She turns to Brayden, whose gaze is searing into me so intensely, it feels as if he's branding my soul. "Want to watch a movie?"

He finally drops our stare and looks to her, shifting on his feet and pawing the back of his neck. "I...uh...can't actually. I've been summoned by the wicked witch over here." He tosses a thumb at me.

Normally, I would put up a fight, but the way envy swirls through Dorothy's features has me biting my tongue. Besides, it's true. I need him to go with me to check on someone.

"Sorry about your luck," she says, scrunching up her nose. "Dad wants me to do something for him anyway. You know... business stuff."

Irritation winds its way through my middle at the fact that Dad has her doing something, *again*, and I don't know what it is beforehand. Or maybe she's lying just to get a rise out of me. With Dorothy, you can never be too sure.

"What kind of business stuff?" I push.

She grins. "If Dad didn't tell you, then why should I?"

"I tell you what," Brayden says suddenly. "Once I'm done doing my *obligations*, I'll come grab you for a late-night snack. You can tell me all about your day and your important 'business.'"

Her face lights up and anger floods through me like a broken dam.

I close my eyes as the rage makes my hands shake, and I count back.

Ten. Nine. Eight...

CHAPTER 18

Nicholas

I STARE OVER AT EVELINA, A THOUSAND DIFFERENT questions on the tip of my tongue but not knowing how to ask any of them. I can tell she's upset, and I'd like to assume it's because I was flirting with her sister, but more than likely it's because she's just a miserable person who can't stand to be around me.

She's made it more than clear where we stand, and as much fun as it is to rile her up, keeping our distance is for the best. For both my sanity and my job. I can pretend I'm using her for information all I want; the truth is there's something about her that drives me fucking wild.

Her sister is easy and will be all too willing to share any secrets she knows.

But none of it changes the fact that I'm still stuck as Evelina's shadow for the foreseeable future.

I glance over at her again when we stop at a red light, the green skyscrapers from downtown Kinland having disappeared as we make our way to whatever destination she plugged into the

GPS. Now there are boarded-up windows over dilapidated buildings, cracked pavement sidewalks overgrown with weeds.

"What's really in the notebook?" I ask, partly out of curiosity and partly because I'm trying to gauge if it's something important I should try to get my hands on.

She sighs, running a hand through her hair. "Poetry."

Surprise swims through me, my brows skyrocketing. "Who's your favorite?"

"I like the classics."

"Hmm." I nod. "'She dwells with Beauty. Beauty that must die; and joy, whose hand is ever at his lips. Bidding adieu; and aching pleasure nigh, turning to poison while the bee-mouth sips.'"

She blinks, her mouth parting.

"What?" I grin, turning left onto a side street that leads into Kinland Heights, one of the roughest neighborhoods in the city. "You don't know it?"

"No, I…" She shakes her head. "I do. Keats is my favorite. I just…how do *you* know it?"

"I know lots of things, sweetheart." I wink.

Her lips purse. "Well, *pretty* words don't impress me. And neither does your poor attempt at avoiding actual conversation."

My grip tightens on the steering wheel, and a sharp pain swirls through me. "My mom liked poetry."

The hole in my chest aches when I say the words, and I don't even know *why* I'm saying them. I don't talk about my mom. Ever. And especially not with someone who's the living embodiment of why I don't have her anymore.

"Oh," she whispers. "She's dead, right?"

"Who fucking knows," I bite out.

She tilts her head, her lips thinning. Eventually she says, "You're mad at her."

My stomach twists. "No, I…I don't know what I am. I don't feel much of anything anymore, to be honest. It was a long time ago."

She lifts a shoulder. "My mom left a long time ago too, and I'd still be the first person in line to spit on her grave."

My lips twitch. "My mom had issues. She wasn't around much, and when she was, she was sick."

Dope sick usually, but I don't add in that bit.

Evelina rests her head against the car window, and I don't know if that means she's listening or she doesn't care, but now that I've started talking, I don't really want to stop. The memory surges through my insides and plays like a movie, so potent and visceral it's like it's happening in front of my face.

"She had this collection of old books. They were small, red, and warped around the edges. I don't even know where the hell she got them, but when I was little, she'd sneak to my room in the middle of the night and read them to help me sleep." I park the car on the side street lined with small, worn-down houses wrapped in broken chain-link fences. "When I got older and she stopped coming around as much, I don't know…I guess they helped me feel close to her or something. It's stupid."

She reaches across the console, locking our fingers together, the metal from her rings cool against my palm. "It's *not* stupid."

My chest throbs with stuttered beats as I stare at her small hand and the way it fits so perfectly in mine.

"They comforted you," she states.

She's comforting me. I swallow around the knot in my throat. "Words were my calm in a life filled with chaos."

A beautiful grin spreads across her face, and the sight of it knocks the breath from my lungs. "Mine too."

My hand shoots out before I can think twice, and I cup her jaw, my thumb rubbing across her pouty lip, sparks flying through my fingers. "Jesus, pretty girl. You could ruin lives with a smile like that."

Her grin drops as she stares at me, and my heart slams against my rib cage so hard I swear it's trying to break free and fall to her feet.

I grit my teeth, annoyed at the unwelcome feeling.

"Anyway." I snap my hand back. "I don't really like to talk about it."

My words are harsh, but it has the desired effect, her face molding back into the sharp angles of a grumpy girl with a short temper. "Good, because I'm not your fucking therapist."

"Thank god for that." I laugh.

She crosses her arms.

"You know, you're a real piece of work," I bark, anger dripping through my system like lava burning through rock.

She grips her hair and then slaps her thighs with her hands. "I'm not even *doing* anything. Holy shit, and people say *I* have mood swings?"

"Oh, well, at least you know you're psychotic."

The air thins.

She grins maniacally. "Okay."

I frown. "What do you mean 'okay'?"

She doesn't answer, just swipes her palms down that flowy skirt she always wears and hops out of the car, marching toward the small house at the end of the street.

Closing my eyes, I exhale heavily and pound my fist against the wheel. "*Fuck!*"

Jumping out, I jog after her, not wanting her to walk into a situation she might not be able to get out of. But I shouldn't have worried, because when I finally catch up, she's already inside the house, a guy on his knees in the center of the room, her giant gun pressed against his head.

And maybe if she didn't drive me so crazy, I would realize that I've made a mistake.

Because while it's true that I don't know if my mom is alive, Brayden Walsh's mom died of cancer.

CHAPTER 19

Evelina

CILLIAN IS ONE OF OUR DRUG DEALERS. HE'S NOT high enough for access to my father or into our daily business dealings, but he *is* Liam's little cousin, and with Liam acting incredibly on edge lately, I figured it was a good time to pay him a visit. Introduce myself and make sure there isn't anything funny going on we need to know about.

I walk in the door without knocking—idiot keeps it unlocked—and head straight toward Cillian, who jumps up from the ratty couch, his baggy jeans practically falling down his legs.

Anger pulses through my veins from my fight with Brayden and I use it to fuel me, knowing that I wouldn't normally be coming in so strong but not finding it in me to care.

"Hi, Cillian. Nice place you've got." Bringing up my leg, I kick his knee out until he drops to the floor and press my gun to his head.

"What the *fuck*?" he yells.

"Shut up," I hiss, pushing it harder into his temple.

From the corner of my eye, I see Brayden rushing in the door behind me and my grin widens as he takes in the scene.

The house itself is nothing special. An old couch with a brown blanket draped over the back and mismatched tables that have lamps with no shades. There's a tiny kitchen to the left and a small circular breakfast table directly in front of it where a woman sits, her mouth gaping open as she watches what's happening. My eyes scan the room, noticing for the first time the bricks of heroin—*my* heroin—cut open and being rebagged.

I tilt my head, surprise flowing through me. "Brayden, be a doll and go tell me what's on that table."

Brayden follows my gaze and walks over, his jaw muscles clenching when he sees it up close. He reaches out, grabbing the cell phone sitting next to the woman and tucking it in his pocket. "Just in case you get any ideas." He winks at her.

"Tell me that's not what I think it is," I say. "Tell me that's not powder being cut and branded as ours?"

Brayden clicks his tongue. "Can't tell you that, sweetheart."

I tsk, glancing back down at Cillian, his blond hair matted against his forehead. "Has someone been a naughty boy?"

"Fuck you. Who the fuck even are you?" he spits.

"Oh, just your resident *psycho.*" I grin. "Isn't that right, Brayden?"

Brayden groans, his face tilting back to the sky. "Christ, you're still on that? Can we focus, please?"

I shrug my shoulders. "I'm perfectly focused."

Cillian snaps his hands out and tries to grab my wrist, and I bring my gun back quickly before slamming it down on the side of his head. He collapses, hitting the wood floor with a crack, and I move my leg, placing my heel into the meat of his side. I feel it pressing in against his ribs, and I lean forward so all my weight is bearing down. He whimpers.

"See?" I smile at Brayden.

The woman sitting at the table has tears in her eyes, her hands covering her mouth.

Brayden shakes his head. "Ridiculous."

I look at Cillian. "If I let you up, will you promise to be a good boy?"

He groans and nods, the palm of his hand still covering the gash in his temple.

I release him and crouch down, my elbows resting on my knees, my gun hanging between my legs. "You know, I just realized I never answered your question. I'm Evelina, and I'm dying to know what the *fuck* you're doing with my drugs."

"I'm not doing shit," he grunts. "Just what you guys told me to."

"Oh?" Standing up, I walk away from him and to the table, brushing by Brayden as I peer over the woman's shoulder.

"Please," she whispers. "I don't—"

"Shh." I place my hand on her shoulder. "It's okay."

Bricks are sliced open, piles of powder being transferred and mixed before being rebagged and branded again with our logo. My eyes squint at the sticker on the new bag. It's identical to mine: the silhouette of a monkey with bat wings. My body shakes from the audacity of their replication. My eyes continue to move along the table, noting the baking soda and *rat poison*.

Blackness creeps into the edges of my vision. Spinning back around, I walk up to Cillian, who is standing now, dabbing a paper towel to the bleeding wound on his head.

"Are you cutting my drugs with rat poison, Cillian?"

He scoffs, glaring down at me. "If you don't know what I'm doing, then maybe you aren't as important as you think."

My chest twists violently and I react before I can stop myself, aiming my gun at his knee and pulling the trigger. The sound is muted from the silencer, but the woman screams, and Cillian goes down fast, his hands flying to his leg. "Jesus *fuck*, you crazy bitch!" he screeches.

Before I can react, Brayden is there, his fist flying into Cillian's face before he drags him up by his shirt. "Watch your mouth."

I grin at him, warmth spreading through me and dousing the anger just slightly. It's cute he's defending my honor, even though he's called me worse himself.

"I'm only doing what I'm fucking *told* to do," Cillian cries.

"By whom?" I tilt my head.

He glares, tears tracking down his face as blood seeps through his fingers. "Fuck you. Why would I tell you shit? So they can kill me when I do?"

"I'll kill you now if you don't," I reply.

Silence.

Cracking my neck, I grin and walk into the kitchen, flinging open his drawers until I find a large kitchen knife. *This will do.*

Silently, I walk up to the woman who's shaking in the chair at the table and I smile softly. "Sorry."

I raise my gun and shoot her in the head. She slumps over the table, red pooling beneath her and spreading over the product they've already ruined.

Brayden's mouth is parted as he takes in the scene, his eyes like stone. Is he shocked? Maybe. But that's not my problem.

Sauntering back toward him, I hand him my gun. "Hold this for me, pup, won't you?"

His eyes narrow at the nickname, but he does as I ask, his gaze flickering between the knife, the dead girl, and then back again before he finally raises the weapon, keeping it aimed on the back of Cillian's head.

I step in close, using the edge of the blade to tip up Cillian's face. "I'm not sure you understood me before, so let me be clear. This isn't a negotiation, and despite what you may think, *I* am your judge, jury, and executioner. Which means you answer to me." I slide the blade in farther, just beneath his jaw, a sick sense of satisfaction melting through me when it meets resistance, then sinks into his skin, blood starting to drip on the metal.

He whines, and the sound sends shivers down my spine.

"What made you think it was okay to cut my drugs?"

"He told me to," he stutters.

"Who? Is it Benny telling you to do this? Your cousin?" I purr. "Tell me and this will all be over."

He presses his lips together.

Sighing, I shake my head, snapping back my hand and withdrawing the blade from under his jaw.

"Fine," I say, walking over to the table and grabbing one of the remade bags before making my way back again. My heels click on the wood floor as I move toward him and nod at Brayden. "Bend him back for me, pup."

Brayden's jaw clenches and he glares at me. My heart starts to pound in my ears when I think he isn't going to listen, that maybe he can't handle what's happened. But then, slowly, he nods and reaches down, wrenching Cillian's matted blond hair until his sliced-up neck is exposed.

"You're not putting up much of a fight, Cillian," I tsk, leaning over him with one of the baggies. I cut it open with the edge of the knife. "It's *almost* a disappointment."

Cillian presses his lips together and my fingers surge forward, digging into his chin and prying them open, his flesh getting stuck under my nails. I dip the bag of cut heroin into his mouth, the powder filling up the empty cavern while he chokes on it and spits. I make sure to angle my face away, not wanting any of it to accidentally enter my nostrils.

I grip his cheeks tight, dropping the bag and bringing the flat of the knife up to cover his mouth. "Swallow."

Tears track down his face and he jolts against Brayden's grip. Brayden squeezes his eyes shut but holds him in place.

Finally, Cillian's throat bobs as he eats the dry powder.

"Think that was enough to make you feel good, baby?" I purr, gliding the blade down until it rests against his jugular. "I'm going to ask you one more time," I whisper. "Who?"

"Liam. He want...wanted to start putting some cash aside. So we could get away from this shit. From all you fucking Westerly assholes."

My hand twitches on his back and he jerks forward, catching me off guard. My knife slides into his throat, blood spurting, the warm liquid spraying my skin. His eyes roll back in his head before his body weight sags, the soul leaving his body.

I stare in shock for long moments, the silence around us thick and heavy. Then I step back and sigh, looking at the mess, my hands stained in red. "Well, this is unfortunate."

Brayden drops Cillian's body and stands, his eyes empty as he stares at me like he's never seen me before.

My stomach twists but I push the odd feeling away. It's not a new thing for people to not like what they see, and having him realize that I'm not the girl he created in his head is a good thing. Maybe it will make him leave me alone, let me get my head on straight. I have other things to focus on, *better* things to focus on, like figuring out if Liam's the rat or finding a way to kill Dorothy without breaking my father's heart.

"Call Ezekiel," I instruct. "Tell him we need to meet at the cleaners."

Brayden swallows, his Adam's apple bobbing.

I snap my fingers in his face. "Hello? You alive in there? Do it. He'll know what it means."

And then I spin around and walk out the door, marching back to the car and sliding inside, reaching into the glove compartment with shaky hands, grabbing the baby wipes to try and scrub off the blood.

CHAPTER 20

Nicholas

I DON'T SPEAK ON THE DRIVE BACK TO THE ESTATE.

Evelina doesn't either, her stained hands trembling slightly where they're sitting in her lap. I can't figure out whether it's from adrenaline or if it's because she isn't as cold-blooded as she tries to appear. I hate myself for caring either way.

My mind is flying in a thousand different directions. Regret for not stopping her. Unease because I've already half convinced myself it's okay. That it was *necessary* for me to stand by and do nothing.

If I had stepped in and saved them, it would have blown my cover, and to be completely honest, saving two drug dealers is low on my priority list. The vengeful part of me believes they got what they deserved.

Even worse is that through it all, I don't feel angry with Evelina. All I really want is to make sure she's okay. And that's bullshit, because *she's* the one who caused everything in the first place.

I don't want to face what that means about me, because while not showing emotion is important to the job, I'm still a federal agent. I'm *supposed* to care. But when it comes to degenerates who willingly put poison in drugs, causing overdoses and death, I'm finding it hard to.

Evelina jumps out of the car the second we hit the circular drive, flying up the steps and into her home. I idle, my fingers tight on the steering wheel, warring with myself over what I know I should do and what I want to do.

What I *should* do is go to Seth and call it in. Let Cap know about the recent developments so we can stockpile more evidence for the case. There are dead bodies piled up in Kinland Heights and blood on Evelina's hands. There's a mound of heroin that could lead us closer to figuring out who the hell we're actually trying to pin.

Instead, I'm stagnant in my car, the rumble of the engine vibrating beneath me and the heat warming my skin as it blasts through the vents. I have no clue why I'm staying, waiting for... who knows what? But regardless, the minutes continue to tick by and here I am. Finally, after what feels like hours, I decide to leave.

To do the right thing.

The *only* thing.

I take the car out of Park, but before I can step on the gas, something catches my attention, creeping along the perimeter of the mansion. I squint my eyes, trying to make it out.

It's a person—a small person—with a messy bun and a black hoodie hiding their figure.

Evelina.

I'm turning off the car and throwing open the door before I can second-guess myself, jogging quickly so I don't lose sight of her as she escapes into the woods lining the back of the house.

The sudden chill in the air stings my face as I hurry after her, the full moon casting an eerie glow on the darkened forest. I shiver, my leather jacket barely enough to keep me warm.

I stay far enough behind that she doesn't see me, and I wonder where the hell she's going, because it seems as if she's walking into the middle of nowhere. Maybe she's more rattled from tonight than she let on. Or maybe that's just wishful thinking on my part, desperately trying to seek a shred of humanity lurking somewhere beneath her dark and violent depths.

I don't know how many minutes tick by as I follow her deeper into the woods, but it's enough to make my legs ache and my mouth go dry, when suddenly, the ground shifts and I stumble, the grass and branches turning into faded yellow bricks.

My lungs squeeze tight as I stare down at my feet.

The bricks themselves are crumbling and covered in overgrown weeds, but they're there nonetheless, and my brain buzzes with theories. Is it a coincidence their strip club is named the Yellow Brick when this is in their backyard?

I make my way forward, following the winding yellow until we reach a small clearing in the trees. Evelina slips inside the front door of a small, run-down cottage.

Holy shit.

I've spent hours poring over architectural blueprints and satellite pictures of this land, but somehow, I had no idea this existed.

Hustling forward, I slip in the door after her. I have no interest in hiding. But I should have known better than to think she wouldn't realize she was being tailed, because the second I step inside, she's on me, her gun in my face as I'm shoved harshly.

"Jesus," I bite out, pain radiating through my skull as it slaps against the wall.

"I should have known it was you following me," she gripes.

"I just wanted to check on you." Heat floods through my veins when her body presses against mine, and my hands shoot out to grasp at her waist.

She purses her lips, relaxing her grip. "Consider me checked."

My cock hardens when I see her bare face without a speck of makeup, and my thumbs caress her skin before I can stop myself. My mind screams at me to *get it the fuck together*, but my body has different ideas, the way it always does when it comes to her.

I can't stand it.

"You're trigger-happy as fuck. Has anyone ever told you that?" I snap.

"Only right before they're dead." She grins wide.

I roll my eyes, my stomach churning from her nonchalance. "What is this place?" I look around.

She drops her gun but stays in my hold. "My escape."

"From?"

She shrugs. "Life."

"You don't like your life?" I'm not sure why I ask, but I'm suddenly desperate to know.

Her tongue swipes across her bottom lip, and she tilts her head. "You don't ever want to just…get away?"

"Not particularly."

She sighs. "Well, I do. I'd leave forever if I could."

My interest is piqued. Does she not enjoy working for her father? "Where would you go?"

"Ireland." She doesn't hesitate for a second. "My dad prides himself on our Irish heritage, but I've never even been there. Can you believe that?"

I don't respond because I'm not sure what to say. Instead,

I soak in how effortlessly beautiful she is. But her beauty is a mirage, a trick of the light. It sucks you in and gives you comfort, only to turn ugly when you peer beneath the surface.

"Why do you lie so much?" she asks.

"I don't lie." I grit my teeth.

Technically, I *do*, but it's irritating to have her constantly call me on it when I've been more honest with her than anyone else. I expect her to have a smart comeback, but she only watches me. *Peers* at me like she's trying to sink under my skin and dig up the buried parts. It makes me itch, and I fidget, my fingers pressing in tightly on her waist. "Is this still about the name thing?"

"You tell me."

Smirking, I swallow around the tightness in my throat and bend down to whisper in her ear, "Sweetheart, you can call me anything you want if it means I get to sink into that sweet pussy again."

She jerks back, ripping herself out of my grasp. "Ugh, you're a disgrace to men everywhere."

I laugh. "Says the girl who just killed two people."

She opens her mouth like she has something else to say, but she turns to walk into the small kitchen instead. I follow her, crowding where she's facing the counter with her head bowed, her fingers pressing tightly against the edge. Caging her in, I move down until my nose skims against her neck.

"It bothers you, doesn't it?" I ask. "What you did?"

"Brayden, *please*. Go fuck yourself," she murmurs.

I couldn't tell you why I do it. Maybe it's because I'm trying like hell to find the girl inside the monster, the one she's trying so desperately to hide. Or maybe it's because *I'm* desperate to hear a reason, just a single fucking reason why I shouldn't report her, even though I know it's what I'll have to do.

My stomach churns and I clench my jaw. I slide my palms down the length of her arms, my cock filling as goose bumps prickle along her skin and her ass presses into my groin. Our fingers intertwine on the Formica counter, and my heart slams against my ribs when her body trembles.

"You can tell me," I rumble against her neck, my tongue slipping out to taste her, just a little bit.

In this moment, I mean it. She *can* tell me. I'm not trying to garner information or see what she'll say. I'm not interested in her bratty mouth or all the ways I can make her squirm. I just want to talk to the girl beneath the mask. The one who smiles so big it softens her eyes and lets me whisper sonnets against her skin.

Her breathing is heavy. "I'm not upset that I killed them."

Disappointment settles in my chest like a boulder, but it feels muted and dull, overshadowed by the fire that lights up my insides whenever I'm so much as within a foot of this woman.

"I'm mad that I lost control," she continues.

My grip on her hands tightens, and I know—I *know*—that I should pull away. That after this is over, I'll spend hours hating myself for falling for someone I'm supposed to stand against.

But when it comes to Evelina Westerly, I'm a fucking fool.

So instead of leaving and reporting in to Seth, I move our interlaced arms and wrap them around her middle before removing my fingers, dragging them down the front of her body as I sink to my knees.

"Then take it back."

CHAPTER 21

Evelina

I KNEW HE WAS FOLLOWING ME.

And I know he's lying about more than he lets on, even if I'm not sure *what* it is he's lying about. So do I trust him? Absolutely not.

But *I* wasn't lying when I said I'm upset I lost control. After Nessa's death, I've worked incredibly hard on maintaining my temper—on making sure my impulse issue is under lock and key. I never mastered it while she was alive, and doing so after her death is one of the ways I've tried to honor her memory.

Lately, it's been severely lacking, which makes me feel as though I'm disrespecting her. *Disappointing* her, the way I do everyone else.

But then there's him.

This man. This complete stranger. And he's on his knees for *me*.

I'm under no illusion that him giving up control is easy. The entire reason we're at each other's throats is because there's a constant struggle of me trying to keep it while he takes it away. But there's something there, in between the vitriol and the animosity. A silver lining that's warm and soft around the edges, urging me to sink into what he's giving.

His fingers dig into my waist and my arms tremble as they push against the backs of his hands. I close my eyes, my heart beating so quickly I feel it in my neck. Lips press into my lower back and chills skirt up my spine, arousal sending a shot of adrenaline through my center.

And I know this isn't right. I hate him, and he tolerates me at best. But my nerves are ricocheting off the edges of my body, sending a prickling anxiety stabbing through my insides, and when he touches me, it soothes the sting.

So I'll indulge. Just for a bit.

I twist my body until I'm facing him and my stomach tenses when our eyes meet. My hoodie is bunched up slightly from his hands, and his breath coasts across the sliver of skin that's peeking from beneath the fabric. I reach down, lifting the hem of the sweatshirt and my tank top underneath, raising them over my head and dropping them on the floor. I'm not wearing a bra, and my nipples harden from having his eyes on me.

His dark-brown curls are wild, one wayward strand falling across the top of his forehead, and I run my fingers over it, pushing it off his face and tangling my fingers through his silky strands.

"*Beautiful*," he rasps, leaning in and sucking one of my breasts into his mouth.

I gasp at the wet sensation, his tongue swirling around the nipple, his teeth biting down until pain turns into pleasure.

"Take off my pants," I demand.

He releases my breast with a slick pop, the cool air causing goose bumps to spread across my body. His hands move languidly, dragging down my sides and over my hips until he hooks his fingers beneath the waistband of my leggings and tugs. The fabric scrapes against my thighs as he pushes them down, and I stand still, arousal clouding my vision as he strips me bare. They pool around my ankles and he surges back up, lifting me by the waist and planting me next to the sink. The cold of the counter bites into the skin of my ass and I suck in a breath at the sudden chill against my heated skin.

Brayden's gaze is locked between my legs. He removes my shoes and discards my leggings before tracing his palms back up, squeezing my inner thighs.

I open them wider to give him a good view.

"'Flesh stays no further reason than rising at thy name,'" he murmurs, rubbing his nose along my slit.

My abs tense. "Are you quoting Shakespeare to my pussy?"

He presses a soft kiss to the top of my clit. "You love it."

"I don't." *I do.*

He moves back, a devilish smirk gracing his face. "'I lie with her, and she with me.'" He pauses, and then suddenly his tongue is on me, swirling in small circles around the sensitive nerves.

I whimper, heat shooting down my legs.

His tongue disappears. "'And in our faults by lies we flattered be.'"

My chest warms, desire winding like a rope around my core and up my spine. I think I like him this way.

"You don't have to trust me, Evelina. But words are your safe space, the same way that they're mine."

My fingers thread through his hair.

"Let me be your calm in the chaos, pretty girl."

Emotion swarms through my chest and slams behind my eyes so quickly it makes me lose my breath, but before I can process the feeling, his mouth is on me again, *devouring* me like a man desperate to prove his worth.

My muscles tighten, tingles sprinkling across my abdomen and pooling between my legs. My body jerks when he licks my clit, his fingers massaging the insides of my thighs.

"Yes," I moan, throwing my head back. "Suck it."

He does, closing his lips around me and pulling the bundle of nerves into his mouth, the tip of his tongue torturing me, slow suction mixed with languid licks, over and over until the tension spreads so thin it's about to snap.

And then I come apart, exploding on his tongue and crying out, grinding myself against his face while my vision goes black. He doesn't stop his ministrations and I rip his head away once I become too sensitive. He grins, his mouth glistening from the mess he's made.

"Come here," I say.

His arms cage me in immediately as he stands and I pull his face to mine, licking along his lips before dipping in his mouth.

"That's right, pretty girl," he groans. "Suck yourself off my tongue and see how good you really taste."

My core throbs from his words and I meld our lips together, the musky taste of *me* mixed with everything *him* making my eyes roll.

His arms wrap around me tightly, his hips moving between my legs until his jean-covered erection presses against my bare pussy.

I pull away, hopping down from the counter and pressing my hand against his torso to push him back until his legs hit a kitchen chair.

"Sit."

He does.

"You're right. You *do* follow directions incredibly well." Smiling, I bend over him and lift his shirt, tossing it to the side, my eyes drinking in the sharp lines and muscles of his torso. I grab at his belt, undoing the buckle and sliding it from the loops. "Put your hands behind the chair."

His brow lifts but he does as I ask. I walk behind him, slipping my fingers over his and turning his palms to face each other before wrapping his belt around the outside and tying them together. Anticipation lights up my middle, desire blossoming from how much power he's giving me.

Sauntering back to his front, I kneel between his legs, sliding my hands up his thighs until I get to the top of his pants and undo the button. He lifts his hips, helping me undress him. My heart beats out of my chest as I pull down his clothes, allowing his cock to bob free. It's so hard and thick that it's physically pulsing, and my mouth waters at the sight.

"Do your wrists feel okay?" I ask.

I don't want him to be in pain, especially since I know he's only doing this for me. His tongue swipes along his bottom lip and he nods, his eyes blazing as they stare into mine. I reach out and grip him. He jerks in my hand and I grin, stroking from base to tip, wanting to make him feel as crazy as I do for him.

"Do you trust me?"

He grunts, a bead of precum leaking from his head. "I'm not sure."

"It's smarter if you don't," I reply honestly.

My chest twists and I rise up slightly, just enough to press a light kiss on his lips. It's tender and, quite frankly, unwelcome, but I allow the softer moment, wanting to show my gratitude for what he's giving.

There's something so attractive about one person submitting completely to another, being at their mercy, accepting whatever they see fit to give you.

I want to consume him and revel in his surrender.

His gaze never leaves mine as I bend down over his rigid dick, blowing small puffs of air against him until his muscles tense and his hips buck.

"You like watching me, don't you?" I ask.

"Yes."

My tongue slips out and runs along the length of his shaft, and I know that if he really wanted to, he could easily escape his restraint and take control.

The fact that he doesn't makes me desperate to reward him.

Another lick. This time, I make sure the flat of my tongue with my piercing hits his head, and I circle the sensitive flesh, hoping the added sensation drives him wild.

He groans and thrusts his hips, his cock slapping against my parted lips. I grip him at the base and move back slightly, staring at the thick vein that runs along the length of him, feeling the pressure grow heavy deep in my abdomen. I lower myself again, applying the lightest pressure as I move my face down, the insides of my cheeks barely brushing against his skin. I reach up, my nails scratching against his balls. They immediately tense up, his cock jumping in my mouth.

He groans when I pull away, tossing his head back. "You're fucking *killing* me."

"These things must be done delicately," I say. "But I like having you at my mercy."

He stares down at me, his eyes wild and his jaw clenching. Still, he doesn't try to jerk himself free.

"You're being such a good boy." I smile. "Should I suck your cock as a reward?"

"Please," he whispers, moving his hips as much as he can while his arms are tied behind his back.

I lower my mouth and swallow him until he hits the back of my throat, my cheeks hollowing out as I suck. The salty taste of him makes wetness drip down the insides of my thighs, and I moan, which causes him to jolt forward. I gag when he hits the back of my mouth, and his cock throbs on my tongue. I push farther until he breaks the resistance and slips down my throat, my eyes watering. My lips reach his base and I move my tongue, pressing it against his shaft, trying not to cough as he starves me of my air.

"Goddamn," he groans.

When I can't take anymore, I move back, thin lines of saliva connecting the tip of his dick to my lips, spit dripping down my chin and onto the top of my chest. My esophagus burns but the pain makes my pussy throb, so I breathe in deep and dive back down, starting a quick motion of jerking him off with my mouth and tongue until I feel him swell and his balls tense in my hands.

I pull off quickly, and he moans, his chest heaving with his heavy breaths.

"Naughty boy, trying to come before I tell you to." I move from my knees, running my palms up his heated skin until my arms are wrapped around his neck and my ass is in his lap, his thick cock pressed against my slick pussy. "Do you want to come, baby?" I whisper against his lips, grinding down on top of him.

"*Fuck*, yes," he grits out.

"Tell me."

He surges forward, his breath ghosting across my neck and sending a chill down the length of my body. "I want you to use me up until you've had your fill, then let me come inside you."

My core contracts painfully, and I grip his face in my hands, smashing our lips together until our teeth clack and our tongues collide.

His cock is there, *right* there at my entrance, and I lift my hips slightly.

We moan into each other's mouths when he slips inside, and my walls clench around him. I feel so fucking *full.*

I move my hips back and forth, matching the rhythm of our sloppy kiss, my clit rubbing against his groin with every pass.

"Fuck," he whispers against my lips. "I'm close."

Moving my hand down the front of my body, I start to bounce up and down, my muscles tightening until it feels like I'll burst from the tension. And then I shatter, my pussy milking him as I cry out. He captures the moan and swallows it for himself.

He follows shortly after, his hips slamming into mine as he holds himself deep, his cock pulsing wildly as he pumps his cum deep inside.

I collapse against him, my ears ringing and my vision hazy. Reaching around the back of the chair, I fumble with his belt until his wrists are free. Immediately, they wrap around me, pulling me tighter to him. I rest my face against his chest as he presses a kiss against the top of my head, and I feel…content.

Almost like happiness is *right* here, waiting for me to reach out and grab it.

So I sink into the moment, closing my eyes to the sound of his beating heart.

And when he leaves an hour later, saying he has to go grab Dorothy because he'd hate to break his promise, that feeling I was so close to holding evaporates into dust.

CHAPTER 22

Nicholas

I'M BORED.

I should be focused and attentive since going out with Dorothy and trying to garner some information is the entire reason I'm in Kinland and pretending to be something I'm not. But be that as it may, my mind keeps spinning on its axis, rotating back to the girl with black hair and a violent streak.

"Sucks that you're stuck with Evie all the time," Dorothy says, dipping her fork into a piece of cherry cheesecake.

I snap out of my reverie, moving my gaze to her over the low lit candle flickering on top of the white linen table. We're at some fancy Italian restaurant where Dorothy said she wanted to eat, and we've *been* here for the past two hours, but I've gotten no information out of her. *Yet.*

Forcing a grin, I hum, then sip from my wine, quirking a brow as I lean back in my seat. "I'm not stuck with her now."

The words are bitter on my tongue.

A blush creeps along Dorothy's face and she swallows, dabbing a napkin on her lips before placing it back in her lap.

I take the moment to look at her fully. She's a beautiful woman, but there's an innocence about her that seems almost superficial. As though her features allow her to bat her lashes, widen her doe-like eyes, and fool the world.

In a weird way, it makes me think of my sister. When Rose was in the throes of her addiction, there wasn't a single thing she wouldn't do to get her next fix, and as a result, she became a master of manipulation. My heart pinches as I wonder how she's doing without me. If she's staying strong and staying clean.

"You're right," Dorothy says. "You should do this more often…spend time with me, I mean." Her voice drops, becoming low and breathy.

My stomach curdles, hating that I have to lead her on in order to get information, feeling almost like I'm betraying her sister. But that's ridiculous because I haven't actually *promised* Evelina anything, nor would I.

I'm not here for her.

Clearing my throat, I shake my head to rid myself of the intrusive thoughts, forcing myself to be the agent I've always been. "According to your sister, you're a hard woman to track down. Do you even *have* time to spend with me, sweetheart?"

Dorothy licks her lips and cocks her head to the side. "Evie's just mad that she can't watch me like a guard dog anymore."

"Oh?"

She leans over the table. "She's *obsessed* with me."

I chuckle, and it's genuine, because the version of Evelina in Dorothy's head couldn't be further from who I know her to be.

"In any case," she continues, "I like to actually have a social life, which is more than I can say for her."

"So you're not working for your father like she thinks?"

Internally, I cringe at the question, worried that I'm being blatantly obvious in my snooping, but Dorothy doesn't flinch.

She lifts a shoulder. "No, I am. Our dad wants me to be more involved, and I want to do whatever makes him happy."

"So you have a good relationship then?" I take another sip of wine, letting the oaky notes coat my tongue and warm my throat. "You and your dad?"

Dorothy's grin spreads wide across her face. "Yeah. It took a long time for him to see me, you know? But he finally does, after a lot of blood, sweat, and tears on my end."

"It wasn't always that way?" I press.

Her eyes shutter, and I know from that look alone that I've hit a sore spot, something she won't be willing to talk about.

"I don't like to talk about how things *used* to be. What matters is that now, he loves me the most. He *trusts* me the most. There isn't anything he wouldn't tell me." She dusts off a piece of invisible lint from the skirt of her pale blue dress. "And I'm tired. Can we go?"

The sudden shift in her attitude shocks me, but I blanket the expression on my face and nod, making a mental note and filing it away.

Dorothy doesn't like to talk about the past.

And she wasn't always her father's favorite.

It's been four days since I've seen Evelina.

I left shortly after she tied me up and flipped my world upside down, and I've been spiraling into bottomless depths ever since. She made me come harder than I ever have with *any* woman, and then she lay on my chest and cuddled up to me like I was her man.

But then something happened.

A thought whispered in my brain. That I would give it all up in a heartbeat if I could stay like that forever.

And thoughts like that are unacceptable to me, so I used the one thing I knew would hurt her and left to find her sister.

It had the intended result.

Her eyes, which up until that point had been soft and vulnerable, slammed shut. And when she looked at me again, there was nothing left but an icy tundra where nothing could survive.

I debated on confronting her the next day but fought against the urge.

Then I ran into her on day two. She wouldn't even look at me, making a quick excuse about needing to talk to her dad.

By day three, I realized that pussy was fucking with my head, and no matter how good it is, she's still my enemy. We have absolutely nothing in common outside our sexual compatibility.

And now it's day four. I'm sitting across from her dad in the back office of the Yellow Brick, and my mind can't focus. I'm too busy wondering where she is, what she's doing. If she still hates me as much as I know I should hate her.

"We're going to Chicago."

I focus in quickly on Farrell, his words shocking me into the present.

It's always been a possibility, having to go back to Chicago while I'm pretending to be someone else. Working an undercover case in the same state where you live is risky at best. But the pros outweigh the cons. They needed someone local who could be convincing in their knowledge of the area. The Irish mob isn't exactly known for welcoming outsiders.

Maybe I can sneak away and see Rose.

"What for?" Ezekiel asks, his eyes glancing to me and then back.

"A charity auction, of course." Farrell grins around his cigar. "I'm a phila...phi...someone who does good deeds, and the mayor's reelection is coming up."

"What's in Chicago for the mayor of Kinland?" I ask.

"It's a night on the water," Farrell says behind a cloud of smoke. "For an important cause."

"What's that?" Ezekiel laughs. "Sucking rich people's dicks and lining their pockets?"

"There will be a lot of important guests there," Farrell replies.

Ezekiel scoffs. "Oscar hasn't done anything for us in years. It would serve him right to get kicked out of office."

Farrell shakes his head. "He was friends with my daughter. I don't blame him for keeping his distance after she died on *his* boat, right in front of his and Dorothy's eyes, can you?"

I sit straighter in my chair. *This* is a surprising twist. I hadn't known Nessa died on the mayor's boat. Or that Dorothy saw it happen.

"In any case," he continues, "Oscar *is* working with us now. He's set up something for us with the Cantanellis."

"The Italians?" I ask. "They're trying to work together now?"

His eyes sharpen. "Unsurprisingly, they're tired of not being able to compete with our product. They've been...less than accommodating with their requests that we stop distributing in their areas."

Unease wraps around my chest. "You're moving in on *their* territory?"

He shrugs. "I'm simply sitting down to negotiate terms."

"Are you planning to give them your supplier?" I ask, leaning forward in my seat.

Farrell's smile drops and his thick two fingers come up to take the Black & Mild from his mouth, tapping it into the crystal ashtray, his eyes narrowing. "Let me worry about my supplier. It will be there, and that's what matters. You worry about keeping Dorothy safe."

My heart stutters.

"No Evie?" Ezekiel questions.

"Evie's busy," Farrell snaps.

My middle pulls tight, my mind once again wondering where she is and what she's doing.

The door bursts open, a sweaty Liam rushing in, his eyes bloodshot and his outfit crumpled.

"Skip," he pants.

Farrell laughs, pointing his finger at Liam. "Look at this out-of-shape motherfucker. What's got you running?"

"Cillian's missing." His voice is flat, but I sense the mania in his tone.

Farrell's face grows serious, all amusement draining away. "And my product?"

Liam's fists clench and he shakes his head.

Ezekiel tenses next to me, our eyes meeting for the briefest of moments. I never mentioned that Evelina murdered Cillian, and apparently neither did he.

Farrell sits back in his seat, picking up his Black & Mild, the smoke swirling around his head and evaporating in the air. He removes the cigar from his mouth and waves his fingers back and forth, running his tongue over the front of his teeth. "Walk this back for me, Liam. You come to me." He points to his own chest. "You tell me you've got someone we can trust. Someone loyal. Someone who can make us *more* than what we've been getting. Am I right so far?"

"Yeah, but—" Liam starts.

My senses sharpen, and everything that's been plaguing my mind up to this moment disappears. This conversation seems important.

"But nothing." Farrell shakes his head. "You know, Evie says you're the rat. You been talking to the cops?"

Liam's face blanches. "What? No, I—"

Farrell jumps up from his seat, grabbing a gun from underneath his desk and popping Liam twice, right in the head. His body drops to the floor, eyes wide and staring.

Slowly, Farrell walks forward until he's towering over Liam's corpse. He spits on his chest. "I can't stand a fucking liar."

My stomach heaves.

The wind whips across the water of Lake Michigan and rolls through the city, making the cold sting my cheeks and freeze my hands. My breaths come in visible clouds of air, and I rest against the graffiti-covered concrete wall, watching Seth pace back and forth in the back alley.

It wasn't easy to get away once we got to Chicago, but here I am.

"When's the meeting?" he asks.

"This weekend. Saturday night." I rub my hands together before stuffing them in the pockets of my jacket. "Figured we could set something up. No way he isn't going to bring product for them to sample."

Seth blows out a breath. "Man…you know that's not what we're after."

"Listen," I continue, frustration squeezing my insides. "No

one's gonna tell me shit. Ezekiel's been there for years, and he still has no clue. Let's bring them in, shake them down. We can get Farrell to crack." I pause.

Seth purses his lips. "We can set you up with the PD again, but Cap doesn't want to make any stupid moves."

I shake my head. "PD is compromised as fuck. Farrell definitely has leaks in Kinland, which means he probably does here too."

"What about his daughters?" he asks.

"Yeah," I say, the icy tendrils of dread wrapping around my neck. "They might know something."

He groans, pinching the bridge of his nose. "You know a 'might' isn't enough. Galen wants the big dog, and if we move too early, we could lose it all."

"I'm dying here, Seth," I plead, desperation pushing the words from my tongue. "Do you know what it's like to stand by and watch people get hurt, watch laws be broken, and do *nothing*?" I press my fingers to my temple. "It fucks with your head."

"You've never had a problem before," he states.

"Yeah, well, I'm having a problem now," I bite back.

"Is this because of the girl?"

I jerk away from him. "What?"

"Evelina Westerly." He steps toward me, cocking his head. His hand reaches out and rests on my shoulder, and I grit my teeth, pushing down the urge to shove him away. "Are you in too deep, Nick?"

A burst of anger explodes through me and I grip his shirt, twisting until he's slammed against the wall. Red clouds my vision. "How many fucking times do I gotta tell you not to call me that? Jesus *Christ*. You trying to get me killed?"

"But that's who you are," Seth seethes. "You're Nicholas Woodsworth." He shoves my chest, and my hold loosens. "Born August seventeenth. You had a shit childhood with a junkie mom who made you grow up too fast, and you've got a sister waiting at home. One who loves you and asks about you *every* day."

I release my grip on his shirt, stumbling back as I stare down at my hands, my stomach rolling.

What the fuck is happening to me?

"I—"

"You know," Seth cuts me off, "you even talk like them now."

I'm still staring at my hands.

"I get it, man. I know it's hard, and in my heart of hearts, I believe no one can do this job like you. You've got the gift." He hesitates. "But the reason you're so good is because you don't *feel* things the way other people do. You're a machine. You don't get attached."

I snap up my head, meeting his worried gaze.

"So if you're starting to?" he continues. "That's something we need to address."

Licking my lips, I shake my head, ignoring the way an ache is spreading between my temples. "No, I–I'm fine. Just stressed. I'm sorry." Flexing my shaky fingers, I swallow, determination settling like a heavy brick in the center of my gut. "I think Dorothy may know something."

Seth's eyes shoot up. "You sure about that?"

I shake my head, huffing out an exasperated laugh. "No, but if she does…if we offer her immunity, she might take it. Just—just give me some time with her."

CHAPTER 23

Evelina

THE MAYOR'S DESK IS LARGER THAN IT LOOKS ON camera.

I grab a Cuban from his fancy case and lean back in the chair, placing my heels up on the ostentatious oak and lighting the end of the cigar. There's nobody in here right now, but after a quick talk with his secretary up front, I convinced her to take an early lunch and let me wait in his office.

We're old family friends, after all, the mayor and I, although in the end years of Nessa's life, I was spending more time practicing my botany and producing our drugs than I was out to soiree's representing the Westerly name.

Guilt slams into me, whooshing the breath from my lungs, the grief following quickly after. Because maybe if I *had* tried harder, put forth more of an effort in those last days, she'd still be here.

If I had said yes to attending dinner on his boat and gone with her and Dorothy, I could have stopped what happened.

I push the thought away, refocusing my attention on what I'm here for. I'm tired of Oscar pretending like we don't run this town, pretending as though everything he's accomplished isn't because of Nessa and everything she's done for him. I'm here to ensure that he realigns his loyalties.

This is the perfect time to meet with him. Everyone else has gone to Chicago early, my dad claiming he wants his guys to "enjoy the town" before Oscar's event, but I stayed behind, saying I needed to be here with the poppies.

It isn't a lie. Botany is a very time-consuming thing, and I do need to check on them frequently to ensure we have a constant stream of opium to make Flying Monkey.

But that's not why I didn't go.

The office door swings open, and in walks Oscar. He has a look of concentration on his pale face, and his jet-black hair is stiff and perfectly coiffed, slicked back with a politician's gleam. His footsteps falter when he sees me, his hand pausing from where it was loosening the knot in his tie.

"Well, well, well. If it isn't little Evelina Westerly." His eyes drag up my body. "All grown up."

"Hello, Oscar," I reply, blowing out a cloud of smoke.

"Your father send you?" He walks closer.

I click my tongue, placing the Cuban down on the corner of his desk. His eyes follow the movement, narrowing when some of the ash falls onto his fancy purple-and-gold Persian carpet.

"I'm here on my sister's behalf."

"Which one?"

I tilt my head, watching his face carefully. I hadn't expected him to say that. "Which one do you *think*?"

His eyes squint, and there are a few moments of awkward silence where we're locked in a heated stare. Finally, a grin spreads across his face. "Are you fucking with me?"

"You know." I ignore his question, running the tips of my fingers along the wood of his desk. "This is a nice piece of furniture. Strong. Sturdy." The chair creaks as I move forward, knocking my knuckles on the top. "You could do a lot of things on a desk like this."

"Hmm." His smile grows. "Is that why you've come to see me? To test out how *sturdy* my desk can be?"

"Oh, Oscar." I laugh, standing up and walking toward him. His eyes are half-lidded and the strong smell of cologne wafts into my nostrils as I get near. I wrap my fingers around his tie, smoothing it down and straightening the knot before craning my neck to meet his gaze. "There's some talk about you, you know? Thought you might want to know."

"Really?" His brow quirks. "About?"

"You being in bed with the Cantanellis."

He scoffs. "Please."

"You were close with Nessa, so consider this a favor...a visit to remind you where you came from." I pat my palms on the lapels of his suit. "I'd hate for someone as *important* as you to get caught up in nasty rumors."

His body tenses. "Are you threatening a public official, Miss Westerly?"

"Just a chat with an old friend." I shrug.

"Well, as fun as this *chat* is," he drawls, "it isn't a good time. I have a city council meeting in thirty minutes."

"Of course, I'll let you get to it." I step around him to walk toward the door, my heels clicking on the wood floor and echoing off the plain beige walls. My fingers wrap around the metal knob and I twist, but before I leave completely, I pause, turning back to face him.

He's watching me with his hands in his pockets and a look of consternation on his face.

"You know…it *is* a shame we don't have time to test out that desk." I sigh. "I guess I'll just ask Commissioner Boq how it holds up."

I wink and his nostrils flare. "Get the fuck out of my office."

Laughing, I spin back around and leave, the rush of threatening someone flooding through my veins like a drug.

Three hours later and I'm back with my poppies, breathing in the earthy scents while I write. Scratch that, while I *attempt* to write. I've been blocked for six days, ever since I let Brayden whisper poetry into my skin while I came around his tongue.

Words are your safe space.

I flick the pen back and forth again and again, the end tapping the edges of my knuckles and then the page, creating an agitated rhythm.

Does he whisper poetry to Dorothy too?

My insides sour at the thought and I groan, slamming my notebook on the ground at my side. Closing my eyes, I count backward, focusing on my breathing and trying to find my center. But flashes of Brayden and Dorothy filter through my brain. *Are they having fun together in Chicago?*

I feel…used. Pathetic. Weak. I should have known better than to give in. And it's not only that. I continually give in, over and over, reveling in the way he makes my body sing. I should have listened to my inner voice when it waved its giant red flag like a warning sign from day one, screaming in my psyche.

But for the first time since Nessa, someone *else's* voice snuck into the cracks, and I started listening to him instead of myself. Like Pavlov's dog, he trained me effortlessly to accept the bare minimum. To crave the back-and-forth, the animosity morphing into excitement whenever he was near simply because he paid me some attention.

And whether it was negative or positive, at least he was *seeing* me.

Plus, I can grudgingly admit he's the best fuck I've ever had.

Let me be your calm in the chaos.

Bullshit.

Sighing, I run my fingers through my knotted hair, pulling at the roots until the sting clears my thoughts. It doesn't work. In fact, the longer I sit in the silence, the more I replay every single encounter Brayden and I have ever had, searching for some reason beyond the physical that explains the pull I feel.

And when I get to the other night, when he was telling me about his mom, an epiphany goes off like a light bulb exploding in my brain.

Scrambling from my place on the floor, I practically sprint over to my phone, picking it up and speed-dialing Cody. He answers on the third ring.

"Not a good time, babe."

"How did Brayden's mom die?" I rush out.

"I…who?"

"The guy I had you look into. Didn't you say his mom died?"

"Uhh…yeah. Cancer. When he was eighteen. Listen, can I call you back?"

I drop the phone, a pounding ache spreading through my head and through every limb of my body, followed closely by anger.

Pure, unadulterated rage.

That motherfucker lied to me. Again.

CHAPTER 24

Nicholas

I ASSUMED "WATCH OUT FOR MY DAUGHTER" meant keeping an eye on her during the event, but clearly that isn't the case. I've been put on babysitting duty, wining and dining Dorothy while the other guys could be getting up to anything. It puts me on edge, makes me wonder *why* I'm not with them.

Dorothy, on the other hand, doesn't seem upset that she isn't being included, which isn't wholly surprising because she doesn't fit the mold for this life. It's as if she *wants* to be part of the business but doesn't truly understand what that business entails. Although according to her, Farrell tells her everything.

But I'm not convinced on how true that is. From what I've seen, Farrell is far too protective to allow her to truly hold any power. Showing your enemies—even the ones you're doing deals with—who's important to you is a surefire way to give them ammunition against you later.

Relationships are a weakness, and when you play dangerous games, you have to be a fortress of strength.

So here I am with Dorothy, *again*, eating bruschetta-wrapped appetizers and drinking wine in the hotel restaurant. It's a swanky place, and while I know I should be focused on gaining her trust so she's easier to flip, I can't keep from wishing it wasn't *her* across the table.

Her hair is silky and smooth, a beautiful brown any man would kill to sink their fingers into.

But I'd rather see it tangled and black.

Her eyes are soft and open, serene, like dipping in calm water on a sunny day.

But I ache to feel them raging like a storm.

And when she throws back her head and laughs, my mind wonders what it would sound like coming from someone *else's* pouty lips.

"Is that your natural hair color?" I ask, trying like hell to take my mind off things that don't matter.

Dorothy grins and runs a hand over the strands. "Yeah, why?"

I shrug. "Just wondering. Your sister dyes it. I was curious if you did the same."

Her eyes drop the smallest bit but her smile widens. "Evelina started messing with her appearance the second our sister died. Lord knows why. Maybe so her looks would match her black soul."

She giggles like what she said is funny, but it isn't. In fact, it makes me a little sad. I also realize opportunity when I see it, and the fact that she brought up her dead sister has me grabbing onto the lifeline and pressing for more information. "I'm sorry about your sister."

Her lips purse and she reaches out, grabbing a piece of bruschetta-wrapped bacon from the center plate and popping it in her mouth. She chews, then takes a sip of wine before she speaks. "We weren't close."

"But she and Evelina were?"

She takes another sip of cabernet, the toe of her bright-silver shoe tapping against the leg of the table. "Boating accident."

"A crash?"

I already know, of course, but the way Dorothy is fidgeting, her entire demeanor having changed from the carefree girl she was moments before, has curiosity bubbling at my edges. I had a feeling her discomfort with the past had to do with her sister's death, and she's all but confirming it.

She dabs the corner of her mouth with her napkin before placing it back in her lap. "She fell overboard and drowned. Just an unfortunate accident. I was there, you know? Nessa never really paid me any mind, not compared to Evie, but whenever she'd go on the water with Mayor Norman, she'd take me. She always said it was important for it to be a 'family event.'" Her eyes take on an odd gleam, almost as if she's about to cry. Only she never does. "Par for the course for Nessa to only care about me when it comes to keeping up appearances."

"She didn't care?"

Dorothy hums, her eyes narrowing. "She was a jealous hag. Couldn't handle when I grew up and challenged her as the prettiest Westerly sister."

There's a quick flash of bitterness that tinges the edges of Dorothy's words, belying the truth behind her innocent facade.

"You know, they never even found her body," she muses, picking up her wineglass again. "She's just somewhere out there, decomposing at the bottom of Lake Michigan."

"Jesus, Dorothy. That's morbid." I cringe.

She laughs, taking another gulp of her drink. "Like I said... we weren't close."

I smile and nod, but I feel anything but light. There was an odd undercurrent in that conversation, something that has my intuition jabbing at my spine, and I make a mental note to look deeper into Vanessa Westerly's death.

Suddenly I feel the leg of my pants jostle, Dorothy's shoe running up the length of my shin and then back down.

"You know, all this talk is boring me," she purrs. "Want to get out of here?"

No.

I can't fuck her.

I have zero interest in fucking her.

"Sure." I clear my throat.

We get the check and charge it to my room before walking through the lobby and taking the elevator to the twenty-first floor where her room is. I stop in front of her door, and when she opens it to step inside, I stay behind in the hall.

She spins toward me, her brows drawing in. "Aren't you coming?"

I shake my head. "As tempting as that offer is, I'd rather not end up on your dad's shit list."

She drops her gaze, slowly sliding it back up my body. "I won't tell."

Nausea teases my stomach as I lean in, pressing a kiss to her cheek. "Rain check."

For the next two hours, I pace in my room, my mind warring between staying put in case someone comes by or taking the risk by going to see my sister. It's stupid, but I'm losing my mind sitting here and doing nothing.

Rose wins.

I slip out of my room, using the back stairwell and hurrying down four flights until I reach the back exit.

Our apartment isn't in this part of town, but it's not *too* far, and I can be there within twenty minutes on foot. I haven't let myself think about her while I'm undercover on the case. It's too much to try and separate the people in *Nick's* life from who I need to be when I'm Brayden. But I can't resist the temptation to check in while I'm here.

Just for a minute. Just to make sure.

When I'm about three blocks away, I find an old pay phone hidden in the back of the Gas 'N Go. I rush to it, glancing around before moving into the small glass stall and fishing out some change from my pocket.

"Pick up, pick up, pick up," I mutter, jumping on my toes to keep my body from feeling the chilly Chicago air.

Her voice mail clicks on.

Damn it.

I try one more time and then give up, hanging the phone back on the receiver before making my way down the last three blocks, checking behind me every few feet. There's no one around, but I can't shake the eerie tingles occasionally creeping up my back.

The apartment building is tall and beige, a four-story shithole that has just enough working equipment to be considered "livable." I skip over every other stair as I walk up the front steps and enter the door, my stomach tensing with nerves, although I'm not sure why I'm nervous. I haven't seen her in a few months, but she's still my sister.

The elevator to the right has caution tape slapped across the doors, the same way it has for the past two years, and I walk by it without a second thought, heading toward the stairwell that leads to our second-floor apartment.

My footsteps echo off the concrete walls as I hustle up the steps.

I reach our door, the large 4A gleaming against the muted red paint, and I lift my hand to knock, rapping my knuckles until they ache.

Nobody answers.

Anxiety tightens my stomach.

It's eleven at night. Where the fuck could she be?

I knock again, this time pressing my ear to the door and jiggling the doorknob. I knew I should have brought my key, but I didn't want anything on my person that could be taken. You never know when your items will end up in the wrong hands.

Still, no one answers.

Sighing, I rest my forehead against the door, sadness welling through my middle at the missed opportunity. I don't know how much longer this case will last, but I'm halfway desperate to see Rose, hoping she'd get my head on straight.

Without her to ground me, I'm just a hollow, rusted shell playing the part of a living, breathing man.

A noise from down the hall makes me raise my head, and before I can turn around, the click of a safety switch is in my ear, then the harsh press of metal against the back of my skull.

"Care to explain why the hell you're here?"

CHAPTER 25

Evelina

IT WAS A SPUR-OF-THE-MOMENT DECISION TO come to Chicago. I knew where they were staying—I was the one who made the reservations. So I waited in the wings, ready to hunt down Brayden and either shoot him or cut his dick off for lying to me.

But then I saw him leading my sister to her room, pulling on her hair and pressing soft kisses to her cheek, and my stomach turned in on itself, nausea burning through my insides like battery acid.

I went to his hotel door afterward, but the sharp one-eighty of my emotions kept me from entering. I wanted to hold on to my rage when I saw him, not feel like a sick puppy that watched its owners give them up and find another dog.

When he reappeared, his body radiating the worst type of anxious energy, I followed him. And now we're here, with him looking defeated as my Desert Eagle presses against his head.

"You know," I start, "you almost had me."

His entire body stiffens and he turns around. I allow him

to, moving my gun from his head down to his chest once we're face-to-face. The muscles in my arms are already aching from the weight of the weapon and how tensely I'm holding it, but I don't falter in my poise. And then, for the first time since I've met Brayden Walsh, I see emotion in his gaze. Genuine fear bleeds into his eyes, just a flash, and then it's gone.

"And you call *me* the stalker," he jokes. But there's no humor in his tone.

"Shut up," I hiss through clenched teeth. "Explain what you're doing."

He nods, placing his hands in his pockets and looking at where the barrel is pressed against his chest. "I didn't know you were in Chicago."

"Surprise." I grin.

He glances behind him at the closed door and blows out a breath, his cheeks puffing slightly when he does. "If you're planning to shoot me, I'd rather not bleed out all over my friend's doorstep. It's rude."

I tilt my head. "What friend?"

"I'll tell you anything you want to know about her, sweetheart. Just put the gun down and let's go back outside."

My hands shake, thick gusts of green whipping through me when he confirms it's a woman, and then I want to kill myself for feeling any jealousy at all.

"I swear to god, Brayden, if you have a girlfriend..."

He smirks, those stupid fucking dimples lighting up his face, and he steps into me, the end of my gun touching his chest. "Jealous?"

"Just not interested in community dick."

His hand grasps the side of my face, cupping my cheek. He

opens his mouth but hesitates, his eyes shuttering like he's trying to figure out what to say. "It's not a girlfriend…it's my sister."

I squint my eyes. "You don't have a sister."

"I do."

Slowly, I lower the gun.

He grabs my palm immediately, tangling our fingers together and dragging me behind him. I follow, too stunned from his tender touches and his revelations to argue.

My mind races as we walk down the hallway and through the stairwell. He maneuvers around the building as if he knows it intimately, and my heart squeezes tight, wondering if he's lying.

Cody said he had no relatives.

He opens a side door to the outside, and the cool air smacks my face, but even then he doesn't stop until he's pulled me around the side of the building into a small, dark alley. He yanks back his hand like I lit him on fire.

I shake my head, raising my gun again. "You're lying to me."

His eyes darken and he snaps forward, twisting my arm quickly, my tendons stretching as he steals the Eagle from my hand and points it at me. His other palm grasps my wrists tightly, binding them with his strong grip and shoving them above my head and against the wall.

"Let me lay something out for you, sweetheart." He runs the barrel along the side of my face, the metal scraping against my cheek, my heart surging into my throat. "I may be working for your father right now because I'm ready for a change of pace, but I've been a thief for years. And in that time, I've stolen from very dangerous men. *Important* men. You think I'd do all that without ensuring the safety of people important to me?"

I grind my teeth and push against his hold.

He tightens his grip. "I know you're not stupid enough to believe you're the only one with access to government files."

Confusion swims through my head even though everything he's saying makes sense. In fact, if I were in his situation, I would probably do the same. "My guy would know if your documents were fake."

He smirks, pressing his hips farther into me. "You sure about that?"

"No," I admit grudgingly. "Get my gun out of my face."

"Doesn't feel so good when it's on the other side, does it?" The barrel is cold as he glides it along the skin of my neck, dragging it down at a torturous pace until it caresses my collarbone. "I scrubbed the fact that I had a sister. Made up some stories about a lonely kid who lived a normal life until he lost his mom. Congratulations, you fell for it. Just like everybody else."

My heart rate speeds, adrenaline thrumming through every single vein. "Let me go."

"You're hardly in the position to be demanding."

My fingers are starting to go numb from his grip around my wrists, and I shift, the brick scratching against my back even through my clothes. If I wanted to fight, if I *truly* wanted to, then I know I could, but for whatever reason, I don't.

If I'm honest, this is why I showed up, isn't it? Why I jumped in my car, gun half-cocked, ready to get in Brayden's face and piss him off. It wasn't to demand answers, not entirely anyway. It was because my emotions were exploding, and the only one who takes the hits, the only one who lets me *feel*...is him. He doesn't tell me to get it together or to not be exactly who I am. Instead, he cushions the blow, making sure my pieces don't scatter in the wind. And maybe that's why I revel in his attention, lusting for the way his jaw muscles tick and his eyes grow dark when he puts me in my place. Or when he gives up his control.

He may have given Dorothy soft kisses and fancy dinners, but he doesn't give her this.

I slacken in his hold, becoming pliant, his breath skating across my cheek as he maneuvers my gun along the planes of my body. He notices the shift and moves in closer until his body is flush with mine.

My teeth sink into my lower lip, and his eyes drop to follow the movement.

"You like this, don't you, pretty girl," he rasps, pressing the weapon against the side of my neck. "Does it excite you?"

"Stop flattering yourself." My voice comes out breathy.

"It does." He smiles, dipping his head down until his lips graze against my skin. "I'll tell you a secret. The thought of doing things to you right here in this dirty alley has me so fucking hard."

My insides quake at his words and I push half-heartedly against him, trying like hell to hold on to my anger from a few minutes ago and failing miserably.

"*You* have me so. Fucking. Hard."

He keeps my arms pinned as he works his way over my breasts with the Eagle, slipping the barrel between my cleavage. My nipples tighten, aching for his touch.

"I want to fuck you here," he says, pulling the gun back so my shirt peels away from my skin. "I spent *days* memorizing the curves of your body just to go home and take out my cock, stroking it to the vision of you in my head."

My teeth sink harder into my lip, the flesh splitting until the tang of warm copper hits my taste buds.

He moves again, gliding the metal down my sides, goose bumps sprouting in every place he roams.

Voices shout from down the street, echoing off the buildings and growing louder as the seconds pass, but he doesn't stop. In fact, his erection throbs against me, like the thought of them seeing us turns him on.

"You and these skirts," he groans, finally releasing my wrists and reaching down to slip his free hand underneath the fabric.

My fingertips tingle as blood rushes back and I fling my arms around his neck, my body too shaky to stand on my own.

"Give me your words, pretty girl." The gun presses against my ribs and his left hand ghosts across my pussy, his fingers stroking my clit through the soaked fabric of my underwear. "I want your little love spells."

The voices are so close now, it would be a miracle if they *don't* see us, and my stomach somersaults when I visualize what we'll look like when they do. He wants poetry, but I can't give him mine. It's too personal, and I'm already giving too much.

"'My life had stood, a loaded gun,'" I force out between heavy breaths.

The tips of his fingers slip beneath my panties now, sliding through my lips, collecting the wetness seeping from my hole.

His tongue snakes out and licks up the column of my neck, sending a shiver racking through my body.

"Keep going," he demands.

"'In corners till a day.'"

As if in slow motion, his hand stops rubbing against me, moving the gun down my side until it too disappears beneath my skirt. He presses the barrel against my clit.

My head flies back, cracking against the wall, my nails digging into his neck.

"'The owner passed,'" I cry out. "'Identified, and carried me away.'"

The cool metal pushes into my pussy, and my hips have a mind of their own, sliding along the rail, the evenly spaced deep slots on the top creating a sensation that has heat winding through my core and shooting down my legs.

"Oh *god*," I moan when he moves the gun back and forth.

He leans in, his lips so close that his breath is my air. "I know, sweetheart. I know."

"'And…and now we roam in sovereign woods, and now we hunt…hunt the doe,'" I stutter. "'And every time I speak for him, the mountains straight reply.'" I'm full on grinding against the weapon now, so lost in the fog of what's happening, I forget about anything else. "'And do I sm-smile, such cordial light, upon the valley glow. It is as a Vesuvian face had let its pleasure through.'"

"They're watching us, Evelina." He presses a soft kiss to my lips. "Standing right outside the alley, seeing every depraved thing I do to you."

The way he says my full name makes my face flush and my back bow, my hips working harder against the top of the rail.

"Do you think they like it?" His other hand grips at the fabric and pulls just enough to make my underwear slide halfway down my thighs. "You think their cocks are thick and hard, their minds spinning with jealousy that they can look but never touch?"

A noise escapes me while he paints the lewd picture, and I squeeze my eyes closed.

"I'd kill them if they touched you. *This* is mine," he growls. "There's a woman too. Do you think she'll go home tonight and lie down in her bed, fucking herself to the thought of what I'm doing to you?"

I moan as I move on top of my gun, chasing the orgasm I *need.*

"Spread your legs for me."

I do, without thought. I'm too busy imagining the look on strangers' faces as they watch, the men clenching their fists to keep from taking out their cocks and stroking to the sight. The woman gripping onto one of their arms, her pussy swollen and drenched, throbbing as she watches me get tortured with pleasure.

"Keep going, pretty girl. You're doing so well."

My abdomen clenches, muscles tightening until they feel as if they'll burst through my skin. "'And…and when at night, our good day done, I guard my master's head.'"

His free hand reaches around, gripping a handful of my ass, forcing me harder into both the gun and his body.

I open my mouth, and Brayden dips down, catching the moan with his tongue. He slides the Eagle against my core, then drags it back so the front sight—the small protruding piece on the tip—presses into my clit. I soar even higher, the pressure between my legs growing.

He breaks the kiss and speaks the next line against my lips, his voice deep and strained. "''Tis better than the eider duck's deep pillow to have shared.'"

My pussy contracts. *He knows Emily Dickinson.*

"'To foe of his, I'm deadly…*fuck*…I'm deadly foe,'" I force out, squeezing my eyes shut tighter as I try and formulate words. "'None stir the second time. On whom I lay a yellow eye or an emphatic thumb.'"

Brayden's teeth sink into my throat, hard enough to break the skin as he continues to get me off with *my* gun, and I gasp, my legs shaking.

"Please," I beg, my nails destroying the back of his neck. "*Please.*"

His grip is bruising on my ass cheek as he controls my movements, pushing me forward and dragging me back, and then he changes the angle of his hand until the tip of the gun circles against my entrance.

Sparks ricochet off every single part of me, my body buzzing like I'm high on drugs.

"Finish the poem," he whispers, pulling back to gaze into my eyes.

My heart stutters as I stare at him, something breaking in my chest, allowing warmth to flood through every crack. "'Though I than he may longer live, he longer must than I,'" I pant.

Is the safety switch on? Arousal rushes through me like a storm surge, my back flying off the wall as I hold on to him like I'm drowning.

"'For I have but the power to kill,'" he rumbles, his arm tensing around me.

"'Without the power to die,'" I finish.

He slips the tip of the gun inside me, the metal scratching against my opening, sending pricks of pain, and I'm coming, blinding lights shooting across my vision like fireworks.

His mouth is back on me quickly, holding me tightly as I shatter to pieces, my pussy spasming around the barrel of my weapon, sensation so intense my bones ache.

I black out entirely, and when I come to, I'm panting, collapsed against him with his lips pressing soft kisses to my head. I pry myself off, my body trembling as I look around.

There's no one there.

That fucking liar.

He chuckles, and I meet his eyes, my cunt still throbbing from the aftershocks of the most intense orgasm of my life.

His hand cups my cheek and he tilts my head up to meet his eyes. "Spend the night with me."

I try to talk. I really do. I search every nook and cranny of my being to find the anger that I was hell-bent on holding on to when I first came here, but I come up empty. I pry my tongue from the roof of my mouth and search for more words to give. But they've all disappeared. And I'm tired of fighting, so I press my face into the palm of his hand and I nod, letting him be the calm to my chaos.

CHAPTER 26

Nicholas

I FUCKED UP.

And I keep fucking up. Over and over again, I think I'll get my head on straight, and then *she* shows up and it all goes to shit. It was stupid to try and see Rose without the proper planning beforehand.

So I panicked.

If I lie again, who knows what will happen? And I'm not willing to gamble with my sister's life that way. I shouldn't have gone in the first place.

But if I told the truth…

I took a risk. Showed my hand so Evelina doesn't search for the rest, and then I slammed her against the wall and fucked her with her gun as a means to distract her. But like usual, any time it involves Evelina Westerly, I get lost in the moment.

She's fucking insane. But having her at my mercy does something to me, sparks a match to forgotten embers, creating a blazing inferno whenever she's near. She makes me feel alive.

Now she's in the bathroom of my hotel room, and I'm once

again panicking, my heart beating out of my chest as I fumble with my burner phone and send a text to Seth.

Get Rose out. Now.

I wish I could say I trust Evelina, but I'm not stupid.

What the fuck am I doing?

The restroom door opens right as I shove the throwaway cell into the top drawer of the side table, sloppily hidden underneath the hotel Bible. Lying back in the bed, I pull the sheet up to my waist and place my hands behind my head, smiling at her.

"How was your shower?"

She sighs, rubbing her wet hair with a towel. "Fine."

My eyes track down her damp body, and my cock twitches as I take her in. She always does it for me, but something about seeing her like this, bare and stripped down of all her extras, makes me feel like a caveman.

I clear my throat. "Hungry? I can order us some breakfast."

She tilts her head, dropping both towels to the floor until she's completely naked. My mouth dries.

"You're being weird," she says, slipping beneath the covers.

"Because I'm asking if you want something to eat?"

She shrugs. "I don't know, this is weird, isn't it? Us not arguing? I mean, I was definitely planning on causing you serious bodily harm when I came here. I'm still not one-hundred-percent sure I won't."

"Wow. Romantic." I place my hand over my heart.

"Is that what you want me to be?" She tilts her head. "Romantic?"

Her question punches me in the stomach, and the lighthearted energy in the room evaporates into a black abyss, leaving something heavier behind. It's the kind of air that sits on your shoulders and presses down, making you feel weary from the weight.

"I don't really buy into the whole romance thing." I reach out my hand, tucking her damp hair behind her ear. "But I like the way you make me feel."

The corner of her mouth tilts. "Even when I'm trying to kill you?"

I laugh. "Especially then. Gives me a reason to fuck the brat out of you."

Her tongue ring peeks out as she runs it over the top of her bottom lip. "So this is just…sex?"

My stomach heaves with nerves, and everything is urging me to tell her it can't even be that. The truth is, if I keep fucking her, it isn't going to be for the case or to get an angle. It's going to be because I can.

Because I want to.

Because I'm not sure if I can stand to be around her and *not* touch her.

I grab her small hand in mine, my fingertips tracing along the backs of hers. "You know it's not."

"Do I?" she utters.

Leaning in, I press a kiss to the side of her jaw, moving my palms to just beneath her ribs. I feel her smile as she fidgets.

My fingers trace up her sides and she laughs.

It's just for a moment, but the sound is jolting, a thousand volts of electricity lighting me up inside.

"Do that again," I demand.

She lifts a brow. "Do what?"

I don't reply, digging my fingers into her torso instead, trying to force the noise from her mouth. She thrashes at my attack, yelping as her hands push against me, laughter pouring out of her as she fights against my hold. I dive down, peppering her neck with kisses, my entire fucking body *floating* from the way her giggles soar through the air and settle in the center of my chest.

Finally, I pull back, and she calms down, her eyes gleaming as she stares up at me with a smile on her face.

And I'm fucking reeling, no breath in my lungs, dizzy from the height type of spin.

It's *that* smile again, her real one. Rare and so beautiful.

My eyes are ravenous as I stare, burning this moment into my memory in case I never see her look this way again. Knowing that soon, I'll no longer have the chance.

"I never realized you had freckles," I say.

She scrunches her nose, her hand running across her face. "Yeah, makeup usually covers them."

I grab her hand, bringing it away from her cheeks, my stomach flipping as I do. "You don't like them?"

"They remind me of my mother." Her voice is monotone.

"And that's a bad thing?"

"To look in the mirror and see a woman who couldn't stand that I existed? Uh, it doesn't exactly feel like sunshine and roses, no."

Her body language changes then, arms stiffening as she crosses them over her chest. She's curling in on herself. Stowing herself away.

"Do you always do that?"

"Ugh," she complains. "If I knew you were planning on asking so many questions, I wouldn't have agreed to spend the night."

I grin. "I'm just trying to get to know you."

She rolls to her side, resting her hands beneath her face as she lies on the pillow, her eyes flickering over every inch of me. "My mom was…she just wasn't meant to be a mom, I don't think. Not *mine*, anyway."

My middle burns because I've never related to a comment more.

"I'm the youngest kid, you know? Nessa and Dorothy, they were both planned, but…not me. I was a mistake. An 'unfortunate accident.'" She pauses, her eyes losing focus. "When I was little, back when I was forced to go to Mass every Sunday, I used to listen to the priest wax poetic about God, and I'd go home and lie in bed wondering, if we were all made in His image, why my mother couldn't love me the way I ached to be loved."

"I think," I say carefully, "the only love you can count on is the way you love yourself."

She hums, chewing on her bottom lip. "Yeah. Maybe. I'm over it now, you know? She's been gone for a long time. My dad went to prison and she dipped out quick. Left Nessa to raise us even though she was still just a kid herself."

The quiet stretches between us.

"My mom didn't really die of cancer." The truth feels good as it rolls off my tongue, and I keep going, knowing I'm yet again jeopardizing my cover but not really giving a fuck. She knows my files are fake as it is, and it feels shitty to not give her something real when she just gave something to me.

She rolls her eyes. "No shit."

Chuckling, I reach out and pull her body into me before moving to my back, my hands tracing lines up and down her spine while she rests her head on my chest.

I wonder if she can hear how my heart is racing.

"She was a junkie, actually. She never..." Emotion works its way into my throat and I swallow around it, forcing the words out. "She wasn't around much, and when she was, it wasn't great. But there were moments."

I think back to the last time I saw her. How clear her eyes were, her face looking more alive than it had in years. I was convinced she was getting better.

"Like the poetry?" Her fingertips send goose bumps skating down my skin as she draws circles on my pec.

"Like the poetry," I repeat. "Then one day she dropped us off at her sister's trailer and disappeared."

"She didn't come back," Evelina states.

I shake my head, the scabbed-up wound in my chest being picked open until it bleeds.

"My mom never had moments," she muses. "Not with me anyway. I used to spend countless hours trying to figure out why she hated me so much, and then one day, I realized I didn't care."

Moving my hands up her sides until my fingers hit her chin, I lift her face so she meets my gaze. "I don't know how anyone could hate you."

"Don't *you* hate me?"

I shake my head, my middle squeezing tight. "About as much as you hate me."

She rises up and presses her lips to mine, and for the rest of the morning, I'm lost.

CHAPTER 27

Evelina

I'M STARING INTO MY FATHER'S FACE, TRYING TO figure out what he's thinking and coming up blank.

A thousand different things are racing through *my* mind though. Mainly about the close call I had with Brayden earlier today. I knew it was stupid to stay in his room, and when Ezekiel came by and knocked on his hotel room door in the afternoon, I ran and hid in the bathroom like a kid caught stealing candy.

Not because we're doing anything wrong but because I have no interest in sharing Brayden with the rest of the world. What happens is between us, no one else.

I left shortly after, heading back to my own room to make myself presentable before heading to where I know my father's staying.

"I thought you weren't coming," Dad grunts.

"Changed my mind." I smile, although my lungs squeeze tight at the thought of going to the On the Water event.

"Well, good. I've been meaning to talk to you anyway," he continues, lighting the end of his Black & Mild. "I've got a gift for the Cantanellis."

It takes a minute for his words to register. "For the who?"

"Come on, Bug. You knew I was planning to expand. I can't do that without help. We need the Italians on our side or they'll come after us." He looks at me. "We're the little guys here."

"They're *already* coming after us. You know they're about to bid on that new construction site in downtown Kinland?"

He scoffs. "They can't touch our city."

"They *can* if they've got the mayor in their pocket." I shake my head. "You need to be smart about this."

His fist slams down on the table. "Don't you lecture me. I'm doing what's best for us, for our *family*. If we supply the Cantanellis, we're valuable."

I let out a disbelieving laugh. "No, Dad. If we supply the Cantanellis, we're their bitches. Plus, we piss off the García cartel, who, in case you've forgotten, are the largest drug traffickers in Chicago, and I don't know about you, but I don't want anything to do with that. We're doing just fine in our own little corner of the world." I press my hand into the table until it aches. "Not to mention I don't even have the capacity to produce enough for that level of distribution."

"We'll bring on more people."

"*Fuck*. That." I blow out a frustrated breath. "Look...we've got enough problems as it is. Remember how I caught Liam's piece of shit cousin cutting our drugs and keeping the profit? Who knows what other little shit is doing the same?"

Irritation wells inside me, bubbling like a cauldron about to overflow. I pinch the bridge of my nose and close my eyes.

Ten. Nine. Eight...

Once I'm back under control, I open them again. "The *point* is, you're making a mistake. And on the off chance the

Cantanellis *do* take you up on this offer, you're asking me to do the impossible."

He shrugs. "Then I suggest you figure it out."

"Nessa would have never done this," I snap.

His eyes flash as he puffs on his cigar, watching me. He brings the Black & Mild down, tapping his front two fingertips on the table. "Maybe if she had, then we wouldn't be little fish in a big fucking pond."

My fingernails dig into my palms to keep from lashing out and doing something I'll regret. "She was cautious."

"She was stupid," he hits back. "And a laughingstock. You know how much work it took to get our name in good standing after the shit she did? The mistakes she made? She was a woman trying to do a man's job, and it wasn't easy rebuilding relationships that she floundered while she pranced around touting the Westerly name."

My veins heat, fury rushing through them, and I shoot up from my chair. "Shut up."

"Excuse me?" He rises just as fast, leaning over the table and gripping my face tightly in his hands. I wince at the pain. "Watch the way you fucking speak to me."

"You don't know her," I grit out through clenched teeth. My voice wobbles as emotion sprouts up and bleeds into my tone. "You *never* knew her."

He laughs, tossing my face away from him. "Quit being dramatic. The best thing your sister ever did was take care of you. I'm sorry if that hurts your feelings, Bug, and I know you loved her. I know you miss her. But she wasn't the hero you have her painted as in your head."

My nostrils flare, a burn searing through my throat.

There's no place like home, and there's nothing like family. Stick together.

My vision grows hazy in the corners, the urge to lash out and make him feel a tenth of the pain I do filling up my stomach and expanding to my chest. But a knock on the door holds me in place. He goes to answer it and I'm standing stock-still, my fingernails still piercing into my palms and my chair knocked on its side behind me. My jaw aches from where I'm sure red fingerprints are left behind.

Voices filter in through the hall and get closer as they come toward the center of the room, but I don't look. I can't move, my body frozen with the rage I'm trying like hell to stuff back down and hide.

"What's wrong with you?" Dorothy says, stepping close and waving her hand in front of my face.

I look up.

My father's staring at me, Ezekiel isn't paying me any attention at all, and Brayden is scanning the room, a frown pulling at his features. My stomach flips when our eyes meet and he quirks a brow. He drops his gaze to my cheeks and his body stiffens.

It disgusts me how badly I want to walk over and wrap myself around him. Let him comfort me through the pain my dad just wrought from the darkest parts of my soul. I've been nothing but loyal to this family, yet *this* is how he repays me?

"Everything okay?" Brayden asks, his gaze never leaving mine.

"Everything's fine," my father replies, walking over and slinging an arm across my shoulders.

My body tenses, not liking the touch. I shrug out from under his grip.

"I thought you weren't coming," Dorothy sighs.

"Plans changed." I grin at her, trying to find enjoyment in her distaste for me being here.

"Where have you been?" Dad snaps at her.

Her eyes grow wide. "I went down to the hotel spa and got a massage. I didn't think you'd need me."

He grunts, and I tilt my head, watching the way her fingers latch together and twist as though she's nervous.

Brayden moves across the room while the attention isn't on us until he's standing close. He looks at me from his peripheral vision. "You all right?"

It's such a small question. Inconsequential, really. Still, my heart flutters at the fact that he's asking.

"No," I answer. "But I will be."

CHAPTER 28

Nicholas

WHEN I CHECK MY BURNER, I SEE A TEXT FROM Seth.

She's safe. At my place and asking to see you.

Relief flows through me and gratitude filters into the cracks for Seth. I've been a shitty partner, but more than that, I've been an awful friend, taking out my personal issues on him when out of everyone in my life, he's the *only* one who has my back.

He's never done me dirty, and I'm repaying him by exploding in fits of anger and going behind his back, hooking up with the one girl I promised him wasn't a problem.

She *is* a problem. And that's never been as clear as an hour ago when I walked into her father's hotel room and saw marks on her skin.

My vision bled red, and it took everything inside me not to cause a scene. I know she can take care of herself, but it doesn't mean she should have to.

I turn to Ezekiel just as he flips the key in the ignition, the rumble of his car coming to life. We're making a quick run to the store, grabbing some food and more cigars for Farrell.

"I need you to take me somewhere."

He glares at me, his hand pausing on the gearshift. "Sorry?"

"It's been a minute since I've checked in with my guys, so I need you to take me there," I repeat.

His cheeks grow ruddy as he looks at me incredulously. "The fuck I am."

Impatience wrings my muscles. "It's not a suggestion."

Ever since my failed attempt, the need to see Rose in person has only grown stronger. To see with my own two eyes that she's thriving without me.

That she's still sober.

Grabbing the phone, I call Seth, who picks up on the second ring.

"Yo."

"I'm coming over."

"Hey, buddy. Nice to hear from you. I'm good, thanks."

I pinch the bridge of my nose. "Shit, sorry. I'm in a bit of a time crunch, but I need to… I need to see her."

The line grows silent. "You sure that's a good idea?"

"No," I reply. "But you said to tell you if shit was getting real. Shit's getting real and I need to talk to her."

"All right, man. We'll be here."

Nodding, I blow out a breath. "Thank you."

Ten minutes later, I have Ezekiel pull into a gas station three blocks from Seth's house. He may be working for us, but that doesn't mean I trust him with knowledge of where a federal agent lives. "You can wait here. I'll be quick."

"When is this shit gonna be over?" he questions.

I had already started to get out of the car, but I sit back down, turning toward him. "When you get me the supplier."

His face drops. "Oh, fuck off. The deal was to get you an in, and I did that. Besides, you know what? Even if I did know, I wouldn't tell you." He slams his fist against the steering wheel, the horn beeping so loudly it makes my insides jump. "I feel like shit, okay? The guilt's fuckin' eating me alive."

I shrug, even though I relate to his words more than I care to admit. "That sounds like a personal problem, Ezekiel."

He breathes out an empty laugh. "You can pretend you don't care. Play the part of the big federal agent coming in to put away the bad guys. But I see you."

My heart stalls. "See what exactly?"

"You know why Skip came to me all those years ago, wanting to team up and rebuild my father's legacy? It wasn't because of who I was…not fully anyway. My father was king of the jungle, not me. I never got that gene, the one where you can climb to the top and not be afraid of the fall." He taps his fingers to his temple. "But I'm perceptive, and that shit's valuable in this life."

I shift in my seat.

"Turnin' on the Westerlys?" He shakes his head, his tongue pressing against the front of his teeth. "I'll have to live with that shit for the rest of my life. And you can say I'm doing the right thing all you want, but the truth is it doesn't *feel* right. It feels like the easy way out." He stares at me. "And whatever it is you're doin'? There won't *be* an easy way out for you. You understand? You're fuckin' with the wrong woman."

And I know without a doubt, right then, he's talking about Evelina.

I smirk, but my insides are reeling. "Stay in the car. I won't be long."

"Yeah, whatever." He focuses out the driver's side window.

I jump up from the seat, slamming the door behind me. I don't have time to worry about Evelina and the mistakes I'm making when it comes to her or how things will end. Right now, I need to focus on my *real* life, the one that's looking blurry, like I'm staring in a rearview mirror.

The walk is quick, and before long I'm standing at the base of a hill with a steep drive, a small ranch-style home with blue shutters on the windowsill staring back at me. I make my way up the steps and Seth opens the door before I even knock, reaching out and dragging me in for a hug. "What's good, bro?"

"Where is she?" I ask, pulling back.

He nods toward the back hallway, rubbing his neck. "In the spare room."

My stomach flips as I make my way to where Rose is, and I push open the door, my muscles relaxing when I see her, legs crossed in the middle of the bed. She has headphones in her ears, and when she opens her eyes and locks them on me, they narrow.

Before I can get a word out, she stands up, walks over, and slaps me across the face.

Pain shoots up my cheek and I cover the spot, trying to soothe the burn. "Ouch. What the fuck?"

She points a skinny finger at me. "That's for making me come here."

I groan. "Please don't start with your shit, Rose. I need you to do this for me, just until I'm back."

She rips the headphones from her ears and tosses them on

the bed before throwing her hands on her hips. "And how long will that be, Nick?"

The name is a jolt to my system, and I blink at her as I absorb the blow.

Her brows rise, the anger fading from her features, being replaced with something softer, something more like concern.

"Are you all right?" she asks.

I nod, gritting my teeth. *No.* "Yeah."

Her eyes flit over my face and she bobs her head. "Okay. I'll stay."

Relief pours through me and I move to the left wall, shoving my hands in my pockets. "I want to know how *you're* doing. You seeing your sponsor?"

She sighs, reaching behind her and grabbing a pillow to throw at my head. "I haven't seen you in three months and this is the first thing out of your mouth?"

"You *smacked* me." I duck, chuckling. "I just worry is all."

"Yeah…I know." She nods, her fingers traipsing up her arm. "I actually found a new job."

"No shit?"

Her face perks up. "Just basic level data entry for some rich guy who has a bunch of apps, but it's nice." She grins. "It feels good."

Contentment flows through me, happy that *she* seems to be happy. I glance behind her, seeing it's been thirty minutes since I left Ezekiel. My stomach cramps, knowing I need to get back.

"I gotta go, kid."

She crosses her arms. "You just got here."

"Yeah, well…it's a miracle I could even stop by in the first place."

She brings her fingers up to her mouth, chewing on the ends of her nails as she walks over to me, linking our arms together and walking us back out to the front room.

I'm only there for another ten minutes, just long enough to brief Seth and say a quick goodbye.

When Rose falls into my arms, she hugs me tighter than normal, resting her head against my chest. "Promise me you're safe?"

I swallow, hating that I have to lie to her. Hating that I have to lie to *everyone*. "I promise."

"Love you." She squeezes tight and then lets go.

"Love you too, kid." I smile down at her.

She rolls her eyes. "I'm your *elder*."

I shrug, grabbing her into a headlock and giving her a noogie, joy sparking in my chest when she fights against my hold.

This is what I needed. A reminder that while I feel like a fraud in a sea full of people, she's here, waiting for me to come back home.

CHAPTER 29

Evelina

I DON'T LIKE DRESSING UP, BUT I DO LOVE WEARING heels. I'll admit they aren't the most practical of shoes, but when you're five foot two and in the realm of dangerous men, it's important to have everything you can use at your disposal. And stilettos hurt when you stab them into flesh.

I've been nauseous since I woke up, knowing tonight is the charity gala On the Water. The name alone has panic churning through my insides, not to mention it will be on the same yacht where my sister was last seen alive. I haven't been anywhere near the water since Nessa's death, and even before then, I've always felt uneasy.

My stomach rolls like choppy waves, my left hand holding the side of my emerald-green dress from trailing on the ground. I feel naked, both because of the strapless gown but also because it's so tight, there's no room for my Desert Eagle.

The MY *Toto* is large—pristine with its sparkling black trim. It bobs in the water serenely, soft waves crashing against its sides as the Chicago skyline twinkles in the background. It's picturesque, and the sight makes me want to puke.

My hands shake as I hold my purse close to my body and walk up the ramp to board. I hurry past the front deck and into the dining hall where I know the auction is taking place, pressing past people dressed in their best, anxious to get to a room where I can pretend I'm still on land.

I've just entered the main area, my skin shivering from the cold, when a rough grip wraps around my arm. I spin, my body already on edge, but I falter when I realize it's Ezekiel.

He looks down on me and smiles. "What're you doin' up here? Come on. Let's go to the basement."

"Oh, I didn't know where to go." Because of course my father didn't think to include me in the details.

I peer around as Ezekiel pulls me along, and I spot Dorothy standing in the far right corner, a glass of champagne in her hand as she talks with Oscar. I squint my eyes, remembering he asked *which* sister I was talking about. I hadn't known they interacted after Nessa's death, and now I'm kicking myself for not paying closer attention. Especially considering they were together the night Nessa died. Is Oscar who she's been disappearing with?

Ezekiel's body is on full alert as we walk down the carpeted hallway and past the restrooms, hitting a staircase leading to the lower level. My spine stiffens with every step, anxiety squeezing my middle when the yacht jolts as it starts to move. My fingers twist together and I tap my tongue ring on the back of my teeth.

"Where are they meeting, in the fucking dungeons?" I hiss.

Ezekiel looks at me, stopping us in front of a steel door and turning to face me. "You gonna make it?"

I force a smile even though I think I might pass out. "I'm fine. Just annoyed that you guys didn't tell me what time to be here."

"Okay," he says, lifting his chin. "Don't do anything stupid in here, you know? These guys…just sit back and let your dad handle things."

My stomach drops to the floor, his words forming into knives as they carve out my skin.

I stiffen my jaw and nod sharply.

He opens the door and we walk into a room filled with boxes and crates. Wire shelving runs along the sides, stocked with cleaning supplies. The walls have little circle windows evenly spaced throughout, and if I listen close, I can hear waves crashing against the boat as we move across the lake. Beads of sweat break across my hairline, my heart slamming against my chest.

If we sink, this will be the first room to go.

"Hey," a voice whispers. I swallow, looking up and meeting Brayden's eyes. He's gazing at me with concern, like he's worried I might get sick and he doesn't know what to do.

But all of it gets pushed to the back burner when I see Giacomo Cantanelli sitting at a small folding table in the center of the room, smoking a cigar with my father like they're old friends. They're definitely not friends. In fact, they've widely avoided each other, staying out of the other's territory, an unspoken truce. It's part of the reason why I'm so uneasy with my dad's sudden need to expand.

Neither of them acknowledges me when I enter, but the two goons standing at Giacomo's back sure do.

"You know," Giacomo says, pointing his gold-ringed finger in my father's face. "Your flying whatever-the-fuck product's really causing me a headache."

My dad grins. "There's a solution to every problem, Giacomo."

Giacomo hums, swirling the cigar in his mouth, his thick silver and black strands slicked back with pomade and a sharp three-piece suit fitted to him perfectly. He looks like a god, and when I stare at my father with his tattoos and his rough around the edges exterior, there's no comparison.

The Cantanellis are rivals, but at the end of the day, they're still big fish in the pond. Their reach is far greater than ours, and if they wanted to, they could kill us all right now and be at church tomorrow morning with nobody asking questions.

That's the power my dad wishes he had but will never reach.

That's the type of desperation that makes people do stupid, stupid things.

"You and I, we think alike." Giacomo smiles and it sends alarm bells ringing in my head. "No need to be enemies when we can be *friends*. Of course, you understand, if you work for me, I need to know everything."

My chest tightens when I step forward. "Who says we'll be working *for* you?"

The eyes of everyone in the room snap to mine, as if they're just now realizing I'm here. Brayden sighs heavily but steps closer to my side.

"Evelina. Quiet," my dad demands.

"Evelina Westerly," Giacomo purrs, his gaze glossing up and down my form. "What a pleasure."

I smile at him, making sure to show all my teeth.

He waves his hand in the air, calling me over. "Come here, doll. Let me get a good look at you."

I move toward the table, keeping my eyes on him the entire time. In my peripheral vision, I can see my father's disapproving stare.

"You look tense, Evelina," Giacomo notes. "You aren't afraid, are you?"

Laughing, I shake my head, sitting down next to my father and grabbing a cigar from the table. Giacomo is there with his lighter before I can even ask. I take my time puffing on the end, allowing the smoke to billow in my mouth before I blow it back out in the air. No one speaks while they wait, and surprisingly, I don't mind the attention.

"No," I finally say. "I'm not afraid. I'd just appreciate it if everyone stopped acting like I was a meek girl incapable of taking part in the conversation."

"You are a prize, aren't you?" Giacomo grins, his eyes searing through my dress again. "Farrell, surely she isn't here to do business?"

Movement catches my attention, and Brayden moves from near the door until he's closer to the center of the room, where he leans against a pillar with his arms crossed.

He looks calm, cool, and collected. But I know better. His stare never strays from me.

"If you're going to work *with* us, then I'd like to be part of it, yes," I reply.

My dad clears his throat. "Evelina does a lot for me. She knows a lot about our business. Family's important to her, so she can get a little...passionate. You understand."

"I do." Giacomo nods. "Interesting you let a woman hold such prestige. I'd never allow such a ridiculous thing."

Fire burns through my middle but I bite back the retort, pressing my fingernails into my palms until they break the skin.

"I assume you brought some product for us to test?" he continues.

My father inclines his head. "Of course." He snaps his fingers.

Brayden and Ezekiel both move, walking to the corner of the

room where there're five large black duffel bags. They lug them over and drop them down on the tabletop.

"Consider this a gift in good faith," Dad says.

Giacomo scans his eyes over me one more time. "Is she a gift too?"

My smile drops, black starting to edge in around my vision. I tilt my head, placing the cigar into the ashtray. "My sister might be more to your liking."

My father stiffens and satisfaction runs through me. That's what he gets for making deals about my production without me.

"Somehow I doubt she holds a candle to you." Giacomo laughs before tipping his chin at Dad. "We'll try the product and you'll hear from us soon, but you should know if we agree, *you* work for *us*." He stands, buttoning his suit jacket before staring down at both of us. "That means I want to know who I'm working with. Who I'm buying from."

There's no way my dad will agree. Years I've been doing this for him, and in all that time, not a word. That's the deal. It keeps me protected, out of the spotlight, and it gives us leverage where otherwise we would fall short.

My father grins and shakes his hand. "You have my word."

CHAPTER 30

Nicholas

I ADJUST THE CUFF LINKS ON MY ARMS, TRYING TO ease the tension that's been racking my body since stepping onto this ridiculous fucking boat. I hadn't expected Evelina to show up to the meeting, and when she did, my stomach flew to my throat, praying like hell she wouldn't fly off the handle.

She didn't, but now I'm pissed for a different reason. That motherfucker had his eyes all over her, and his hands were *way* too grabby. A possessive fire pulses through my veins as I walk past the auction in the dining hall and head to the back deck. I walk to the wall of French doors and step outside, immediately thankful there's no one else here except for one lone figure.

Evelina.

Now that the immediate threat has passed, I have time to soak in what she's wearing, and when I do, my lungs cramp and my cock springs to life. She's flawless in a green gown that flows along the curves of her body. Her hair is curly and off her neck, and while I know she doesn't act like the rest of the Illinois elite, *damn* can she dress the part.

Her back is to me, and I drink up the view of her naked skin, the gown backless and draping along the curve of her ass. I move forward without thought. Her hands are wrapped around the metal railing that lines the back of the ship. The wind whips off the water, swirling across the deck, and the bottom of her dress rustles, small wisps of her hair fluttering around her neck.

"Don't jump."

Her body tenses and I walk closer, wondering why she doesn't have a quick comeback the way she normally would.

I step up next to her, noticing her closed eyes, then moving my gaze down her goose bump–covered arms and finally to where her knuckles are blanched from her tight grip on the railing.

"You okay?"

"Shut up," she snaps, squeezing her eyes tighter.

She peels one lid open timidly, staring down at the dark lake. Her chest rises and falls faster, and she slams it closed again.

Is she scared of water?

I move without thinking, partially because she needs me and the other part because I'm desperate to touch her, just to prove I can after watching another man lust over her and being unable to stop him. I step behind her, not quite flush against her but close enough that the heat of her body radiates off her back.

She's out here all alone, and her entire family is inside like they don't realize she could be struggling. Like they don't even know she's afraid.

Maybe they don't.

It's an off-putting feeling seeing her this way.

I press a soft kiss to the small freckle on her left shoulder and remove my jacket, draping it over her. Then I cage her in, my body surrounding her and my hands resting on the railing.

Her breathing stutters, but she doesn't open her eyes. I pry her grip from the metal, threading my fingers through hers so she can hold on to me instead.

"'Bright star, would I were steadfast as thou art—not in lone splendor hung aloft the night. And watching, with eternal lids apart, like nature's patient, sleepless eremite.'" I whisper the words softly into her ear.

Her body presses back into mine.

"'The moving waters at their priestlike task, of pure ablution round earth's human shores, or gazing on the new soft-fallen mask, of snow upon the mountains and the moors—'"

Her breathing evens out and her head relaxes against my chest, and I probably should care about who could see, about where we are and what we're doing, but I don't. The *only* thing that matters is her.

"'Pillow'd upon my fair love's ripening breast, no—yet still steadfast, still unchangeable, to feel forever its soft fall and swell.'" I bend my head down until my lips graze her neck, and I breathe her in, my cock hard and my heart pounding. "'Awake forever in a sweet unrest, still.'"

She presses into me, a soft moan leaving her lips when she feels my hips tightly against her.

"'Still to hear her tender-taken breath, and so live ever—or else swoon to death.'"

The tension swirling around our bodies is overwhelming, and I don't know what it is I'm feeling, only that nothing else has ever felt like it. Opening her eyes, she twists in my arms to look up at my face.

She smiles.

And my chest feels like it will explode.

"Keats is my favorite," she sighs.

"I remember." I tighten my arms around her, bringing one of our tangled fingers up to press a kiss to the back of her hand.

"For someone who doesn't believe in romance, you're irritatingly good at it."

"Is this what romance is?" I chuckle.

"You're quoting Keats and comforting me." She shrugs. "And not just any Keats. He was writing about wanting to die if he couldn't live forever with his love. I don't think it gets more romantic than that."

She glances down at the water, her body tensing again.

"Don't be afraid," I whisper, the wind sending a strong gust of air whipping around us, making her shiver. "I've got you."

She sucks in a breath, moving her gaze back to me. "Promise?"

I want, with every single bone in my body, to give her the truth. But I can't.

So I lie instead.

"I promise."

"This is cute," a high-pitched voice interrupts.

Evelina shoves me off her before spinning around and adopting a blank look as she stares at her sister.

"What are you two doing?" Dorothy looks between the two of us.

"Just admiring the view," I reply, placing my hands in my pockets.

"Hmm," she hums, sipping from a champagne flute as she walks toward the edge of the deck. She rests against it, her bright-red nails tapping against her glass as she looks at us, then glancing into the dark waters below. "People really do come and go so quickly here, don't they?"

My brows furrow, but Evelina jolts next to me.

When Dorothy looks back up, there's a manic look in her eye and a wide smile on her face. It surprises me how much it reminds me of the way Evelina looks right before she snaps.

I guess the gene runs in the family after all.

"You're a fucking bitch," Evelina spits.

Dorothy chuckles as she looks at the two of us.

I've never seen her this way before, as if she's transformed into an entirely different person. But I've had my suspicions, moments when I took her out where the veil was thinned and I could peek behind the innocent daughter who loves to be in the public, hiding this sinister woman who was lurking underneath.

"I'm just stating a fact," she says.

Sighing, I run a hand over my face. This family is exhausting. "What are you talking about, Dorothy?"

"Oh, didn't you know? This is where our sister died."

Shock hits me in the chest, and I swing my eyes to Evelina. But they aren't paying any attention to me at all. She's laser-focused on Dorothy.

Evelina cocks her head. "Want to refresh my memory on how exactly that happened again?"

The left side of Dorothy's red mouth lifts. "She slipped."

Evelina sneers, and I feel the shift in energy before it happens. Still, I'm not quick enough to grab her. She lunges forward, gripping Dorothy around the throat, both of them tumbling to the deck floor, Dorothy's champagne flute shattering beside them.

Dorothy is flailing, her nails scratching at the back of my jacket as it slips off Evelina's shoulders, and I rush toward them, grabbing Evelina around the waist and tearing her off.

Dorothy's hand shoots to her throat. "Jesus, Evie. You need to be institutionalized."

"Take *off* those shoes!" Evelina yells, her face blotchy and tears streaming down her cheeks. "How fucking dare you wear those here."

My eyes drop to Dorothy's feet, where bright-silver sparkly heels are gleaming in the moonlight.

Dorothy scoffs. "You're always so dramatic. It's not like they'd even fit you."

Evelina's head twitches and she turns to me, her gaze feral. "Do you have your gun on you?"

I do, but I'm extremely uncomfortable telling her that right now. She notices my hesitation.

"May I see it?" she asks sweetly.

Stepping back from her, I shake my head. "I'll let you do anything you want with it once we leave."

Dorothy sighs loudly, dusting off the front of her dress before toeing off the shoes and picking them up in her hand. "Fine, you want them so bad? They're yours."

She holds them out, and Evelina steps forward, reaching out to grab them. Then Dorothy flings them over the side of the boat. I can barely hear when they plop into the water.

"*No!*" Evelina cries, throwing her body into the railing. As soon as her eyes hit the water, she freezes, and I'm after her, gripping her by the waist and pulling her into me, her body trembling as I sink us down to the deck floor.

"Maybe if you dive in after them, they'll take you home to her," Dorothy quips.

My eyes narrow as my head snaps up. "Dorothy, shut the fuck up before I shoot you myself."

She laughs. "God, imagine I wanted to sleep with you. Pathetic." Her footsteps are loud even without her heels as she walks closer, and she crouches down in front of us. "I'll tell you a secret though, Evie."

Evelina looks up, mascara streaking down her face, her lips swollen and red. I've never seen her look so defeated, and my chest cracks at the sight. This isn't how it's supposed to be. This isn't who *she's* supposed to be.

"I didn't mean to kill her," Dorothy whispers. "But I'm happy I did."

She stands and saunters away, and my grip tightens until I'm sure it will bruise around Evelina's waist, wanting to let her go so badly but knowing if she harms her sister here, in front of all these people, even *I* won't be able to save her.

CHAPTER 31

Nicholas

WE LEAVE BEFORE THE AUCTION IS OVER, AND I don't wait around to tell anyone we've gone. My insides are going wild, my brain trying to slot new pieces of the puzzle into appropriate places. Dorothy murdered Vanessa Westerly, and I had to *keep* Evelina from murdering her.

I'm not surprised with Evelina's violence, and if I'm honest with myself, I'm not wholly shocked that Dorothy admitted she was behind her sister's death. Not after the way she was always on edge when we brought up the past.

Evelina doesn't fight me when I carry her off the back deck of the boat, and as soon as we're on solid land, her body relaxes, the debilitating fear she was carrying washing away like memories drawn in sand.

"I'm still going to kill her," she states calmly.

I grin, placing her in the passenger seat of my car and reaching over her front, buckling her in place. "I know."

It doesn't bother me the way it probably should.

Evelina has *years* of wounds that haven't been healed, just bandaged with sarcasm and sadness, forming mutilated scar tissue that still oozes when pricked.

And maybe my morals are dulled when it comes to her. Because as long as *she's* taken care of, it's hard for me to give a damn what happens to anyone else. I lean in and press a soft kiss to her forehead, breathing in her earthy, floral scent.

"Take me home," she whispers.

I nod, sending a text to Ezekiel telling him to grab my stuff from the hotel room, and then I drive us back to Kinland. We don't talk on the way, and I let us sit in silence because sometimes words *can't* help. For two hours, I hold her hand and don't let go, my thumb rubbing methodically over her knuckles, and it isn't until we pull into the front gates of the Westerly estate that I loosen my grip.

I'm not sure how to handle this part of her. This vulnerable, sad girl who misses her sister and hates the people who took her away.

She doesn't look at me as she exits the car, moving to walk up the front steps to the large double oak doors. I follow behind her, unsure if she wants me to stay or go.

"Evelina."

She pauses, twisting around to look at me. Her hair is mussed, frizzy strands falling haphazardly around her face. Mascara streaks down her cheeks, black tears reflecting the stains marred on her soul.

And through everything, she's still the most stunning thing I've ever seen.

"Do you want me to go?" I move up the stairs until I'm standing in front of her.

She sighs, running the back of her hand over her mouth,

smearing some of her already muddled red lipstick. "I don't want you to leave."

I thread my fingers through the roots of her hair and tilt her chin up with my thumb, my stomach flipping when I soak her in. "Damn, you're beautiful."

She's on me in a flash, her mouth meeting mine. I press into her, grabbing her waist and taking everything she has to give.

She's overwhelming.

Devastating.

She's going to ruin my fucking life.

Breaking away, she reaches blindly behind her to open the door, dragging me in with her. My hands are wild, unable to stop touching her skin for a second, all the possessiveness from before—when I saw another man think he could have her—roaring back.

We stumble in through the foyer, the mansion empty and dark other than the sparkle from the unlit chandelier hanging high above our heads. There's a large round table in the center of the room, wedged between the split stairwell, and I throw her down on top of it, not caring that the vase of flowers falls off the edge and shatters on the floor.

I skim my teeth along her jaw, my lips already swollen and bruised from her assault, but I don't care. I want her to brand every piece of me. My hand roams down her throat, and I press my mouth against hers.

"Tell me you're mine," I demand against her lips.

Her hand jumps up to my face, scratching the stubble as she stares into my eyes. "I'm yours."

My fingers grab the front of her dress and pull until it tears, her perfect breasts on display just for me. I dip down and draw a nipple into my mouth, feeling it stiffen under my tongue.

She moans and I suck harder before releasing it when her fingers tug on my hair and pull me back up to her mouth.

We've already fucked countless times. I've taken her in every position, filled her with my cock in a thousand different ways.

But right now it all pales in comparison to the way kissing her feels.

It's all-consuming, as if she's ripped through my middle and placed her heart inside my chest, forcing it to beat.

I move down her body, pressing my lips to every bare inch of skin I can find, and then I sink to my knees, sliding the green fabric up her legs until it's bunched around her hips.

She's not wearing any underwear, and my cock pulses when her dripping cunt is in my face, needy and demanding, begging me to devour her fucking whole. I waste no time dipping between her thighs. I stare up at her while I lick her out, her taste flooding my tongue and making desire tear through me.

"That's right, baby," she moans, propping herself up on her elbows as she grinds her pussy against my face. "Lick my clit."

She comes violently, clenching around me as she cries out, her body collapsing on the table. And then I'm moving to a stand, diving into her mouth so she can taste herself on me, the way I know she loves to do. She groans as we kiss, and her hands roam down my shirt until she grabs my belt and clumsily undoes my slacks. Her feet move up, resting on the waistband, and she pushes them down with her toes until my cock bobs free, the head almost purple from how fucking hard I am for her.

Her hand grips me and she strokes from base to tip, making my body jerk into her, arousal racing up my spine. She sucks on my tongue and then breaks away, hopping from the table, spinning around and pushing my chest until I'm the one flat on my back, my dick throbbing as it stands straight up in the air.

Grinning, she grabs her tits, rolling her nipples between her fingers, her eyes rolling back in her head.

"You're so fucking sexy when you touch yourself," I pant, stroking my cock while I watch her.

Her lips purse as she spits, saliva dribbling out of her mouth and dripping down, hitting the top of her cleavage, rolling along the curve until it sinks between the valley of her breasts.

Goddamn.

Leaning forward, she wraps them around me, her hands pushing them together as she starts to move her chest up and down.

"Oh, *fuck*."

She spits again, this time letting it fall onto the head of my dick, and the feel of it slipping down the side of my shaft while her sticky skin slides up is enough to make my balls tighten.

It's one of the hottest things I've ever seen. She bends her head and sticks out her tongue. My hand grips her jaw and I sit up until her face is beneath me, my cock still wedged in her cleavage. I let my own saliva dribble down until it hits her mouth, and the filthiness of it all turns me on so fucking much I can hardly breathe. I capture her lips with mine, her breath hot and sweet as she moans, moving her breasts to jerk me off. Heat collects at the base of my spine, and I know if I don't stop, I'll come all over her tits.

"Tell me again." I thrust into her.

"Yours."

Fire blazes through me, dulling everything except the need to get closer. I let go of her face and flip her over until she's prone beneath me. Fisting my cock, I line up to her entrance, both of us still half-clothed and fucking desperate, and I sink deep inside her, my dick jerking as her walls contract around me.

Shit.

This feels different. This feels like more.

Rough and messy and a thousand different shades of wrong.

But if I'm her calm, then *she* is my chaos, and if I can't live with her forever, then I don't want to live at all.

I capture her lips as I start a punishing rhythm, my hips slapping against hers with every stroke. I feel insane, completely overwhelmed by everything she is, by whatever the hell she's doing to me. She's *changing* me. Or maybe she's simply making me feel alive.

She arches into me, her nails digging into my skin as she comes apart, the pulses of her cunt making me swell and explode inside her.

My vision goes black and my body gives out as I paint the walls of her pussy, and I collapse on top of her, sweat dripping down the side of my face, my cheek resting against her breast. She runs her fingers through my hair, and I close my eyes, trying to catch my breath while I listen to the rapid beats of her heart.

My body trembles with aftershocks.

"Brayden," she murmurs.

I freeze, my chest splitting down the middle and falling to the floor.

Brayden.

She's Brayden's.

Which means she'll never be mine.

CHAPTER 32

Evelina

NOBODY ASKED WHAT HAPPENED TO THE VASE IN the foyer, and I didn't offer an explanation. But it's been four days and I've been reeling with my emotions ever since. Truthfully, I've been cowering away in the cottage, because the next batch of pods are ready for lancing and it's a perfect excuse to hide from the world and keep my *impulses* in check.

"Bug."

My father's voice rings out through the greenhouse and I pause, taking a deep breath before spinning to face him. I'm glad he's here. Part of the reason why I've been locking myself away is to figure out how to approach the situation, to let him know I'm not okay with expanding. I don't want to work with the Cantanellis. I don't crave change the way he seems to need it.

Instead of meeting his eyes, I meet the sparkling browns of Dorothy.

My heart nosedives to the floor, cracking and splitting in two. *How could he bring her here?*

I school the look on my face, not wanting her to know it

bothers me. The very sight of her makes me rage, and it takes all my willpower not to take the straightedge from the table and dig it into her eyeballs so she can never look at me again.

This is my place. My sanctuary. The one spot I had to just be without worrying that others would come and find me.

And my father just ruined that.

The anger creeps in and I close my eyes, counting back from ten.

When I reopen them, I lick my lips. "What is she doing here?"

A large smile beams across her face. "I told you before, didn't I? Dad's showing me the ropes."

"You said you couldn't handle production," he chimes in. "Meet your new protégé."

"No thanks," I bite. "I don't need any help."

The warmth on his face disappears entirely and he takes a step closer to me. "It wasn't up for debate. Don't forget who runs this, Evelina."

His words are knives that slice through my middle like paper cuts.

"I'm not expanding."

He blows out a deep breath and walks toward me. My spine stiffens as I stand my ground.

"Listen, I get what you want, I really do, but you need to understand where I'm—"

Crack.

Blood coats the inside of my mouth, my cheek throbbing as my face is thrown to the side from the back of his hand.

He bends down close. "Now, because I love you and you're my daughter, I'm going to let this…*incident* slide. But if you try me again, you'll force my hand. You do a lot for me, but let's not pretend you aren't replaceable."

My chest squeezes so tight I lose my breath.

"Understand?"

I close my eyes and nod, my body trembling from the rage that's begging to escape. I've bided my time with Dorothy for years, stayed my hand when all I've longed for is to see her die, and I did it all because of my loyalty to *him*. But it's clearer now than ever that the feeling isn't mutual.

And I don't have it in me anymore to care.

"Good. I've added Dorothy to the security scanner. She'll be back tomorrow to learn the ropes."

I blink, and my vision blurs, but not enough to miss the way Dorothy grins before she turns around and follows our father as he leaves.

Ten. Nine. Eight...

"I need your help."

Cody spins around in his chair, headphones wrapping his neck and blond hair spiked in a hundred different directions, the same way he always is when we're in his hacker paradise of a basement. "What else is new?"

He smiles, but I don't, and his face morphs into something more serious.

I shake my head, not knowing where to begin and honestly not sure how much I should tell him. After Dorothy and my dad left my greenhouse, I wanted to grab my Desert Eagle and shoot them both in the head.

The idea still holds merit.

But I'd rather see my dad's face as everything goes up in flames.

And Dorothy? I want to watch her burn.

"Are you okay?" he asks.

My legs shake, making the desk chair I'm sitting on swivel back and forth. "How long have we been friends?"

Cody rolls his eyes. "Feels like forever."

"Can you be serious, please? I'm trying to open up to you here, which is what you've been *asking* me to do since you moved back—"

"Three years ago."

I nod. "Right. Three years."

"Longer if you count high school," he notes.

"So I can trust you, right?"

His brows furrow and he uses his heels to push his chair forward, rolling across the ground until he's close enough to take my hands in his.

My insides tense, not liking the touch, but I don't pull away.

"You're my best friend, babe."

Swallowing, I nod. "I haven't been *completely* honest with you."

He gasps, throwing a hand to his heart. "I'm shocked. Let me guess, you're fucking that Brayden guy?"

"I—what? No..." I shake my head. "Well, yes, but that's not what I'm talking about."

He snaps his fingers, chuckling. "I knew it. I knew he was twisting you up."

"That's not what this is about," I say. "I need you to hack into a security system for me."

His brows rise at that, and he crosses his leg over the opposite knee, resting his chin in his hand. "Go on."

"There are things important to me. Things I'd rather not allow my father or my sister to be able to access anymore until I'm ready for them to."

"Like a safe?"

"Does it matter?"

He tilts his head. "Kind of."

I exhale, my stomach somersaulting as I push the words off my lips. "It's a greenhouse."

He nods. "You want me to help keep your plants safe?"

"Yeah. It's for…they're poppies."

He moves forward in his chair. "And why would there be a security system for some poppies, Evie?"

"It isn't necessarily for the *poppies.*" I glance up at him. "It's for the lab."

He blinks, then his face changes, surprise filtering through his features. "You're the flying monkey?"

"I'm the *creator* of Flying Monkey," I correct.

He whistles, shaking his head. "Damn. I should have known. Okay… Tell me everything about it, and then I'll get to work."

CHAPTER 33

Evelina

I'VE JUST GOTTEN BACK TO THE COTTAGE, AND now I'm waiting on Brayden to get here. I realized that I didn't have his number, which is insane considering his dick has spent numerous hours inside me, so I got it from Ezekiel and texted, asking him to stop by.

It feels weird having what I guess you would consider guests. Nessa gifted me this cottage right before she passed, and when my dad realized we needed a space to grow, he built the underground greenhouse, chock-full of security and insulation so that even thermal cameras wouldn't pick it up.

I can't help wondering why the hell he went through the trouble just to be so willing to give it all up in the end.

For years, it was just the two of us. Now there's Brayden, Dorothy, and Cody to add to the list of people in the know. Although considering I plan to kill Dorothy in the immediate future, she doesn't truly count.

Regardless, I refuse to sit and wait around for him to invite the Cantanellis too.

There's a knock, and although I'm sure it's Brayden, I grip my Desert Eagle anyway, swinging open the door and aiming. I'm anxious, and it's making me feel a little manic.

Brayden grins, stepping through the doorway, his chest brushing against the barrel. "Is this your way of asking me to fuck you with it again?"

I drop the gun and move to the side, closing the door behind him.

"Are you ever *not* annoying?" I snap.

He smirks, brushing his lips across mine. "Nice to see you too."

I press my hands against his chest, my fingers rubbing the leather of his jacket. "Is this real leather?"

"Uhh…yeah. Why?"

Yuck. I scrunch my nose, looking up at him. "Doesn't matter. Listen, can I trust you?"

His Adam's apple bobs. "I don't know, sweetheart. Can *I* trust *you*?"

I rub my tongue against the back of my teeth before biting my lip. He steps in close, running his hand through my hair and pulling me to him. I breathe in deep, enjoying the way he brings me comfort and hating myself for needing it.

"What's wrong?" he asks.

Nerves race through me, making my palms sweat. It's a risk to lay it all on the line for him. But I want to tell him everything, and in order to do that, I need to make sure he feels for me the way I feel for him. I'm terrified he won't. After all, *he's* the one who said he didn't believe in romance.

My heart stutters.

I pull him into me and press my lips to his before shoving him away.

His brows rise and he grins again, those dimples on full display. "So you *don't* want to fuck?"

"I don't want to fuck. I mean, I do, obviously, but not right now."

That's not what this is about. We always get distracted by the physical, and right now, when my mind is so *twisted*, feeling like a captive with no way out, I need his attention, not his touch.

"I love you," I blurt.

The words are surprisingly easy to say, and I hold my breath, waiting for his response.

His body locks up tight, every single one of his muscles tensing as he stares at me blankly.

I laugh, running a hand through my hair. "I know, that's crazy, right? I didn't mean for it to happen. I don't even know when the hell it *did* happen, but I just know it's there and it's big. Like, can't breathe when you're around kind of big. And it's..." I pause, throwing my hands up in frustration. "Fucking annoying. The same way everything *always* annoys me with you. And it's stupid. Because I don't know little things like your favorite color or how you did in school or your middle name. And to be honest, I really don't care." I start pacing because with every word I vomit out, his body coils tighter. "But it's there. And it fucking sucks, and I *hate* myself for loving you."

He takes a step closer. I stop moving, dropping my hands to my sides.

"But I hate the thought of not having you more."

The silence rings louder than any noise ever has, my words strewn out and tattered in the space between us. The urge to take it all back is strong, but I don't.

"All this time, and I couldn't pay you to shut up, and *now* you choose to go quiet?" I complain.

The corner of his mouth lifts, and then he moves.

He's on me quick, grabbing the back of my head and stealing my breath for himself, his lips and tongue claiming with a kiss that tops every other kiss in existence. My heart skips, my stomach flips, and for the first time in my life, I feel just like any other girl.

A girl who finally has someone to love her back.

He breaks away from my mouth and presses his lips to my ear, his hands gripping my face tightly. "My favorite color is blue." He trails a light smattering of kisses along my jaw and down my neck.

My chest feels like it might cave in.

"I did okay in school. Good at sports. Bad at homework. Hated college."

Something tings in the back of my mind, but then his lips meet mine again and I'm gone, lost in what he's giving me.

"And what's in a name?" he continues. "That which we call a rose by any other name would smell as sweet."

I grin against his mouth.

"Thank you for loving me," he whispers, pulling back just enough to look me in the eye.

His thumb brushes across my cheek and I melt into the moment, waiting with bated breath to hear whatever he'll say next.

But then his phone rings.

"It's Ezekiel." He cringes. "Hold that thought."

Before I can blink, he's out the door, taking my heart with him.

CHAPTER 34

Nicholas

GUILTY. THE FEELING OF SHAME OR REGRET FOR your misconduct.

I've never thought about the word much, but the guilt I feel for every single thing involving Evelina is a tornado, whirling quick and strong, destroying everything it touches. And then it compounds because I know, without a doubt, if I went back and had a chance to do it all over, I wouldn't change a thing.

Not knowing her—not existing in her world—is a far greater tragedy than playing a small part within it.

She loves me.

She *loves* me.

But she doesn't know who I am, and I have no doubts that when she learns the truth, everything will be over for us.

And fuck, it hurts like a bitch.

I silence Ezekiel's call, having only used him as an excuse to leave before I did something stupid, like blow my cover and beg her for understanding or lie completely and say I feel nothing at all. I was on the spot, and I don't *like* being on the spot, so I fled.

The sky is cloudy and gray, the smell of the first upcoming snow in the air, dead leaves and debris crunching under my feet as I speed walk the yellow brick path. I'm staring down at my phone and sending off a quick text to Ezekiel, letting him know I'm busy, which is why I don't see the person standing in front of me before I run into her.

My body jostles, the phone flying from my hand, the screen cracking when it hits the ground.

"*Shit.*" I bend down to pick it up. When I rise from grabbing it, I come face-to-face with Dorothy.

She purses her lips. "So you know then."

It isn't a question and my forehead scrunches, trying to figure out what the hell she's talking about. *Know what? That Evelina is planning to kill her?*

She crosses her arms, her nails tapping against the insides of her elbow. "Typical. I'm always the last person to find out anything."

"What?" I brush off the chips of glass from my screen.

She throws her hand at the cottage. "About the greenhouse."

My hands pause from where I was trying—and failing—to fix my phone. "Oh," I say carefully, my stomach twisting. *Greenhouse?* "Right. You mean you didn't know about that until now?"

She scoffs. "You know it's just like Evie to not include me. She and Nessa were *always* leaving me out, and she hates that our dad doesn't do the same."

My heart speeds, pieces of a puzzle clicking into place, creating a picture I had no idea existed.

"Well." I lick my lips, glancing behind me. "Seems like you know now at least."

"Yeah." She sighs. "But it kind of sucks, right? I mean, who wants to learn about plants?"

My stomach sinks, her words repeating in my head like a mantra. "What exactly are you learning?"

"How to make Evie's product, obviously."

My ears go numb and my mouth runs dry.

She tilts her head, eyes narrowing, and I try to school my features, but I don't think I'm successful.

"You know," she continues, "I didn't mean to hold you up from whatever. I'll let you go. Just…forget I said anything, yeah?"

She moves around me in a hurry and I let her pass, my heart slamming against my ribs.

Shock trickles through my limbs like ice.

Evelina is the supplier.

Holy shit.

I spin around, my body trembling as I hurry to my car, sliding into the seat and numbly leaving the estate. I don't pay attention to my surroundings, and I have no clue if the guard at the gate even waves goodbye. All I know is I'm supposed to meet Seth at the motel in three hours for our weekly check-in, and now I actually have something to tell him.

Something big.

Because this time I've found our guy. But I didn't expect it to be her.

My mind is on autopilot as I drive through the outskirts of Kinland, pulling around to the back lot of the motel. I park, but I don't get out. Instead, I sit in my car, watching the digital numbers on my dashboard click over, one minute after the next, until the sun dips beneath the horizon and the moon rises to take its place.

The thought of turning over Evelina makes bile climb up the back of my throat, the nausea feeling like I'm being tossed at sea.

I blow out a breath, my elbows resting on the steering wheel as I rub my eyes.

What the fuck am I supposed to do?

Leaning back in my seat, I remind myself of all the reasons why I became a DEA agent in the first place. To put criminals like *her* behind bars. It's been my goal ever since I was old enough to realize that drugs and the people who put them on the streets are what cost me my childhood.

My family.

My innocence.

It's all I've ever known, and while the things I feel for her are so strong they dull everything around me...they're still new. And my hatred for what she stands for is just as strong. *Isn't it?*

My hand flies to my chest from the throbbing pain, spreading outward like ivy and wrapping around every piece of me until I feel like I'll buckle beneath its weight. I don't want to do this, but I also don't know if I could ever look her in the eyes again and not see all the trauma from my past.

Both options are painful, clamping down on either side of me and tearing until I split in two, jagged pieces that won't ever fit together again.

Emotion clogs up my throat, tears burning behind my eyes. I exhale, my cheeks puffing out as I try to shake off the sadness.

I know that in my heart of hearts, this is what I have to do.

So I turn off the car, open the door, and walk to the motel room to see Seth.

The way I always have.

CHAPTER 35

Evelina

I STOOD IN THE COTTAGE FOR ABOUT TWO minutes, staring at the spot where Brayden was before he stormed out. And then I snapped out of it and ran after him, ready to demand he look me in the face and tell me how he feels. Because he doesn't get to do that. He doesn't get to make me *feel* so much and then just walk away like Ezekiel was more important than me.

Leaving out the front door, I run smack-dab into Dorothy. She says something, but if I talk to her, then I'm going to murder her, and I want to make it hurt when I do, so I shove her to the side and run past, hoping it's not too late to catch Brayden.

When I make it back to the estate, I see him in his car, getting ready to leave. My chest pulls tight, because if he was talking to Ezekiel, why would he be leaving entirely? So I jump in my Range Rover and follow, because I'm going to make him face me whether he wants to or not.

He drives through neighborhood streets until we hit the heart of downtown, then continues on, and eventually I realize he's heading toward the outskirts of Kinland.

Does he live out here?

When he pulls into the motel, I drive around to the other side, parking far enough away where he won't see. My hackles rise from not knowing why he's here, and I don't want to rush in and demand answers. I just want to sit back and see what the hell he's doing.

Turns out he's doing nothing.

He sits. And sits. And sits.

The longer he does, the more unease starts to billow in my chest because there's no good reason why someone would be in the most dangerous part of Kinland acting shady as fuck.

It grows dark outside and my eyes start to droop, exhaustion wringing its way through my bones. But then, *finally*, he moves to get out of his car. I perk up, my heart stuttering as it bleeds anxiety through my veins.

I grab my Eagle from the glove compartment when I see him slip around the corner of the building, and once again I follow, making sure to walk slow and light so my footsteps don't ring out in the dead of the night.

Creeping along the motel doors, I hit the edge of the wall and peer around the corner.

He's at the last door, knocking three times and running a hand through his curly brown hair.

Is he meeting someone? If he's meeting a prostitute, I think I'll be sick.

Someone answers, and a slight breath of relief hits me when it's a man's voice. Brayden gives him a one-armed hug and then they both disappear inside the room. I sprint around the corner, trying to catch the door before it locks, but there's no need because the *Do Not Disturb* sign hanging on the handle is lodged between the crack, making it easy for me to push it back open, just a bit. Just enough to see inside.

My eyes scan what I can from my limited vantage point, and I take in Brayden and the other man, who's standing behind a makeshift desk, coffee cups and double-monitored computers in front of him. There's a gun lying on the table and the two of them are at ease, talking like they're old friends.

They definitely know each other.

I squint my eyes as I stare at the stranger, trying to place him. He looks so familiar and it sends a twinge down my spine, something prodding at my brain urging me to just *think*. And then it clicks.

The night all those months ago at the bar.

"I got put on a new job today that's taking me out of town. We're celebrating one last time."

A job. Okay...maybe they're just friends catching up.

"Galen wants to talk to Ezekiel," the stranger says.

Brayden laughs. "Good luck. Ezekiel is fucking done. It's a miracle that motherfucker hasn't given me up yet."

My forehead scrunches, something heavy dragging its sharpened tip through my middle.

"I can't fucking do this anymore," Brayden continues, his voice low and tortured.

His friend watches Brayden with dark eyes, his hands on his hips. He puffs out his cheeks and shakes his head. "Nick..."

The name is a sucker punch to my chest, the breath forcefully pushed from my lungs. *Nick.*

My middle spins on its axis as I replay every single moment we've had together, breaking apart the memories and staring at them from different angles.

My eyes fly back to Brayden—*Nick*—and I watch him pace back and forth in front of the desk.

The way he carries himself right now is different, the way he talks is different, his name is different, *everything* about him is different, and I have to throw the back of my hand up to my mouth to keep from puking.

The truth brands against my skin, flaying me open and sinking into my bones. It's a familiar feeling, but I've never felt it burn quite so deep.

I am *so* sick of people using me. Lying to me. And I'm done because I have nothing left to give. Black slips in the edges of my vision.

My grip on my Eagle tightens as I stand up, my knees cracking as I do, and I kick the door open so it slams against the wall before swinging back. I catch it with my shoulder when I step into the room.

Both of them draw their weapons and spin around toward me.

I cackle as I take them in, realizing that besides when he was torturing me with my own, this is the first time I've ever seen Brayden hold a gun. His form is flawless. Like he's been trained to perfection.

His eyes widen, arms immediately falling to his sides, the weapon dropping on the floor. "Evelina."

My eyes move to the gun and back to him and I jerk my chin. "You should probably pick that back up. Shoot me now so you have a better chance."

His mouth parts and he takes a step forward.

My fingers tighten around the Eagle, my gaze flicking to the man behind him. "I don't think we've been introduced," I say, my voice tight.

He glares. "Oh, I know all about you, Evelina Westerly."

My nostrils flare, sharp prongs of betrayal tightening around my middle.

Brayden turns around and sees him. "Man, put the gun down, Jesus."

"Nick, I—"

Brayden freezes and everything in me goes ice cold at the name, even though I've already heard it said.

I shake my head, and *Nick* puts his hands up in front of him, like he's approaching a predator. "Evelina, I can explain."

"I don't want to hear your explanations," I hiss. My vision blurs with tears and I grit my teeth, shaking my head, so fucking *mad* that I'm showing everything he's making me feel.

"Evelina," his friend says calmly. "Drop your weapon."

"Seth," Nick snaps. "Shut the fuck up. I can handle this."

I huff out a laugh. He can *handle* this. My chest burns, and then something else dawns on me, the phrasing of the words hitting me like a dagger straight to the heart.

My mouth drops, and I squeeze my eyes shut, trying to keep my focus so I don't lose it completely. I take a moment and breathe deep to find my center. When I pry my lids back open, my gaze meets concerned green.

But they don't have the same effect on me as they did before.

My hands tremble so much the gun shakes in my grip. "Are you a cop?"

His face twitches and his mouth parts, but then he closes it again, his head shaking as he takes moves toward me.

I back up, bringing the barrel higher. "Take another step and I swear to god, Brayden, I will empty this entire clip in your lying fucking mouth."

He swallows, his eyes growing glassy. But he doesn't move again. "Evelina."

"Don't." My teeth ache from how tightly I'm clenching them. "Just…tell me the fucking truth for once in your life." My tone rises with every word.

He presses his lips together, his nostrils flaring and chin lifting as he watches me with watery eyes. "I'm a federal agent."

It would have hurt less if he shot me.

My eyes close and my face turns to the side, hot *disgusting* tears flowing down my cheeks like tangible heartbreak.

"Please," his voice cracks. "Please, pretty girl…let me explain."

I breathe through my nose, trying to count back from ten, but the numbers don't come.

All that comes is anger.

Slowly, I open my eyes and straighten my spine, letting the salty wetness drip from my chin and onto the ground.

I move my aim from him to his partner.

It happens in slow motion after that. Brayden—Nick—drops down and picks up his weapon, his hands as steady as his empty chest must be.

"Don't do this, Evelina," he says, bringing up his pistol.

"You would shoot me?" Another traitorous tear falls to the floor.

His jaw clenches but he doesn't move his aim. "I won't let you kill *him*."

"So it's like that then?" My mouth tilts up.

He steps to the side, blocking Seth. "Yeah, pretty girl. It's like that."

My finger sits on the trigger, and I step toward him until the end of the barrel is pointing directly at his chest. He lowers his arms, like he's accepting death if I choose to give it.

"Drop your weapon!" his friend yells. "I won't tell you again."

But I ignore him, craning my neck and staring into eyes I've never really known. "Will you let him kill *me*?" I whisper.

He looks down at me, his Adam's apple bobbing with his swallow.

His silence is all the answer I need.

"Do it then." I turn around and walk away, my heart in my throat, half of me wishing he'd just finish the job now and shoot me in the back. But nothing happens. So I leave, a heavy type of numb dropping into place like a curtain, shielding me from anything other than darkness.

CHAPTER 36

Nicholas

MY COVER'S BLOWN.

Obviously. So I'm officially pulled from the case, and now I'm sulking in my apartment—my *real* apartment—the decision on whether to tell my department everything I know sitting so heavy on my chest that I can't breathe.

Last night, I made the decision, sure I was doing the right thing no matter how much it hurt. No matter how much it tasted like I was betraying the only person who had never let me down. But when I stared Seth in the face, I couldn't push the words off my tongue. And when Evelina busted down the door and looked at me as though *I* had killed her spirit?

That was when I knew.

I would pick her a thousand times over, even if it meant rotting in hell.

I let her walk back out the door because I don't deserve to keep her, and I broke down telling Seth everything. Everything *except* who the supplier is. Then I came home to my sister, not knowing where else to go.

Rose sits at the small round table across from me, a steaming cup of tea in her hands. She purses her lips as she watches me. "You look like shit."

"Feel worse," I grunt.

She sets down the mug, reaching out to grab the top of my hand. "Well, it's good to have you home."

I run my fingers through my hair, the cavity in my chest rattling. "Yeah. Feels good to be here."

Except it *doesn't* feel good, because this doesn't feel like home anymore. I don't think I knew what home was until I found it in *her*.

"You wanna talk about it?" Rose asks.

"Have you ever been in love?" I blurt.

She sits back in her chair, her red brows shooting up. "Uh… yeah."

I look up at her. "What's it feel like?"

"So that's what this is," she breathes. "A broken heart."

Is it? I laugh, bending until my forehead rests on the table. "No, I just…I don't know."

She takes a sip of her tea. "I get it, dude. Love fucking sucks."

"How do you know it's real?" I whisper, stomach twisting.

"Does it hurt?"

"Like a bitch."

She smacks her lips. "Then it's real."

I don't say anything, just roll my head back and forth against the cool wood, hoping somehow it will reach inside me and soothe the burn.

"So who fucked it up, you or her?"

"Her. Me." Another empty laugh pours from my mouth and I sit back up, tugging on the roots of my hair. "I don't fucking know."

Rose sips from her tea. "Who is she?"

"She's this woman—"

"Yeah, I got that," she cuts in.

I smile softly, biting down the pain that's breaking me apart when I picture Evelina's face.

"She's…she's *everything*." I shake my head. "But she's not a good person."

Rose hums. "I find it hard to believe my brother would fall for someone who isn't worth loving."

The back of my throat swells until it burns.

"Does she love you?"

"She said she does…*did*. But I don't know." I shrug. "It's fast."

Rose's nails tap against the side of her cup. "You know, I've never thanked you for saving me."

"Don't thank me," I mutter.

She swipes her hand in the air. "Don't do that martyr shit with me, Nicholas."

"I'm *not*," I scoff.

"You always do," she says. "You've shouldered the blame for every single thing that's happened in our lives when *none* of it was your fault." She leans in, her eyes sharp as they stare into mine. "Do you hear me? None of it."

I press my lips together, trying to hold back the sob that wants to escape.

Her eyes water. "*I'm* the older sibling. I'm supposed to be the one to protect *you*. And if you don't know what it feels like to be loved, then clearly, I failed in that."

"No," I say. "The people who put that poison on the streets failed us both. You did the best you could."

"And you're doing the best you can too," she replies.

"Am I? It's my *job* to stop them. How can I live with myself for loving someone who represents everything I lost?"

"Oh, Nick," Rose sighs, resting her chin in her hand. "Did you know I sold once upon a time?"

The breath whooshes out of me and I collapse against the back of my chair. "You…what?"

She nods. "Yeah. I was fucked up and desperate, and sometimes it was the only way I could keep enough in my pockets to survive."

"You were sick. It wasn't your fault."

"I knew exactly what I was doing." She wipes the tears from her cheeks. "Do you hate *me* now?"

Grabbing her fingers across the table, I squeeze. "Of course not."

"Right. Because I'm still *me*." She sniffs. "We're all just out here living, you know? Roaming under clouds that are a thousand different shades of gray. But you can't help who you love, Nick."

Nodding, I stare down at the table, my rusted heart trying like hell to pump in my chest.

"I've watched you exist for a long time now. You go through the motions and you…you pour yourself into your career, trying to make up for mistakes that were never your weight to bear in the first place."

My bottom lip trembles and I grit my teeth.

"You aren't to blame for the decisions other people made. The decisions *I* made."

I meet her gaze.

"And neither is she."

"You sure about this?" Seth asks, his tone low and deep.

I blink at him, not saying a word—not *having* any words—because what else is there?

What's left for me to say?

I spin around in the desk chair I haven't sat in for months, staring down at the few framed accolades and the screen saver dancing across the monitor. It feels foreign, as though Nick Woodsworth doesn't really exist. Like he never really did.

It's funny how something that felt so intrinsic to who I was for so many years now feels like a stranger.

"I'm sure," I reply.

Seth leans on the edge of the gray cubicle wall, nodding. "You know it won't change much. We won't stop the case, not until we find what we're looking for."

I swallow around the knowledge I'm keeping close to my chest, and I stand up, grabbing my badge and my gun, knowing they'll need them back when I resign. "I know."

"Want me to come with you to tell him?" he asks.

"Woodsworth. Adams. My office, now," Cap's voice yells out.

I grin at Seth. "Looks like you don't have a choice."

Seth's hand meets my shoulder and squeezes, holding me in place. "I'm your partner, but more than anything, I'm your friend. Professionally, I can't condone what you're doing." He pauses, a slight smile lining the corners of his mouth. "But personally…it makes me happy as hell to see the man behind the machine."

He walks away before I can say anything back, but his words ache in the deepest parts of me. I'd give anything to go back to how I used to be, because this feeling now? It fucking sucks.

And I don't know if it will ever go away.

I follow Seth down the narrow aisle through the cubicles and head into Cap's office, stopping short when I see Oscar Norman, mayor of Kinland, sitting next to another man in a gray suit and mussed-up hair.

Cap smiles when we walk in. "Fantastic news, boys. Turns out it doesn't matter that you fucked up."

I frown, confused.

"Gentlemen, meet Agent Baum." Cap nods toward Oscar. "And this is Mayor Norman."

Agent Baum stands from his chair, reaching out his hand to shake mine, his wire-framed glasses falling slightly down his face. "Nice to meet you."

"What's going on?" Seth asks, looking around with a furrowed brow.

Cap nods toward the men. "Agent Baum is with the Chicago division of the FBI. They've been building a case against the Westerlys for the past few years, and they've had a big break."

My stomach drops. *Fucking FBI.*

"And you're here because?" I jerk my chin toward Oscar.

Agent Baum clears his throat. "The mayor *and* the commissioner of Kinland recently decided they'd rather cooperate with us than not." He grins over at him. "Isn't that right, Oscar?"

Oscar's lips are pressed tight as he nods.

"He's been integral in getting us what we need against both the Cantanellis and the Westerlys."

A light bulb explodes in my brain. The charity on Oscar's yacht. The meeting. *Holy shit.*

I whoosh out a breath, sinking into a chair in the corner of the room, my elbows going to my knees as I take in what this means, what they're saying.

Agent Baum bobs his head. "We appreciate all you've done

up to this point. I'm here as a favor to let you know your hard work won't be forgotten. As soon as you can get us access to all your evidence, the better."

Seth laughs. "There's not much we can offer." He glances at me. "Our focus was on finding the supplier, not building a case for petty crimes. Agent Woodsworth was made before we could find them."

My leg taps out a nervous rhythm.

Agent Baum grins. "But we did."

CHAPTER 37

Evelina

IT'S BEEN TWO DAYS SINCE MY WORLD WAS ONCE again turned upside down and I found out that Brayden is a lie. That everything *between* us was a lie.

I feel dirty.

Used.

And more than anything, I feel really, really fucking stupid. I've always prided myself on being the brains of the family, but how smart can I be if I let this happen?

Closing my eyes, I lean back against Nessa's tombstone. "You lied to me, Ness," I whisper into the wind. "You said family's all I need, that we have to stick together. Turns out that's bullshit."

I shake my head, my fingers threading through the grass beneath me. My lower lip trembles and I snap my eyes back open, staring at the notebook in my lap. I open it, scanning over the messy handwriting and scratched-out words that blur together on the pages. I run a fingertip down the last poem I was able to write. Now every single letter reminds me of *him*.

My palm tenses and I grip the page, tearing it from the book. It feels good, so I do it again. And again.

Rip. Tear. Rip.

I don't stop until every single thing is torn from the binding and in pieces on the ground. My eyes scan the space around me and I grab the shredded pages, placing them on the base of Nessa's marker in a little pile on the stone. Reaching into my pocket, I grip the matchbook from Winkies that I brought, just in case, and I move forward on my knees, my fingers shaky.

Every word feels like a confession now instead of an escape. Sappy poems from a broken, lonely girl pretending to be something strong.

The wind whips across my face, strands of my hair tickling my cheeks, and I breathe in deep, striking the match against the cardboard and dropping it into the torn-up parts of me, watching the words go up in flames.

With every second they burn, my soul throbs with an ache I'm sure I'll wear for the rest of my life. And I hate *Nick* just a little bit more for stealing the one thing that felt like mine.

He was the king of pretty words, so now I'll make him king of the ashes.

The fire burns quickly and then goes out when there's nothing left.

Here lies one whose name was writ in water.

I reach forward, blowing on the ash until it scatters, floating away over the graves of a hundred different people. Maybe my little love spells can be *their* calm in the chaos.

"My whole life I've lived for other people, and I'm done." I look at Nessa's tombstone one last time. "That means I have to stop living for you too, Ness. I hope you understand."

Sadness weaves its way through me, and although it's hard, it feels oddly cathartic too, as if deep underground chains are snapping from my body, freeing me from the constraint the blood in my veins and my last name have always caused.

"No matter where I go in life, Nessa, no matter who I love and lose... I think I'll always miss you the most."

Smacking a kiss to the palm of my hand, I press it to her tombstone before backing up and walking away, leaving a single poppy flower at the base of her grave.

I head straight back to the estate, bypassing the main entrance and walking around to the back, going to the cottage instead. Honestly, I don't plan on staying after everything is destroyed, but in the meantime, I can't stand to see the faces of people who never really cared.

I love my greenhouse and everything in it, but it's tainted now, and I wouldn't be surprised if the feds show up any second to take me in anyway, so getting rid of as much evidence before I disappear is paramount to me being able to be free.

Ezekiel is sitting on the patio, leaned back in a chair, cigarette smoke billowing in the air around him. And in all my grief, all my sadness, I had forgotten a major detail from the other night.

Ezekiel's name was mentioned in a room of federal agents.

I squint my eyes, walking up to him as he looks over at me, then back up at the sky.

"Give me one good reason why I shouldn't kill you, Ezekiel."

He pauses, the cigarette halfway to his mouth. "They told me you found out, you know? Called me last night, trying to convince me to leave. Witness protection or some bullshit."

"So why didn't you?" I slip my hand beneath my skirt, pulling my gun from the holster and resting it on the patio table.

I expected to feel angrier with him, but I guess when I let go of the Westerly name and its importance, the people who betrayed the name start to matter less. Still, it stings knowing he was throwing me under the bus and not caring where I landed.

"How could you?"

He sighs, sitting forward in the chair, looking at me for the first time. "They didn't give me a choice."

"There's *always* a choice."

"You know what happened to my father when he went to prison? He turned into someone's bitch and then was mutilated and hung from the rafters. He still gets mocked to this day." He shakes his head. "You think I want to end up like that? I've been forced to live a life like him. I don't want to die like him too."

"So you made a deal," I add.

He nods. "So I made a deal."

I tap my fingers on the top of my Eagle. "You know, you're really nothing but a coward."

Smoke billows from his nostrils. "You're right. I *am*. And it fuckin' terrifies me. I lived my whole life lookin' up to my dad. He was it, a god to me. And he'd be disgusted by who I've become... But I am who I am."

I don't respond, not having it in me to fight. And while the betrayal is still there, I understand living in your father's shadow and wanting to break free. I can't begrudge him that, as much as I might wish to.

"Are you going to kill me?" he asks when I stand up and grab my gun.

"No," I sigh. "But I never want to see you again. Living with the shame of knowing you'll never be half the man your father was is more painful than any torture I could offer." Moving around the table, I stop in front of him. "One day, Ezekiel, I hope you find your peace."

"I don't deserve your empathy," he whispers, staring down at his lap.

I swallow around the knot in my throat. "No…you don't. But I'm giving it to you anyway."

Reholstering my gun, I walk past him and into the woods. Who cares if he sees where I'm going at this point.

CHAPTER 38

Evelina

I SPENT THREE HOURS SETTING UP THE SPACE before texting my sister and asking her to meet me here so I could "show her the ropes," since I blew her off yesterday. I'm going to enjoy watching her die.

My legs are crossed and my eyes closed as I sit calmly in the center of the hallway, directly outside the greenhouse door. The small pitter-patter of feet walking down the hidden closet's staircase makes my ears perk up, excitement tingling down my spine. I've been waiting *years* for this moment.

I peel my eyes open, grinning as I look up at her. "Hello, Dorothy."

"What are you doing?" she glances around. "Where's Dad?"

"He'll be here," I say calmly, standing up. I move toward the door to press my fingerprint on the scanner, but Dorothy beats me to it. The light turns green, everything unlocking. My forehead wrinkles, realizing Cody must not have been able to hack into the system yet.

Not that it matters anymore.

She traipses into the greenhouse, her nose scrunching up as she looks at all the poppies. "You know, for beautiful flowers, they really don't smell that good, do they?"

"Subjective, I guess," I murmur, my black skirt swishing as I move past her. "This way."

I lead her down the two acres of flowers, flourishing in their various stages, and to the lab in the back, flicking on the lights and making my way to the metal table in the center of the room where my chemistry set is. I already have everything prepared.

"Wow, this is…intense," she muses as she walks around, her eyeball magnified as she stares through a beaker.

"Yep," I reply, pouring water into a small metal bowl as well as some of the raw opium I've recently finished extracting.

"What are you doing?" She hovers over the table to try and get a better look. "You should be explaining things, right? How am I supposed to learn otherwise?"

I smile at her. "Just getting things set up so I can show you how they work."

"Oh. Okay." She lifts a brow. "You're being weird."

"You know," I say, taking the container and placing it over the Bunsen burner, slowly turning up the heat. "I want to apologize to you, Dorothy. I was out of line the other day. I don't know *what* I was thinking."

Her eyes narrow.

I laugh, watching the opium melt into liquid form. "Something you said that night on the boat really stuck with me."

"Really?" Her tone is disbelieving.

"Really," I repeat, removing the liquid from the burner and grabbing the needle at my side. "You said that maybe if I dove in after Nessa's shoes, they'd take me home to her. And in that moment, I was tempted, because nothing's ever felt like home to me the way Nessa did."

"I did us all a favor." She scoffs. "Nessa was a bitch. Always getting in the way, making *everything* about her. Weren't you tired of living in her shadow for so long? I know I was."

I throw back my head and laugh. It's high-pitched and tense, and even to my ears, it sounds piercing.

Dorothy's eyes widen. "You're fucking crazy."

"Yeah." I grin. "That's what they say."

Drawing back the plunger, I suck up the liquid opium, then hold the needle up to the light and flick the side, getting rid of air bubbles.

"Wanna see?" I ask, holding it out to her.

She leans in. "Hmm. Fascinating."

"Anyway," I continue, "I thought about how silly it would be for me to do that…to let you *win*. Even if it was my greatest heart's desire to be with Nessa."

I meander around the table, the needle at my side. Her eyes are flicking to it and then to me and she backs up a step.

"So the next time I ache for something I love? I'm not going out of my own backyard." The toes of my shoes press against the tips of hers. "And I'd really, really *love* to see you die."

Bringing up the needle, I jab it into her neck, sticking the plunger so the opium pours into her bloodstream.

Her eyes grow round, her mouth dropping on a scream as she flails. I reach up, delight swimming through my veins as I cock back my fist and swing it forward, punching her right in the face until she drops to the ground.

Pain spreads through my knuckles and I shake out my hand, grabbing her stupid bouncy brown ponytail, the way I've dreamed of doing for years, ripping it from her scalp as I drag her over to the table. She's crying and flailing, but I've got a good grip, and I turn around, enjoying the way her blood is pouring from her nose and staining her baby-blue top. I kick her in the side, then press my heel on top of her, sinking all my weight until the satisfying *pop* of skin pushes my boot through. She screams again, her hands coming up to dig into my leg, and I reach over quickly, picking up the zip ties I placed there just for this occasion.

As the opium starts to rush through her veins, she slackens.

"That's right," I coo, brushing the back of my hand down her face and then tying her wrists together before moving to her ankles. "Go to sleep for a bit, sweet sister. Don't worry. I won't do anything fun for another couple hours."

"What's another couple hours?" she mumbles, her eyes growing hazy.

I smile. "That's how much longer you have to live."

Sighing, I brush my hair back from my face, allowing the adrenaline to fill me up until I'm ready to burst. This has been a long time coming.

Gripping her once again by the hair, I pull harshly, feeling the give of roots as I drag her out of the back room and through the aisles until I make it all the way up to where I've set the stage for the show. I drop her limp body down while I give my arms a rest. It's poetic, having her unconscious and about to die here in my field of poppies.

My feet are *aching*, sweat drips down my face, and my clothes stick to my skin, but I don't mind the exertion. I've attached a special hook to the end of one of the mobile halide lights, and I pull her underneath it, grunting as I lift her arms up and slip the hook beneath her zip tie. Then I walk over to where I control the height and press a button, raising her up, up, up.

There's a fifty-gallon black plastic barrel I roll into place beneath her feet, and I grin when she moans, her head lolling from side to side. Walking to the far wall, I roll the protective gear up my arms, place the mask on my face, then pick up the Teflon bottles filled with hydrofluoric acid and head back to the barrel, humming to myself as I fill it up.

When it's done, I move to the side, strip off the gear, and send a text to my dad, telling him it's an emergency and I need his help. Then, I grab my Desert Eagle and sit down on the ground, crossing my legs and closing my eyes with my palms up and open.

Now we wait.

It takes thirty minutes for my father to arrive. I know because I counted every single one. I hear the beeping of the security system, so I open my lids, jumping up and heading toward the button that controls the height of the light Dorothy's attached to. The greenhouse door opens, and I smile, soaking in the sight of my father as he takes in the scene.

"Hi, Dad. You're late."

"Bug..." His eyes flick to where Dorothy is unconscious, dried blood around her nostrils from where I broke her nose, mouth gagged as she dangles above the vat of acid. "What the hell are you doing?"

"Just tying up some loose ends." I scratch my temple with the barrel of my Eagle. "I think I've done a lot for you over the years, wouldn't you agree?"

He swallows, and he takes a step closer, his hands reaching behind him.

I tsk, aiming my gun. "Please, for once in your life, don't be stupid. I'd hate to have to kill you before you get to see the show."

"Evelina," he says. "Let's talk about this."

Dorothy groans behind us and his eyes fly back to her, his jaw muscles tensing.

"Oh good, she's waking up!" I grin. "Put your gun on the ground and go sit in the chair I set up just for you."

"*Evel—*"

"Sit!" I yell, my finger jolting against the button. Dorothy's body drops until only her feet are submerged in the acid. I pause, blowing out a breath to collect myself. "In the chair, Father. I don't like to repeat myself."

He does as I ask, his fiery gaze never leaving mine.

Dorothy's eyes blink as she comes to. When she wakes up fully, she starts to flail, the acid solution splashing up her skin.

"I wouldn't do that if I were you," I singsong. "There's only a couple more minutes until you start to feel it. You're just making it worse for yourself." I turn back to Dad. "As I was saying, I feel like I've bent over backward to accommodate you since you came out of prison. I've grown for you. Fixed all your problems. Killed anyone who got in our way. And what do I get as thanks?"

"Bug," he tries again.

I press my finger into the button again, and Dorothy drops, letting out a muffled scream through the gag in her mouth.

Laughing, I scrunch my face. "Yeah, starting to burn? That's hydrofluoric acid for you. Do you want to know what it's doing as it melts through your skin? It has fluoride ions that migrate through the body, destroying tissue until they lodge in your bones."

Dorothy flails more, snot and tears pouring from her eyes.

"Of course, if I'm feeling nice, maybe I'll just drown you first." I tilt my head. "Think Nessa will welcome *you* home?" I point the gun back at Dad. "Any last words for her, *Daddy*?"

His jaw muscles tense and his nostrils flare, but he turns his head to the side, not even looking her in the face.

I click my tongue. "No? Okay. Let me ask you this." I drop Dorothy again until she's waist deep, her face now the shade of a ripe tomato from how hard she screams. "Did you know she killed Nessa?"

He licks his lips and shakes his head. But I can tell by the look on his face that he did.

"You really never cared about us at all, did you? We're all just means to an end. Well, congratulations, Dad. We're at the end of the road now."

A noise distracts me, and I twist toward it, seeing Ezekiel standing in the open doorway of the greenhouse, his eyes wide and his jaw hanging open as he takes in the scene.

Great. He must have followed my dad down here.

And then my body is thrown, my gun slamming into the button as it flies from my hand, dropping Dorothy in the acid entirely. There are hands around my neck, and my air is immediately cut off, my father lying on top of me, the veins on his throat protruding through his tattoos. I flail, my nails digging into the skin of his arm as I try to free myself.

But it's no use. His body size alone puts me at enough of a disadvantage where I'm shit out of luck.

"You stupid fucking bitch. You think you have the power? You've never had *any* real power here." His spit flies onto my cheek, and my lungs are seizing, my heartbeat loud in my ears as my body begs for a breath. My vision blurs and I toss my head back, trying like hell to get out of his strangling hold. I can barely make out Ezekiel, standing still, watching. Doing nothing, the way he always has.

Coward.

My body grows limp, my mind growing hazy, and I give in, realizing this is it. My last moments spent are in a roomful of poppies at the hand of the man I was so desperate to have love me.

A sharp sound rings out, and a heavy weight drops on my chest, air flowing back into my lungs at an alarming rate as my dad's hands relax their grip. Something wet drips down the side of my neck, and the smell of blood hits my nostrils, making me retch. Suddenly, his body is lifted and tossed to the side. I gasp, my hands flying to my throat, which is so tender that I wince at the touch. I'm sucking in greedy gulps of air as I stare up at the blurry face of Ezekiel, a gun at his side.

He reaches out a hand, helping me to stand, and wraps his arm around my waist to keep me steady.

"Thank you," I rasp, my voice barely over a whisper, my vocal cords raw from the trauma. I scan the room, noting the bullet hole in my dad's chest, his eyes staring vacant and wide up at the ceiling, and then over to the barrel of acid, Dorothy's body submerged.

They're both dead.

It's done.

Surprisingly, all I feel is numb.

"Come on," Ezekiel says. "I'll help you clean it up."

CHAPTER 39

Evelina

I'M NOT SURE WHAT EZEKIEL DID WITH THE BODIES of my father or my sister, although there wasn't much left of Dorothy after I melted the skin off her bones. And when I woke up this morning and tried to find Ezekiel, he was nowhere, leaving a note thanking *me* for helping him find his courage.

But I didn't do any of that. It was inside him all along. I hope one day he knows. I'm forever in his debt for saving my life when I needed him most.

No one's questioned my father's disappearance, not yet anyway, but I know it's only a matter of time. Mere hours before people start looking, his lower-level bitch boys coming in to pay him his dues, and I'd rather not be around when shit hits the fan.

Sighing, I move around the cottage bedroom, feeling oddly bittersweet about leaving everything behind. Out of all the places in my life, this was the only one that ever really felt like *mine*, and I'm sad to have to leave. I expected to feel more after killing Dorothy. After all, it's been the only thing I've ached for that was out of reach for so many years, and I assumed, maybe foolishly, that after I avenged Nessa's death, I would feel… different somehow. But I don't. Instead, I feel the same as always, other than a hollow type of resignation that so many years of my life were wasted on things that ended up not truly mattering in the end.

Family.

Loyalty.

Love.

It's time for me to move on and make new memories somewhere else. If only Cody would pick up his fucking phone. I press the cell to my ear, trying him one more time before I show up at his place uninvited.

Music echoes from the other room, and I freeze in place, spinning around as I strain to hear. I frown and follow the noise. My hand holding the phone goes lax.

Another noise, and a muffled curse floats through the air right as I turn the corner and step into the living room, my heart ratcheting up into my throat.

"God, there you are." I breathe out a sigh of relief. "I've been trying to call you all day."

Cody spins to face me, the front door still open behind him, and he smiles. "Hey, babe."

"What are you doing here?" I ask, my eyes trailing down his suit and back up to his mussed-up hair and glasses. "And why are you so dressed up?"

"Thought I'd drop by and see where the magic happens." He wiggles his brows, looking around. "So this is it, huh? The cottage in the woods."

I make a face. "Uh…yeah. I guess it is."

Laughing, he shakes his head. He places his hands on his

hips, the sides of his gray jacket swinging back, and I suck in a breath as I notice the gun clipped to his belt.

"Since when have you had a gun?"

"Since I got jealous of yours." He smirks. "Where's yours? Maybe we can compare."

I peek at the front table by the door where my Desert Eagle is before looking back at him. It didn't even cross my mind to grab it when I came up front. But he's acting weird and dressing differently and making me feel like that was a really stupid thing for me to do.

He smiles, that beaming goofy grin he's always given me, only this time, it doesn't look as genuine as it has in the past.

"I've been worried about you," he says, walking over and drawing me into a hug.

I tense up at the contact, my arms straight as arrows at my sides.

He pulls back the smallest bit, his hands gripping my shoulders. "I really do care about you. I want you to know that."

Confusion races through me, and I tilt my head, shifting in his grip. "Cody, what the fuck is going on?"

His hold tightens, one of his palms leaving for the briefest second as he reaches behind his back.

My mind is still playing catch up, trying to figure out what the hell is happening.

Click.

Something cold presses against my wrist.

"You have the right to remain silent," he whispers.

Oh my god.

I jerk out of his hold but I'm not quick enough, and he catches me again, throwing me onto the ground and straddling my back, grabbing my other hand, and cuffing it.

"Calm down," he grunts.

"You're a fucking cop?" My breath comes in quick pants, and my cheek is squished against the wood floor, pain bleating through my head.

All this time, and I've really only ever been alone.

He gets off me as soon as he has me cuffed, and I flip around, groaning at the discomfort. He leans down, cringing as he helps move me to a sitting position, my back against the old velvet couch.

"You were working with Bray—Nick?" My heart twists at the name.

He shakes his head, running a hand through his hair to fix the wayward strands. "Please. That piece of shit moved in on my territory like he could just stick his dick in you and steal my case. This is *my* case, and I'm not working with some DEA fuck."

"Wow. Two separate undercovers. I had no idea I was so popular." Resting my head back against the couch, I accept my fate for what it is.

But how unfair that after all this time, I end up catching the flak and saving my family from the same fate. Death was too good for them both.

"Where's your backup?" I try to see behind him, out the door, but he's too close to me and it's difficult to move to look around him.

"I came first as a courtesy," he says, like it makes any difference. "They'll be here soon."

"This whole time, huh?" I ask, still not wanting to believe that after everything—after all these years—it was just a lie.

"I was chosen specifically because of our connection in high school."

Realization sinks in, sharp and deep, serrating the bruised and battered pieces of my soul. "You moved back because of me."

"I'll admit, I was starting to lose faith." He chuckles. "You're incredibly cagey, do you know that about yourself?"

"Seems I had a right to be," I snap.

"Fair." He quirks his lips. "Honestly, they were about to pull me. But then you gave me a gift."

Disbelief rains down on me like hail. "I told you about the greenhouse."

"Do you think they'll give me the medal of merit?" His eyes lose focus like he's picturing it right then. "Don't take it personally, babe. We've got stuff on the Cantanellis too, thanks to that recording you suggested we take of the mayor."

The USB drive. I had forgotten that even existed.

"All this time, I thought you were this mysterious guy, living behind a curtain and playing fancy tricks with your computers."

He shrugs. "I'm a man of many talents."

"You're a real piece of shit."

"Come on, there's no ne—" There's a bang, and then his eyes widen, blood spraying from the hole that just appeared in the middle of his head. It drips down his face, and his body drops, the thud loud as it hits the ground.

Nicholas stands behind him, my gun at his side and his eyes like fire as they burn through me.

My mouth drops open, and I stare at him, completely gobsmacked. My heart gallops. "What—"

"Quiet," he demands, closing the door behind him and then rushing forward to lean over Cody's dead body, his hands checking his pockets until he finds a small set of keys.

I snap my mouth closed because, well, I'm not really in a position to do anything other than what he asks right now.

"Is there another way out of here?" he asks.

My brows scrunch, my eyes flinging back and forth between Cody and the blood pooling around his body, then back to Nick. Again and again. *Is this what shock feels like?*

"Evelina." His voice is sharp. "Is there another way for you to go?"

I swallow, snapping out of my daze, my chest heaving as I realize what he just did. "Ye-yeah, there's a tunnel underground that has a back exit."

When he kneels at my side, his cinnamon and pine scent flows through me, making my chest cramp so tight I can hardly breathe. "You need to leave."

He undoes my cuffs, and I bring my hands up, rubbing at my wrists. "You just—"

Grabbing my face, he turns it to him, his hands as steady as they ever were, his thumbs brushing beneath my cheeks. His eyes are dark and worried and so fucking perfect, and it pisses me off that even now, I get distracted by everything he is.

"Listen to me," he rushes out. "You need to go."

"But I—"

He slams his mouth to mine and I can't help but kiss him back, because for everything he's done and everything he's not, I still love him, no matter how much I've tried to stop.

"I love you," he says.

A sob works its way through my body and gets stuck on the back of my tongue.

"I didn't know that I *could* love until you. And you're not perfect, okay? You piss me off and you do things I never thought I'd be all right with, and you're moody as hell. You're actually the furthest fucking thing from perfect I've ever seen. But, Evelina… you're perfect for me."

My heart twists, small bits of it mending back together at the seams.

He kisses me one more time. "In about five minutes, this place is going to swarm with feds, and they're here for *you*. You understand what I'm saying?"

I nod, my stomach flipping, the blood racing through my veins.

He tightens his grip on my face. "Listen to me. I won't ask for your forgiveness." He glances at the door before locking his frantic eyes back on me. "I don't *want* you to forgive me right now. I just want to know you're out there and there's a chance. That one day, maybe we'll meet again, and I'll walk up to you and say I'm Nicholas Tennyson Woodsworth, my favorite color is blue, I hated school, and I am so fucking in love with you that I can't imagine living in a world that doesn't have you in it."

I hiccup, my hands wrapping around his wrists.

"If you don't run, *right now*, then I don't get that chance." His eyes flick back and forth between mine. "Please, let me have it, pretty girl. *Go*."

There's a single moment where I consider staying. I stare over at Cody, sprawled out on the floor, and I wonder how Nicholas will explain it. If he'll be able to.

"I'll be fine," he urges.

He grabs me, presses his lips to mine one more time, and then shoves me away.

I jump up, turn around, and run.

CHAPTER 40

Nicholas

I MADE IT IN TIME.

Honestly, I wasn't sure if I would. I hadn't resigned yet, wanting to keep my eyes and ears open, and thank fucking god I did, considering it was only three hours ago I got the tip that Agent Baum was moving in.

When I heard, there was a moment of clarity, like staring into crystal clear waters for the first time in my life. There was no doubt left, everything I've been battling dissipating into thin air as though it never existed in the first place.

All I knew was that I couldn't let her fall. And maybe that makes me stupid; maybe it makes me weak. Maybe she's manipulated me into becoming something I never wanted to be. Whatever the case, I don't care. Because she's changed me fundamentally. Irrevocably. And there's no going back.

I don't love Evelina in spite of her flaws. I love her *because* of them.

Relief floods through me when she disappears to the back of the cottage, and I close my eyes, praying for the first time in years she makes it out okay. Then I wipe my prints off the gun, setting the scene to corroborate the story I'm about to spin, and make my way out the front door to wait.

Tires crunch over the freshly fallen snow, black sedans pulling through the trees, ready to take the girl I love into custody. To steal her away forever.

And to put it simply, I can't live with that.

A dozen suited-up agents hop from their cars, local police department surrounding them as backup. They crouch behind open doors and aim their guns at me. "Drop your weapon!"

I raise my hands and walk onto the rickety wooden porch, dropping the pistol to the ground.

"I'm Agent Nicholas Woodsworth," I call out. "I've been working this case."

A man with dark hair and steely eyes comes out from behind the door, advancing without taking the target off my chest. "Where's Agent Baum?"

"Dead."

"And the suspect?"

"Gone." My heart stampedes against my chest. "I'm going to reach in my pocket and show you my badge, okay?"

The man lifts his weapon higher. "Keep your hands where I can see them."

"Fine, *you* can come check. I came to offer backup, but I was…" I shake my head, frowning. "I was too late."

I nod toward my jacket pocket and he reaches in, grabbing my badge and flipping it open, scanning it before glancing up at me. Finally, he drops his arm and alerts the others to do the same.

"Agent Woodsworth, sorry about that." He cringes. "Protocol."

I smile. "I get it."

The rest of the night is a blur. I'm brought in to give a statement, and I watch as they load up the first man I've ever killed on a stretcher, placing his bloody body in a bag and rolling him out.

I don't feel regret, and I'm not wrestling with what I had to do. I just feel content knowing I kept the woman I love safe.

The next morning, I walk into my division, bypassing my desk and going straight into Cap's office, placing my gun and my badge on his desk.

He lifts a brow. "What's that?"

"This is me turning in my badge." I shrug. "I'm done, Cap."

He breathes deep, running his tongue over his teeth. "The hell you mean you're done?"

"I mean just that. I'm done. I'm out. I quit." Every time I say it, my shoulders feel lighter.

"That's a big decision," he says. "You sure it's the right one?"

I sit with his question for a minute and then glance at the paper on the top of his desk, a picture of Evelina with the word WANTED stamped underneath in bold letters.

Steeling myself, I nod. "This life's not my dream. Not anymore."

He squints his eyes. "You need to talk to someone about what happened with Agent Baum? We have resources, you know?"

I shake my head. "I'm good, but thank you. I appreciate that."

"Okay." He blows out a breath and walks around his desk, coming up to me and placing his hand on my shoulder. "I should probably try to convince you to stay."

Smiling, a sense of sadness hits me in the chest. After all, being an agent is all I've ever known. For most of my life, it's all I've ever wanted. But then Evelina's face appears in my mind, and there's *nothing* I want more than her.

"Don't waste your breath, Cap."

His brows draw in. "I'm not a fucking captain."

I chuckle, grabbing him into a hug. He stiffens, patting me on the back and pushing me away.

"You'll always be the captain of my heart."

The first month without her was filled with anxiety. She was all over the news. The brains behind Farrell Westerly. Considered armed and extremely dangerous.

Agent Cody Baum was awarded the medal of merit posthumously, and I was called three times by Cap trying to get me back in the field.

Turns out he doesn't hate me so much after all.

The second month rolled around, and the coverage started to ease. She was old news now, and they hadn't had any luck at finding her. Plus, the Cantanellis were being brought in on several different charges, thanks to the wires Mayor Norman wore when doing dirty deals, and they always *were* the bigger fish in the pond.

Mayor Norman got off with nothing, of course. Not that I blame him for working with the FBI. I know how easy it is to scare a dirty politician into doing whatever it takes to stay out of prison.

By month three, I was restless. I took up woodworking and found out I had quite the knack for creating custom furniture. Even started a little business to try and pass the time, but nothing stopped my soul from aching, crying out for its other half.

Month four, I debated calling Seth, seeing if he could track her down. But I never did. I've already put him in enough situations that put his career at risk. I may be a selfish man, but I'm done being a selfish friend. So I hired a PI, one who rides the edges of the law just enough that I won't worry about him turning in the information he gathers to anyone but me. And at first, my hope was renewed.

But the months dragged by.

Then one day, twelve months and seventeen days after I killed Agent Cody Baum and helped Evelina escape, my phone rang.

He found her, living in a small town off the coast of Ireland. Exactly how she always dreamed.

It's been three days since I've heard the news, and I still haven't done shit about it.

Rose sighs, coming over to sit down next to me on the living room couch. "You should go to her."

Swallowing around the knot in my throat, I shake my head. "She's okay without me."

"Well, *I'm* sick of you," she laughs. "And while I appreciate the way you've been filling up our place with beautiful furniture, if you give me another end table, I'll start a goddamn fire just to make some room."

"I don't want to leave you, kid."

She smiles, nudging my shoulder. "I've always wanted to visit Ireland."

That's all it takes. The next morning, I'm on a flight, with a scribbled address on a piece of paper and nothing but nerves and hope exploding in my chest. It takes eight hours and I'm on the edge of my seat the entire time, wondering what I'll say when I see her, if she even *wants* to see me at all.

Time moves slower when you're anxious to start the rest of your life, but eventually it *does* move.

I step out of the cab, staring up at the small bed-and-breakfast in Doolin. The village itself is quaint, colorful buildings lining a beautiful landscape of rolling green hills and a sparkling sea. But I'm not staring at any of that. Not when Evelina's right in front of me.

She's walking out the front door and heading down the street, a notebook in her hand and a black flowy skirt swishing around her knees. She looks the same yet entirely different. Her black hair is gone, the natural brown waves flowing to the middle of her back, and the freckles scattered across her face are visible even from where I'm standing across the street.

My heart stalls in my chest and my hand comes up to rest on top of it.

She takes my fucking breath away.

I follow behind her.

We walk for what feels like hours, but I don't mind the view, soaking in the way she's just *existing*. Eventually, the path narrows and the view changes, going from rolling land into sharp cliffs that drop into the sea.

Waves crash against the rocks and she stops in a small area where no one else is around, staring out at the ocean, the wind making her hair fly in different directions behind her.

Thunder rumbles low and deep in the distance, and I look beyond where we are, noticing the dark-gray clouds rolling in, sheets of rain visible as they crash onto the land.

She sits down, crossing her legs and opening her notebook, and I stand back and watch her like an absolute creep. She scribbles, then scratches and brings the pen up to her lips, her head tilting in thought.

Finally, I make my move.

"You're trying too hard." I take a step closer, my heart slamming against my chest.

Her body freezes and she twists around, her mouth dropping open as she stares at me.

"Excuse me?" she says. "Who says I'm trying?"

She stands, her gaze fierce and her lips turned down, and for just a moment, my chest stalls, thinking maybe she's upset I'm here. That maybe she hasn't forgiven me, and maybe she never will.

But then a grin spreads across her face. A real one, the kind that shows all her teeth and makes her eyes crinkle in the corners.

My heart skips and stutters, then starts beating in a steady rhythm.

And with that single smile, I know I've made it home.

EPILOGUE

Evelina

HE'S HERE.

It's been twelve months, almost to the day, and I had given up hope that he'd find me. I'm glad he didn't until now.

I needed time to breathe, to learn how to be *me* without the added weight of expectation. And I needed time to forgive him.

So I ran from my cottage, went to the streets, and somehow found a pilot who was willing to fly me out of the country. People will do anything for the right amount of money and threats. Then I came to Ireland, and I fell in love, knowing I'd never leave.

Not that I could anyway, considering I'm a fugitive.

Nicholas is standing a few paces away, and he moves forward, not stopping until he's directly in front of me. I breathe deeply, cinnamon and pine rushing through my senses and making my chest flip. It aches from missing him.

"Hi," he says.

"Hi."

He sticks out his hand. "I'm Nicholas Tennyson Woodsworth."

My throat swells, and I place my palm in his. Goose bumps

race up my arms at the contact and I glance down at where we're touching. "Kind of a long name."

He laughs. "Are you gonna tell me yours?"

Shaking my head, I look up at him. "How do I know you're not a stalker?"

"Oh, pretty girl." He steps in close, threading his fingers through my hair and pulling me to him. I go willingly, sinking into his hold. "I'll be whatever you want me to be."

I press my head into his palm, bending slightly to slip my hand beneath my skirt and grab my brand-new gun. It isn't rose gold, and it doesn't have the memories, but it still does the job. I drag it up his torso and place it beneath his chin. "Give me your words, Nicholas. And maybe I'll let you stay."

His eyes flare.

"'You do not know how longingly I look upon you. You must be he I was seeking, or she I was seeking.'" He bends his head down and ghosts his lips across my cheek. "'I have somewhere surely lived a life of joy with you. All is recalled as we flit by each other, fluid, affectionate, chaste, matured.'"

His nose rubs against mine, and my stomach flips and flies.

"'You grew up with me, were a boy with me or a girl with me. I ate with you and slept with you. Your body has become not yours only nor left my body mine only.'"

His fingers move, tracing over my forehead, my nose, my cheeks. I close my eyes, the sound of the ocean almost as loud as the beat of my heart from where it pounds in my chest.

"'You give me the pleasure of your eyes, face, flesh, as we pass. You take of my beard, breast, hands, in return. I am not to speak to you. I am to think of you when I sit alone or wake at night alone.'"

He wraps his hand around mine, moving the gun down until it's at my side instead of under his chin.

"'I am to wait. I do not doubt I am to meet you again.'" His breath skims across my lips. "'I am to see to it that I do not lose you.'"

I look behind him, seeing the storm rolling in and a faint rainbow peeking from its edges and dipping into the water below.

"You know, for not believing in romance—"

"I'm so fucking in love with you, Evelina Westerly," he cuts me off.

I grin, rising up on my tiptoes to press a kiss to his lips. "Every wretched piece?"

He brushes the hair back from my face. "Every single one."

EXTENDED EPILOGUE

Evelina/Nicholas

Evelina

STORMS HAVEN'T BOTHERED ME IN A LONG TIME.

In fact, I find the thunder soothing with the way it rumbles through the sky, sprinkled with flashes of light while rain pelts against everything it touches.

It's nice to know that even Mother Nature unleashes her wrath on anything and everything without regard to who gets hurt when they're in her torrential path.

A small fire crackles in the middle of the living room, the orangey blaze framed by white painted bricks and beautiful pieces of furniture handcrafted by Nicholas over the past few years. The hot tea in my hands warms my fingertips and I breathe in the chamomile scent as I curl my legs beneath me in my favorite oversize chair. I had it placed directly beneath the largest window of our cottage, showcasing the shades of green from the forest that surrounds us.

Today, nature is angry.

And she's beautiful when she gets mad.

I try to remember the last time a storm affected me. Try to pinpoint the exact moment it went from being just another storm to something that makes me want to retreat into solitude and find comfort in.

A memory hits me out of nowhere.

It's different now that Dad is gone and locked up in prison.

Mom has gotten even meaner, if that's possible. Nessa says she's struggling with being a single parent. I say she never really was a parent to begin with. Now, she disappears four to five times a week, trying to get us to believe she's down at the cathedral to pray or spending time with our father during visiting hours. But I see the way she comes home with mussed-up hair and smudged lips. And I watched out the window one night when some random man dropped her off in his fancy black car and she about sucked his face off before walking back in the front door.

Even with Dorothy, she's changed.

And that's done absolutely nothing except make Dorothy ache for her attention even more.

Nessa jostles my arm as she drags me out onto our back porch, the air outside eerily calm and still other than the loud sirens wailing through the quiet.

"I thought tornadoes were supposed to be windy," I say, my hand gripping my journal tight to my side as small tendrils of panic weave their way through my middle.

Nessa doesn't respond, most likely because she's too busy dropping me in place and spinning around to drag Dorothy down the steps and across the grass until we hit the underground shelter about fifty feet away, just before the line of trees start in our backyard.

"God, Evie, do you ever not sound stupid?" Dorothy spits, jerking her head to glare at me.

"Shut up, both of you," Nessa snaps.

Nessa's wearing dark-blue jeans, and when she stands back up after having dropped down to haul the heavy cellar door open, there's dirt and grime and a little bit of blood seeping from the frayed holes across her knees.

Guilt nags at the back of my brain. Maybe I should have helped.

Nessa waves an arm frantically, her brown hair whipping through the air as the wind starts to pick up, the eerie stillness disappearing in an instant. I go underground first, my foot slipping on the narrow metal ladder as I make my way into the space. It smells musty and dank down here, and there's a dim light that casts a warm yellow glow around the small space, controlled by a string.

I rack my brain, trying to remember the last time I've been here. I don't remember it being so small.

It's cold as I make my way over to the corner and huddle against the concrete wall, trying to blot out the noise of the wind as it grows stronger and whips across the ground above me.

Nessa is fighting with Dorothy again, but it's hard to hear over the rest of the noise.

I see Nessa's arm reach out and grip Dorothy's tightly, half shoving her down to the ladder. "I swear to god, Dorothy, if you don't get your skinny ass down in that shelter, I'll kill you myself."

"I'm not going without finding her first." Dorothy's voice, high and panicked, filters through the open cellar door, her feet stumbling on the steps.

Nessa pushes her way into the space, forcing Dorothy to move farther down. "She's fine, Dorothy."

"You don't know that," Dorothy replies, her voice cracking.

They're talking about our mother, of course. There's no one else who Dorothy would be so up in arms about. I didn't even think about her being gone or about her safety through the storm. Maybe that makes me a bad person. But I'm only giving her the same energy she'd give me in return.

Dorothy plops down in the middle of the room against the wall and Nessa sits next to her, reaching out to drag me into her side, hugging me close. She reaches for Dorothy too, but Dorothy jerks back, scoffing.

Something smashes against the top of the door, the cellar rattling like giants are trying to rip open the lock. I lean further into Nessa.

Dorothy lurches forwards, trying to escape up the ladder. "What if Mom's inside looking for us? For me? We need to make sure she's okay!"

Nessa drops me from her side like a sack of hot potatoes, and pain shoots through my arm when my elbow hits the concrete ground. She moves quickly, grabbing Dorothy around the waist and pulling her back down.

Dorothy fights against her for a few seconds, but Nessa is bigger and stronger, and in the end, Dorothy gives up the fight, small hiccups and sobs breaking through her pinched mouth as she sinks into Nessa's hold.

My stomach churns violently as I watch Nessa stroke her hair and rock her back and forth.

Another harsh slap against the cellar door makes my insides jump, and I can't help the little bit of sluggish green jealousy that drips through my muscles when Nessa coos to Dorothy to keep her calm.

I'm here too. I'm scared too.

But like usual, I end up soothing myself.

Eventually, the storm passes and we make our way back up the ladder and into the yard.

The house is still standing, although half the roof is torn off, and there's debris and broken trees everywhere.

The air is silent again, like nature's gone to sleep after having the temper tantrum of a lifetime.

Dorothy immediately runs off, searching for our mother, but of course, she isn't here.

And she doesn't come back. Not that night or the next or the one after that.

But Dorothy never stops waiting.

I snap out of the memory, a small pang of sadness hitting my chest, the way it always does when I think of Nessa.

My view of her has changed in the five years since I've come to Ireland and made a new home and a new life here with Nicholas, but the grief of losing her will never leave. It only changes from day to day, the weight sometimes easier to bear than others. Grief is funny that way.

Both a variable and a constant.

But it's been easier to navigate ever since I forced myself to reflect internally. To recognize the flaws in myself that make it easier for others to hurt me. Turns out I love to put people on pedestals. Even when I know that doing so will make it so much worse when they inevitably fall.

My father pulled the wool over my eyes for years, manipulating my misplaced loyalty, but he wasn't wrong about everything, namely the part that Nessa played in damaging our name in the criminal underworld. I knew it even back then, but I didn't want to admit that the woman who was perfect to me wasn't perfect in everything she did. That she had flaws—cracks and jagged edges that sliced through people if they got too close. Dorothy was one of them, and while I'll never forgive her for killing Nessa, I understand what it's like to long for love and attention and feel anger when you don't get it the way you want.

It took a while for me to be able to admit that to myself.

Still glad she's dead though.

Truth is, nobody's perfect.

Not even me, although if you ask my husband, he'd be inclined to disagree.

My husband.

The words send a thrill through me, desire coursing through my middle and spreading through my core, heating between my legs with a territorial ownership that's both toxic and addicting.

It was a spur-of-the-moment thing, us getting married. And technically, we still aren't. For obvious reasons, trying to legally bind to each other is something we decided would be best to avoid, considering I'm on America's Most Wanted list.

But one day, after we sat on the rocky shores of Ireland and he finger fucked me while I let him read my own poetry for the first time, he dragged me into a small run-down church and had us "married" right then and there.

And although he's not mine in the eyes of the law, Nicholas is mine in every way that matters. I own his heart, his mind, and his soul. And he owns mine right back.

About a year later, we found a small cottage in Northern Ireland, nestled in a forest with ten acres of land surrounding it, and we both fell in love. We've been here for three years now. Nicholas spends his time selling chopped wood to locals and creating beautiful one of a kind furniture that he sells around the world under his business name, the Tin Roof.

And me? I do whatever I please.

It's an odd feeling, having gone from spending the majority of my life pleasing other people to having the freedom and time to figure out who I truly am. Although it's a new discovery every day, because honestly, I'm not sure there's a definite answer to who or what a soul is. We're ever changing.

Right now?

I'm a writer.

A dreamer.

A romantic.

I tend to my garden in the day, bringing in fresh vegetables to eat and fresh flowers to decorate the space, and I spend my nights curled up by the fire with a man who loves every single flawed part of me. And it doesn't get much better than that.

But there are times where an itch starts to scratch beneath the surface of my skin, one that thirsts for an outlet to the darkness that lives inside, and I don't shy away from that either.

Figuring out who you are means knowing every part and accepting every part, no matter what other people may think.

So when the burner phone I have rings and a distant cousin of mine—who I met three years ago by chance when I realized I had actual living family members in Ireland—gives me a name and an address, I slide up the zipper on my knee-high stilettos and I make my way to take care of people who are better off dead.

Anonymously, of course.

I have no interest in having my name affiliated with the Irish mob. Not anymore. And especially not here.

I'm perfectly content with living my quiet life.

The rain finally dies down and I finish my tea, stretching my body until my muscles pop and flex.

Nicholas is out in the woods still in his workshop, most likely waiting for the rain to pass to come back home, and I miss him, so I walk out our front door, down the new yellow brick path that leads to his shop nestled in the middle of the trees.

Nicholas

The smell of cedar is especially strong after the rain, and right now, it's filling the air.

Over the past five years, I've gotten so used to the scents of freshly cut wood and sawdust that coming back here to my workshop and crafting another piece feels like home.

Which it is now, I guess, as long as Evelina's around.

Lifting up my arms, I wipe a bead of sweat from my brow and drop the axe to my side, staring up at the overcast sky. I can't do too much with damp wood, but I had a few pieces I kept inside my workshop that needed to be split, so as soon as the last raindrop fell, I came outside to chop them.

If you had asked me six years ago, before I met Evelina, I never would have imagined living this life: working for myself and living in the middle of Ireland with a woman who fits me like the missing piece of a puzzle. But here I am, and I wouldn't change it for a goddamn thing.

A tree branch crunches behind me and I spin around, squinting my eyes to find the source of the noise.

Evelina traipses through the low hanging leaves, a goddess in her flowy black skirt and worn Vans. Her hair is still that beautiful natural brunette, and I swear to god every time I see her, my heart grows a little bit in size. Beats a little stronger. Hums a little deeper.

A smile blooms across my face as she trips over something on the ground and kicks it to the side, scowling.

I quirk a brow. "You should watch where you walk, pretty girl."

She snaps her head up and frowns. "Nobody asked, stalker."

Her chest rises and falls with her small puffs of air as she makes her way over to where I am, and I cross my arms over my chest, grinning at the way her cheeks are pinking up.

"Besides," she continues as she steps right up to me, craning her neck to meet my eyes. "I wanted to come see you."

I smirk, reaching out to brush a strand of hair off her face. "Damn, you're beautiful."

Her face softens and she rises up on her tiptoes, pressing her pillow-soft lips against mine in a chaste kiss. "Don't forget your sister gets here tomorrow."

My hands reach down and grip her hips, enjoying the way she feels under my touch. Leaning in, my nose skims against the expanse of her neck and I inhale, allowing my lips to brush against her throat. "I don't want to talk about my sister right now."

"Oh no?" she breathes, pushing her body into mine. "What would you rather talk about?"

Arousal strikes through me like a lightning bolt, the way it always does whenever Evelina's around.

"I'd rather you not be talking at all," I rasp, pressing my hips into her.

My cock jerks, filling rapidly. It's always half at attention and ready for her. Living with Evelina has me in a state of constant hardness. It's fucking torture sometimes.

"Have you been a good boy?" she whispers, skimming her lips against the underside of my jaw.

My abs tense as her long black nails scrape against my stomach, over the plaid flannel of my shirt, working their way down until she's cupping my erection through my pants. I bite the inside of my cheek to keep from groaning out loud.

She leans back slightly, removing her touch, and I'm about to protest but then she drops to her knees, right there on the forest floor. My left hand threads through the silky strands of her hair and tugs, bringing her face back just far enough so I can catch her gaze.

"I'm always a good boy."

Her eyes flash and then she has my fly unzipped and I'm in her mouth, her tongue ring doing incredible things against the ridge of my cock.

My other hand flies forward to cup the back of her head as she sucks me down.

"Fuck, pretty girl, you take it so well."

Moving my hips back, I drag my dick out, the feeling of her lips around it enough to send pleasure flooding through my veins. I thrust back in, and her tongue flicks against me while she sucks and my knees buckle the slightest bit from the sensation.

She hums, the vibration coursing down the length of my dick, heat coiling in the base of my spine.

But I'm not ready to let this end yet. I tug on the strands of her hair, yanking her off my cock with a loud pop of her lips.

"What's wrong, pup?" She grins. "Can't handle it?"

Her antagonizing does nothing but make me want to fuck the brat out of her more, and I slide my hands down from the back of her head along the sharp lines of her jaw. I bend down slightly, pulling her face to mine to leave a soft kiss on her lips before I continue to move until my fingers slip beneath her arms on either side of her.

She's light as hell and flies up easily into my arms as I lift her. I spin us around and lie her down on top of the large tree stump where I cut my pieces of wood.

She shrieks. "Fuck, Nick, it's wet!"

I smirk, my hands gliding up the insides of her thighs beneath her skirt, forcing her legs apart as I slip her panties to the side and drag my fingertips through her pussy lips.

"Oh, it's wet all right." I waggle my brows.

She scoffs. "You're ruining the moment."

My grin grows, a happy warmth coasting through my chest as I lean over her, bringing my body to rest on top of hers. "You love it."

Her hand lifts and strokes the side of my jaw, our gazes locked like magnets. "I love you."

The amusement in my chest dissipates, leaving behind something heavier. My chest brushes against hers and I rest my lips a centimeter away until we're breathing the same air, my cock lining up at her center.

I had planned to take my time, lick her sweet cunt until I was full off her taste, but suddenly, my need to be inside her, to be one with her, is overwhelming. I push my hips forward, the tip slipping inside.

She moans, her hand moving from my jaw to wrap around the back of my neck, her nails digging until they break skin.

"'Whoever you are,'" I murmur against her mouth, "'now I place my hand upon you, that you be my poem. I whisper with my lips close to your ear. I have loved many women and men, but I love none better than you.'"

Surging forward, I fill her to the hilt, the whispered words of Walt Whitman lingering in the space between us as the contentment of being inside her fills up my very being.

She moans again, her head flying back and smacking against the tree stump, and I immediately start a punishing rhythm.

My pretty girl has never really been one for the soft and sweet.

Her thighs spread wide around my hips, one of her legs wrapping around the back of my waist, her foot pressing against my ass and pulling me harder into her.

My hand slides down her side and grips the outside of her thigh tightly as I fuck her, pleasure spiraling through me until a sense of euphoria fills up every single pore of my body.

I was already on the edge from her sucking me off, and I know I won't last long now. It's too intense. She is too intense.

"Fuck, pretty girl, I need you to come."

Her eyes are glazed as they latch on to mine, and she wraps her other hand around my head until her fingers intertwine behind my neck. Then she starts moving her hips in tandem with mine, fucking herself on my cock as I thrust into her.

The sensations of her tight cunt gripping me as she works herself is more than I can take, and I lean down, melding our lips together, my teeth biting into her lip to try and hold myself back from coming.

Her muscles tighten beneath me, and she gasps into my mouth, her tongue swirling around mine and sucking, and then her pussy is spasming, and she's drenching my cock with her orgasm.

My eyes roll in the back of my head from how she's gripping me, but just before I come, she shoves me back, my dick sliding out of her pussy and bobbing in the cold air. And then she's in front of me again, on her knees, her cheeks rosy and her eyes wild.

I suck in a breath, taken aback by how fucking beautiful she looks on her knees and freshly fucked, and before I can utter a word, her tongue swipes out, and I'm frozen, watching as she licks herself off the length of me.

My balls tighten.

"Goddamn, Evelina."

Her lips wrap around me and she swallows me down whole, and the vision of it combined with the heat of her mouth is all I can take. My body clenches tight and I explode, shooting my cum down her throat.

My eyes are glued on her, watching the way her throat bobs in time with every spurt of my spasming dick, and the sight is so lewd and so Evelina that I almost collapse from the pleasure.

She does things like this, where she strips me of everything and rebuilds me until I live and breathe just for her.

And I let her because as long as we're together, that's all I need. Giving her control when she needs it doesn't make me feel weak. It makes me feel like more of a man.

Her provider.

Her protector.

It's an intuitive type of relationship that I've never felt with anyone else.

She's my soul mate, my heart mate, and I would do anything for her.

Smiling wide, she wipes the corner of her lips and tucks me back inside my pants before hopping back up to a stand and brushing the debris off her skirt.

I reach out, grabbing her and pulling her flush against me, then lifting her up by the thighs until her legs wrap around my waist.

My nose nuzzles against hers. "You are the most beautiful kind of chaos, Evelina Westerly Woodsworth."

"And you're the best kind of calm," she whispers back. "Let's go home."

I nod but tighten my grip on her legs, deciding I'll carry her back.

The cottage in the woods may be our house, but there's no place in the world like home.

And Evelina is mine.

Here's a sneak peek at book four in the Never After series

TWISTED

PROLOGUE

Julian

MY MOTHER USED TO HAVE ME PICK MY OWN switches. I'd traipse through the small, wooded area at the back of our house and find the smallest branch I could, one that was thick enough to replace the belt but wouldn't hurt quite as bad.

Then she'd whip me until I bled.

"It will only hurt for a little, piccolo," she'd always murmur.

Afterward, she'd apologize and take me for gelato.

Dark chocolate raspberry. Her favorite.

Sometimes, I deserved it. Other times, you had to look deeper for the cause. I was a rowdy boy who rebelled against the idea of following in my father's footsteps: taking over the dry cleaning business started from the ground up by my grandparents when they immigrated from Calabria.

Any time my father would come home after being ridiculed and talked down to by the customers he'd clean stains of, he'd beat my mother black and blue. Our walls were thin, and I'd lie awake to the sounds of a broken woman's whimpers and an angry man's curses. I'd always know that not long after, she'd come into my room, her midnight-black hair pulled back as tight as her smile while she passed along the torture.

My family has always been predictable that way—taking power from those too weak to keep it.

It will only hurt for a little.

I snap out of the memory, my mother's voice fading into the recesses of my mind where I keep her locked up tight, and I straighten from where I'm leaning against the wall in the dimly lit room of my basement.

There's a man currently bound to the chair in the middle of the unfinished floor, the blank off-white walls creating a calming sensation that doesn't truly exist. His breathing is heavy, the sound accompanied only by the hissing of Iesha, my twenty-foot Burmese Python as she slithers her way around his feet and up his legs. The second she hits his calves, he jerks, his once perfectly pressed suit soaked through with perspiration.

Normally, I wouldn't do things like this here, but my choices were limited and this needed to be kept a private affair.

"Careful," I tsk. "She likes when you put up a fight. It *excites* her."

I rub my palm over my jaw, the three-day stubble rough beneath the pads of my fingers, and I sigh, reaching into my pocket and gripping my compact metal staff. Pulling it out, I press a button on the side, and it elongates until it's full size, the silver brass knob shimmering against the black metal. I twirl it in my hand as I step toward him.

"Pl-please," he begs.

A chuckle escapes my chest as Iesha continues to curl her way around his body.

"Your manners are *impeccable*, Samir," I drawl. "But I don't have any use for them."The clack of my steps halts when I stop in front of him, my muscles tight with anticipation. "Do you know why you're here?"

His brows furrow, small beads of sweat trickling down the sides of his ashen face. "I'm just here for the girl," he rasps, his bottom lip trembling. "They told me to come. I—"

"The girl and everything that comes with her are *mine*." My eyes flare. "And *no one* will take her from me."

I snap the staff upward in my grasp, spinning it around sharply, reveling in the fear percolating through his dark eyes.

"Don't worry." I grin. "This will only hurt for a little."

CHAPTER 1

Yasmin

"HE DOESN'T LOOK SICK."

The words slice through my clothes and prick against my chest. If I weren't brought up to remain politically correct and cordial, I'd snap and say something out of turn like…

"Read the room, Debbie. You sound like a clown."

Instead, I bite the inside of my cheek and pick up my water, allowing the weight of the crystal in my palm and the cool bite of liquid against my lip to keep me quiet.

Besides, I'm confident that Debbie, the young, shiny wife of New York's governor, didn't *mean* for me to hear what she said. Or maybe she did. Seems like something she might do.

I follow her stare, down the length of the espresso-stained dining table, until my gaze hits my father at the head, his dark-olive skin looking sallow and worn. Deep bags line his tired eyes, the splotches of purple belaying the fact that he *is*, in fact, quite ill. But I guess if someone hasn't spent years of their life memorizing the miniscule changes of every one of his features, I could see how he might look simply overtired. And for a man who owns and runs a multibillion-dollar company that controls most of the world's jewels, being *overtired* is synonymous with normal.

I'm sure my dad will be thrilled that people can't see the change in his health.

Jealousy squeezes my middle, and for just a moment, I wish I could trade places with someone else in the room, *anyone* else, if it meant I could pretend he was still okay.

The tilapia from our last course threatens to surge back up my throat, nausea tossing my stomach, because I know my wish is impossible to grant. Maybe *they* don't see the difference, but I do.

I see it in the way his movements are stiff and jilted, like there's a concrete grasp on his bones that he can't seem to shake.

I see it in the downturn of his lips when he thinks no one is watching, as he soaks in small inconsequential details that we all take for granted every day.

And most of all, I see it in his absence, every time he locks himself away, sparing me from having to watch as the radiation and chemo burn through his veins, destroying everything in its path.

That's what cancer does. It ravages you from the inside out without care for who you are. It doesn't matter whether you keep the world in the palm of your hand or if you have more money than God.

It just cares for death.

And death always wins one way or another.

My gaze moves from my dad to the French doors that line the far wall and open to the back of our estate. The stars twinkle against the black sky, and I focus on how the deep blue light of the expansive pool creates a haunting glow over everything it touches.

Anything to keep me from focusing on the problems I can't seem to outrun.

Debbie giggles and draws my attention to where she's practically purring at the man sitting next to her.

Julian Faraci.

His dark eyes, as black as bottomless pits, are already on mine, searing through my mask of polite acquiescence and stripping me down until I feel like a small, worthless girl primed and ready to be squished beneath his shoe.

I remember when he first came around, being hired on as the COO of my father's company Sultans when I was fifteen, and like the naive stupid girl that I was eight years ago, I developed a crush. He was a power-hungry twenty-eight-year-old man, and whenever I'd come home from boarding school for the holidays, I'd hero-worship him, blinded by his appearance and sucked in by the commanding nature that bled from his pores.

But he made sure to stomp that to dust once his cold demeanor and slimy personality shone through. Besides, I was already half in love with my best friend anyway.

My gaze narrows at Julian, irritation stabbing at my skin like needles. He smirks, lifting his wine and tilting it toward me, the tattoos on his other hand shifting with the flex of his knuckles as he brushes it through his disheveled black hair.

A small drop of water splashes on the back of my wrist and I set down my glass quickly, tearing my eyes away from his amused gaze while I shove my trembling fingers beneath my thighs.

My phone vibrates in my lap, and I snap my head down, seeing a notification from the boy who's held my heart since we were kids.

Aidan: You look beautiful

My heart flutters and I grin despite myself, glancing around to see where he is. His mom is standing in the corner of the room, her blond hair pulled back in a tight bun, the way every member of the staff in our house is told to wear it, and her gaze is pointed down. *Is he working with her tonight?*

"Yasmin." My father's harsh voice cuts through the fog and I snap my head over, meeting the eyes of the twenty people who are now focused on me around the table.

"I'm sorry." I force a smile and bring my hands up to clutch my silverware. "I must have missed what you said."

"The governor asked what you think about your father's newest acquisition." Julian's voice is cold yet smooth as butter, and a chill skirts down my spine. It's rude for him to have a voice like that and a face like he does when his soul is so rotten.

My fork clacks against the plate as I set it down and turn my attention to Governor Cassum.

"I wouldn't presume to know the ins and outs of *my* father's business," I say, emphasizing the word *my* purely for Julian's benefit. "But if you're asking for my opinion on the moral implications of continuing to trade diamonds in conflict areas, then I'm more than happy to give you my thoughts."

Someone scoffs to my left and my eyes are drawn back to Julian. His sharp jaw twitches, highlighting the five-o'clock shadow that accents his tan face.

My father breaks the tension, chuckling. "These days, kids run off to university and think they're ready to take on the world. This is just another example of why men run the country and women are fit to stay at home and care for the children."

Heat sears my cheeks and I peer back down at my lap even though I'm not truly embarrassed. I'm used to my father's misogynistic rhetoric, and despite what he says, I know he means well. He may not be a *good* man, but he's always been good to me, and I love him despite his outdated ideals and less than savory business tactics.

It's amazing what we're capable of overlooking—what we're willing to do—when it comes to those we love.

My father's eyes soften as they take me in. "You'll make a wonderful mother with that caring heart, *habibti*."

Julian leans in and speaks to my father while the other dignitaries start up their superficial conversations that mean nothing and *do* nothing other than stroke their own egos, and just like that, the attention is off me.

My phone vibrates again.

Aidan: I can't wait to touch you

My fingers drift over my lips, excitement bubbling in my middle as I think of ways to escape this boring dinner and find Aidan. My foot taps against the marble floor of the dining room and I glance around, my insides fidgety.

I could probably leave without anyone even noticing.

But I don't, because no matter how much I want to, the etiquette that's been bludgeoned into my psyche since birth reigns supreme. It isn't until dessert is finished and the men excuse themselves to my father's cigar room that I press a hand against my head and feign a yawn.

"Are you all right, Yasmin?" Debbie asks, her copper brows drawing in.

The few other women left at the table—mostly wives, a few mistresses—look at me in mock concern.

"A headache, I'm afraid. Nothing a good night's sleep won't fix." My eyes glance to the hallway. "If you'll excuse me."

My fingers curl around the wood as I push back from the table, and I walk past the few estate staff clearing the dirty dishes, my eyes scanning to see if Aidan is one of them. He isn't. I pull out my phone the second I'm around the corner, my fingers flying as I type out a message of where to meet, butterflies fluttering in my stomach.

CHAPTER 2

Julian

I SWIRL THE JOHNNIE WALKER BLUE IN MY GLASS, the smell of books and tobacco filling the air as I lean against the ornate wooden table in Ali's cigar room. The clock to the left chimes eleven times. It's late, and everyone has finally left. Blowing out a breath, I sip my whisky, a headache throbbing between my temples at having to wear the face of a dapper host.

Even though it isn't *my* estate and it wasn't *my* dinner, everyone knows that wherever Ali is in name, I'm there in the background, pulling the strings. It's tedious to put on soirees like the one tonight, but they're essential. And never-ending.

This week, it was the governors and the CEOs of the world. Next week it could be the capos or the jefes, depending on who it is we need to have in our immediate pocket. It's a tenuous game we play, being masters of the universe, but it's one I enjoy.

Controlling most of the world's diamonds means you control most of the world, and a diamond is never *just* a diamond.

With Ali's recent health issues, I'm more than happy to take complete control of Sultans in his stead. Besides, no one can deny that I've done more to advance our position both politically and socioeconomically in the past eight years than Ali accomplished in a lifetime.

There's only one issue.

He doesn't *want* me to take the reins. Not officially anyway, which is complete bullshit considering no one else has poured their blood, sweat, and tears into his legacy more than I have.

With his declining health, there's an undercurrent of anxiety that taints the air, specifically when he speaks of his daughter, Yasmin. She came back six months ago, a fresh graduate from whatever university he had her stashed at, and he started calling in suitors for her hand immediately. Like it's the eighteenth century and he's on borrowed time.

It was incredibly suspicious. A quick trip to his personal lawyer and a flip of my staff later, I learned the ins and outs of Ali's will. He's leaving *everything* to his daughter, provided she marry someone "suitable."

Ridiculous.

I can't imagine Yasmin knows of Ali's intentions, but I have no doubt in my mind she'll jump at the chance to take over her father's legacy, to make him happy, even if it means marrying someone she has no interest in.

She'll be its ruin. She'll be *my* ruin.

Unless I become the man she marries.

The thought makes my stomach curdle.

Samir, the poor fool who thought he'd be introduced to Yasmin this evening, was the first of what I assume will be many unfortunate casualties. But after careful consideration, I've decided that until I have a plan in place, no one will get near Yasmin Karam.

Ali lets out a sigh, sinking into the deep burgundy leather of his oversize chair. He coughs suddenly, surging forward. The sound is jagged and rough, as if it were forced from his lungs by steel hands and dragged through barbed wire on its way up his throat.

My brows crease, something tightening in my sternum. "Do you need water, old man?"

His eyes water as he waves me off. "No, no. I'll be fine." He pauses, his finger running over his trimmed salt-and-pepper beard as he stares into space. "Did you find out what happened to Samir?"

I try to adopt a sympathetic face. "Never made it on his flight, I'm afraid. I've tried to get in touch, but no luck so far."

"Hmm," he hums, his body slouching. "And the lamp? Any news?"

Frustration bleeds into my middle, spreading like molasses. This blasted *lamp* is quickly becoming the bane of my existence, especially considering no one knows if it even truly exists. But if it does, then I need it in my hands and under my control. You can wield a lot of power with a lost relic said to have been a spelled lamp of an ancient Egyptian king.

Ludicrous, of course, but the jewels supposedly encrusted on every square inch and the myth alone are enough to make it priceless.

I purse my lips, fingers tapping against the rim of my tumbler. "Still looking."

Ali jerks forward but stops as another harsh cough pours from his mouth.

I blow out a breath, setting down my tumbler of whisky on the table, and walk over to where he sits, reaching out my arm.

"Come on, old man. You don't need to put on a brave face for me. Let's get you to your room so you can rest. Everything else can wait until tomorrow."

His eyes flare and I can see the way I've offended him by the harsh lines that burrow deeper with his frown. But then yet another coughing fit attacks, his thin skin showcasing the bulging blood vessels underneath.

Reaching in my breast pocket, I pull out a handkerchief and pass it to him. He grabs at it quickly, shoving it against his mouth, his eyes crunching in the corners as his free hand curls around his stomach.

I stand by silently, my jaw tensing as the man who I've looked up to for a decade, the only man I'd consider a friend, disintegrates in front of my eyes.

Finally, it eases, and he drops the cloth in his lap.

It's stained with red.

He reaches out and uses my arm as leverage to pull himself to a stand, shaking his head as he pushes past me and into the hall. I don't follow, knowing he needs to maintain every ounce of dignity he has left. I can't say I wouldn't do the same.

Glancing around the room, I walk back to my whisky and drain the last few drops before making my way down the darkened hallway of the expansive estate, following the twists and turns I know by heart so I can go home for the night.

It's a large building, well over twenty thousand square feet, and I parked in the private lot off the staff's quarters, not wanting anyone to see me arrive or leave. I've just hit the hallway that leads to my car when a muffled moan hits my ear.

My footsteps stutter.

I spin on my heels, head tilting as I try to pinpoint where the sound is coming from. Another moan, this time slightly louder, and my abs tense with a delicious sensation. I move toward the noise without a second thought, wanting to see who's responsible for the arousal suddenly spinning through me. The last door at the end of the hall is closed, but I reach out, testing the handle, my heartbeat ratcheting higher in my chest. I continue to twist slowly until it unlatches, creating a sliver of light that filters from the room into the dark hallway.

My eyes scan the scene, blood rushing to fill my cock immediately when I see a naked woman laid out on a small twin bed. It takes a few moments to realize who it is, and by then, I'm too invested to leave, perverse pleasure racing through me and making me rock-hard.

Yasmin.

Her breasts are large and full, dark areolas puckered in the air and begging to be sucked as a young man thrusts into her.

Well, this is interesting.

She moans again, and my dick jerks as I soak up every greedy inch of her skin, seeing her in an entirely different light.

I've known her for years but avoided her like the plague whenever she'd come back from her school. She was young, and I have no use for teenage girls with silly crushes. It wasn't until she arrived home for good that I looked at her fully, appreciating the new soft curves of her body and the sharp angles of her face.

But I have plenty of people to keep me satisfied, so there's never been the slightest temptation, even if she has grown into a stunning woman.

Until right this second.

Now, I'm pretty sure I'll never be able to stroke my cock and imagine anything *but* her.

The idiot above her grunts, his movements growing jerky and then stopping altogether, and amusement filters through my chest when I take in the unsatisfied look that floats across Yasmin's face.

"Did you come, baby?" he asks.

She gives him a small smile and shakes her head. "It's okay."

"Let me take care of you," he murmurs, slipping his purple condom–covered dick from inside her and dipping his face between her legs.

Yasmin lets out a small gasp, but even from here, I can tell his movements are that of a boy, not a man.

She has no clue what it could be like for her. The pleasure that could be wrought from her body. My cock pulses as the image of her tied and bound to my bed, her swollen and bruised cunt on display while she begs for mercy, whips through my mind.

I bite back a groan, palming the front of my pants, pressing the heel of my hand against my erection. It sends a burst of pleasure through me, and my chest spasms when Yasmin's head turns in my direction. I should hide myself before she sees.

Maybe if I were a better man, I would.

But I've never been a gentleman.

Instead, I toe the door open more, just enough to ensure she has a nice view of me standing here. Watching. Waiting.

Her gaze locks on mine and widens, her cheeks flushing, mouth parting into the perfect O.

My balls tighten and my teeth grind as I hold myself back from walking into the room and giving her lips something to latch on to. My stare burns through hers, my cock throbbing with how vulnerable she is, splayed out for another man and unsure of what to do when she sees me watching.

I expect her to scream. To stop the pathetic attempt of her boy toy and cover up.

But she doesn't.

Instead, her back arches and her eyes roll, her chest heaving as she chokes on air. I bite the inside of my cheek because I'm so fucking hard, I can't see straight.

Does it turn her on, knowing that someone who's thirteen years too old for her, someone who's the closest thing to her father's best friend, is watching her get fucked?

That kid may have his tongue inside her, but it's *me* she's thinking of right now, whether she wants to be or not.

Her eyes snap open again, locking on to mine immediately like we're two sides of a magnet drawn together by force.

I smirk, palming my cock lewdly, unable to stop myself, and her gaze drops, her tongue swiping out to run along her bottom lip.

Goddamn.

I'm two seconds away from undoing my belt and stroking myself to the vision of her being licked by another man, but just as my hand brushes against the buckle, my mind catches back up to my body, and I wonder what the *fuck* I'm doing.

Ripping myself away, I spin around and leave, disgust at my lack of control and irritation at the fact that Yasmin's naked body will be burned into my brain forever making me furious.

I have no interest in Ali's daughter, sexually or emotionally.

She's a means to an end, and it's imperative she stay that way.

CHAPTER 3

Yasmin

IS HE GOING TO TELL MY FATHER?

It's the first thought that races through my head after I've come back down from the most intense orgasm of my life.

Julian Faraci was spying on me. And I let him. Liked it even.

"Are you okay?"

Aidan's voice is muddled, both because my ears are fuzzy from how hard I just came and because my mind is in a fog, trying to compartmentalize what just happened. Nausea curdles my stomach when I meet Aidan's deep brown eyes.

Is it considered cheating if I couldn't control it?

I didn't do anything wrong, but the way my thighs are still slick from what *his* eyes caused has betrayal and guilt mixing and sinking like a rock in my gut.

"Baby," Aidan continues.

Shaking my head slightly, I reach up and press my palm against his cheek. "Yeah, I'm fine."

I almost tell him what happened, the words sitting heavy on the tip of my tongue, but at the last second, I swallow them back down, deciding to bury the memory somewhere deep inside me and hope I'll never be able to reach it again.

Julian really has nothing to lose, but if he tells my dad, then I'll be loud too and force him to admit he was watching me. And I can't imagine he'd want anyone to know he was rubbing his dick while watching his boss's daughter get eaten out.

A shot of *something* strikes between my legs and my pussy spasms.

Dammit.

"When can I see you again?" Aidan whispers, leaning in and pressing his sweat-slicked forehead against mine.

Warmth spreads through my chest and I press my lips to his. "As soon as I can sneak away."

Aidan's jaw clenches, a tumultuous emotion flitting through his gaze. "Let me go to your father, Yas."

Panic seizes up my throat and makes my hands clammy, the way it does every time he brings it up. "N-no. Not yet."

Aidan shoves himself back, jumping from the bed and rummaging through the pieces of clothing on the floor until he finds his pants, pulling them roughly up his thighs. I watch him in silence, the guilt feeling like a thousand boulders being tied to my middle, dragging me down until I drown in it.

It isn't until he's fully dressed, throwing his basic white T-shirt over his head, that he speaks again. "You can't let him control your life forever."

A spike of anger flashes through me and I lick my lips, turning my head to the side. "You don't understand."

"Because you won't let me!" He spins to face me fully as his fist hits his open palm.

"He's *sick*, Aidan!" I snap.

He scoffs. "Believe me, I know."

My gaze softens as I stare at him, wishing I could wipe the hurt look from his face. But what Aidan's asking isn't something I'm sure I can give.

Sighing, I run a shaky hand through my tangled hair, the thick, curly black pieces fighting against my fingers. "I don't want to cause him any stress. It's not *good* for him to be stressed."

A little slice of anger wedges its sharp edges into my chest from having to verbalize it. Saying it out loud makes it *real*, and I'm still trying to pretend that it's not.

My dry tongue sticks to the roof of my mouth. "I'll tell him, okay? I just need time."

Aidan stares at me, the smooth planes of his face drawn tight before he finally blows out a breath and walks over, sitting next to me. His hands cup my cheeks, and he wipes a few stray tears I couldn't keep in from trickling down my face. "Baby, how much more time do you *have*?"

His words smash through the grief like a wrecking ball, spreading the shattered pieces into my veins. "Don't use his cancer as a weapon to get your way, Aidan."

"I'm not."

My bottom lip trembles and I pull it between my teeth, twisting my head from his grasp.

His grip tightens and brings me back. "I'm *not*. I just… I've loved you since I was thirteen, and I've respected your wishes, waiting on the sidelines, having you in secret all these years while you figured out a way to tell him. I don't want to lose the chance of getting his blessing. Let me prove to you I'm good enough, Yasmin. For him *and* for you."

My stomach churns.

"I can show you the world. But you have to let me *be* with you in public." He peppers small kisses along my jaw, causing goose bumps to sprout down my neck. "I love you, Yas. Surely, your dad will see that you love me too."

Nodding, I push down the fear and run my fingers through his silky, brown hair. "Okay. I'll talk to him."

But the next morning, when I'm sitting in my father's office…I *don't* talk to him.

Despite what Aidan may think, it isn't that easy. I've tried a thousand times over the years to make the words pass my lips, *"Father, I'm in love with Aidan Lancaster."*

But they never come.

At first there was nothing truly to tell. It was just a deep friendship, two kids who grew up in the same gigantic house, spending their free time together in the summers and sneaking out to make snow angels in the winter. And when it turned into something more, I became protective. Afraid of what I'd do if I lost Aidan all together, and if I'm honest, afraid of making my father upset. There's a need for my dad's approval that spawns deep in my gut, bleeding through every single one of my good intentions until it snuffs out all the light.

I'm not sure where the insecurity stems from. Maybe because my mother died in childbirth, leaving him to be the only one in my orbit, or maybe it's because despite the less-than-ideal vision he has for me, he's loved and supported me every day of my life.

He's never *not* been there.

I would give my dad the world, because it's what he's given me. I'd be selfish to pretend otherwise.

"*Habibti*, are you okay?" My father's voice coasts through

the air, skating along the tops of his dark wood furniture until it settles heavy on my shoulders, forcing me deeper into the rich burgundy leather of his oversize chairs.

We're in his home office, the place he spends most of his days now that he's ill, and flashes of my time as a young child scanning the floor-to-ceiling cedar bookshelves that line the back wall flit through my brain. A warm feeling of love fills me up when I remember the way he'd take phone calls and wink at me out of the corner of his eye as he talked business jargon.

"Yes, Yasmin," Julian cuts in. "You look positively *flushed*. Care to share?"

I cut my gaze over to him, annoyed that he's always here and clearly trying his best to get under my skin. I've always known that he's my father's sidekick, but I didn't realize that meant he would be forever lingering like a bad habit.

He stares at me with challenge, his tall frame fitted in a perfect suit and his shoulder leaned against the wall like he doesn't have a single care in the world. As if he didn't become the world's worst Peeping Tom last night as he watched Aidan fuck me then get me off with his tongue.

"Don't you have your own house to go to?" I snark. "Your own family to bother?"

He chuckles. "Why be there when there's so much to *see* where I am?"

Embarrassment flows through me, my blood pressing beneath the surface of my skin.

"Does me being here bother you?" He tilts his head.

I shrug. "You're like a roach. Always lurking in dark corners."

He smirks, straightening off the wall and sauntering toward me, leaning down slightly as he picks up my hand and presses a small kiss to the back. "I could teach you a lot about what happens in dark corners, *gattina*," he murmurs.

My heart shoots to my throat.

"You two are like siblings," my father says with a laugh.

Julian frowns as he stands up straight. He smooths down the front of his black suit jacket, the veins on his hands pronounced from the black ink that weaves around them.

A tingling sense of foreboding slithers up my spine and wraps my neck.

"Father," I say, tearing my eyes away from Julian. "Can we talk in private?"

I keep my attention on my dad, but the side of my face burns, and I can tell just from the feeling that Julian hasn't moved his gaze off me.

"I was just leaving," Julian states. "Rest up, old man. I'll call you with any important news."

My father nods as he watches Julian leave, and my fingers dig into the sides of the leather chair to temper the urge that's whirling through me, telling me to follow him and make sure he never speaks about what he saw. To ask him who the *hell* he thinks he is.

"I wanted to speak with you too," Dad says. "I'm not sure how much time—"

"No," I cut him off, panic filling up my chest like wet cement. "I don't want to talk about this."

His gaze softens. "We *must* talk about this. There's no cure here, sweetheart, and there are things I need to say before I... before I can't."

I grit my teeth, my fingers curling into fists until my nails break skin. The sharp bite of pain grounds me.

"So I need you to listen with an open mind. Can you do that for me?"

The knot in my throat swells until it feels like it will burst through my esophagus. I swallow around the pain. "I would do any..." I suck in a shaky breath. "Anything for you, Baba."

A dark emotion hits his eyes, and even through the ashen skin and the dried-up lips, I see a spark in him, one that I thought was gone forever.

"Do you mean that?" he asks.

I nod, straightening in my chair, desperate to make him see the truth. "With my whole heart."

"Then I do have one request." He stops, a heavy cough breaking free. It makes *my* lungs cramp tight as I watch him struggle through the harsh sounds and rattly breaths before he pulls himself together. He gives me a sad, small smile. "Consider it a dying man's last wish."

My heart aches.

"Anything," I whisper.

"I need you to marry."

Read on for a look at the first in
Emily McIntire's Never After series

Available now from

Bloom *books*

CHAPTER 1

Wendy

I'VE NEVER BEEN TO MASSACHUSETTS, BUT I'VE heard about the lack of heat. So while the temperature change from Florida is a shock, it isn't wholly unexpected. Still, as I shiver in my tank top, the light breeze blowing across my arms, I can't help but wish I had stayed behind instead of choosing to follow my family to their new home in Bloomsburg.

But I can't stand the thought of not being a phone call away if they need me. My father is a workaholic—even more so after my mother's death—and without me around, my sixteen-year-old brother, Jonathan, would be all alone.

I've always been a daddy's girl, even though he makes it difficult. I'd hoped, after the move, that he'd slow down. Make more time for his family instead of constantly searching for the next big thing to sink his teeth into. But Peter Michaels is never one to settle. His thirst for new ventures overpowers his ache for a family connection. Being named the *Forbes* top businessman for the fifth year in a row means he has a lot of opportunity in that regard. And being the owner of the biggest airline in the Western Hemisphere means he has lots of funding for said opportunities.

NevAirLand. *If you can dream it, we can fly you there.*

"We should go out tonight," my friend Angie says as she wipes down the counters at the Vanilla Bean, the coffee shop where we both work.

"And do what?" I ask. Honestly, I was hoping to just head home and relax. I've only been here for a little over a month, and I've been working so much that I haven't had a night to spend with Jonathan. Although he's in the teen stage of "I don't need anyone or anything," so he may not want me around anyway.

She shrugs. "I don't know. A couple of the girls were talking about heading to the Jolly Roger."

I scrunch my nose. Both at her use of "the girls" and at the name of wherever she's talking about.

"Oh, come on, Wendy. You've been here for almost two months, and you haven't gone out with me once." She sticks out her bottom lip, her hands coming together in prayer.

Shaking my head, I sigh. "I don't think your friends like me."

"That's not true," she insists. "They just don't know you yet. You have to actually come *out* with us for that."

"I don't know, Angie." My teeth sink into my bottom lip. "My dad's out of town, and he doesn't like it when I go out and draw attention."

She rolls her eyes. "You're twenty, girl. Cut the cord."

I give her a half-hearted smile. She, like most people, can't understand what it's like being Peter Michaels's daughter. Even if I wanted to, there *is* no cutting the cord. His power and influence reach every corner of the universe, and there isn't anything or anyone that escapes his control. Or if there is, I've never met them.

The bell above the front door chimes, Angie's friend Maria walking in, her long black hair glinting off the overhead lighting as she saunters to us.

My brows rise as I glance at her, then back to Angie. "What kind of place is gonna let a twenty-year-old in anyway?"

"Don't you have a fake ID?" Maria asks as she reaches the front counter.

"I *definitely* don't have that." I've never snuck into a bar or a club in my life. "My birthday is in a few weeks. I'll just go out with you guys next time." I wave them off.

Maria eyes me up and down. "Angie, don't you have your sister's ID? They look…similar." She reaches out and touches my brown hair. "Just show a little bit of that body and they won't even look at the face on the card."

I laugh as I brush off her words, but my insides tighten, heat surging through my veins and lighting up my cheeks. I'm not a rule breaker. Never have been. But the thought of going tonight, of doing something bad, sends a thrill rushing down my spine.

Maria is one of "the girls," and she hasn't been anywhere close to welcoming. But as I watch her grin and run her fingers through her hair, I wonder if maybe Angie is right. Maybe it's all in my head, and I just haven't given her a chance. I've never really had a close group of girlfriends, so I'm not sure how it's all supposed to work.

"I don't care if you don't want to go." Angie pouts, throwing her damp rag at me. "I'm making the executive decision."

I laugh, shaking my head as I finish restocking the cups for the morning.

"Hmm." Maria pops her gum loudly, her dark eyes searing into the side of my face. "You don't wanna go?"

I shrug. "It's not that. I just—"

"Probably for the best," she interrupts. "I don't think the JR is your kind of place."

My spine bristles and I stand up straighter. "What's that supposed to mean?"

She smirks. "I mean, it's not for *children*."

"Maria, come on. Don't be a bitch," Angie pipes in.

Maria laughs. "I'm not. I'm just saying. What if *he's* there? Can you imagine? She'd be scarred for life from even being in the same building and run home to tell her daddy."

I lift my chin. "My dad isn't even in town."

She cocks her head, her lips thinning. "Your nanny then."

Irritation spikes through my gut, and a need to prove her wrong clicks my decision into place, pushing the words off my tongue. I look at Angie. "I'm in."

"Yes!" Angie claps her hands.

Maria's eyes glint. "Hope you can handle it."

"Give me a break, Maria. She'll be fine. It's a bar, not a sex club," Angie scoffs before turning toward me. "Don't listen to her. Besides, we only go there so she can try and get the attention of her mystery man."

"I *will* get his attention."

Angie tilts her head. "He doesn't even know you exist, girl."

"My luck is bound to change at some point." Maria shrugs.

Confusion makes my brows pull in. "Who are you guys even talking about?"

A slow grin creeps across Maria's face, and a wistful look coasts across Angie's eyes.

"Hook."

CHAPTER 2

James

"THERE'S A NEW PROPOSITION ON THE TABLE."

I pour two fingers of Basil Hayden into the crystal tumbler, adding one ice cube and savoring the flavor before I turn to face Ru. "I wasn't aware we were taking any new propositions."

He shrugs, lighting up the end of his cigar and puffing. "We aren't. But I'm a businessman, and this one has massive potential."

His voice is muffled as he speaks around the roll of tobacco, but years of soaking up his words as gospel make him easy to understand.

Roofus—known to the world as Ru—is the only person in my life worthy of my trust. He saved me from hell, and I'll never be able to repay that debt. But the courtesy only extends to him, which makes it *difficult* when he decides to bring new people into our operation.

He's grown reckless with age.

"One day, your inability to turn down *potential* will get you killed," I tell him.

His eyes narrow. "I have no intention of dying and leaving my legacy to a Brit."

I smirk. All this is mine anyway; he just doesn't like to say it out loud. Doesn't want to admit the student has surpassed the master, that he only holds the reins because I allow him to. It's been the truth since the moment my uncle's blood spilled under my hand eight years ago—the day I turned eighteen. I gutted him like the worthless fish he was, then used the same blade to cut into my steak at dinner, daring anyone to question why my fingers were stained with red.

Ru may have the title of boss, but it's *me* they all fear.

Setting my glass on the edge of the desk, I sit down in one of the wingback chairs. "Your mortality is not something I particularly like to joke about."

Sometimes I truly believe Ru thinks he's untouchable. It makes him sloppy. Makes him trust too easily. Allows people to get too close. Luckily, he has me, and I'll slice my knife deep into the belly of anyone who tries, reveling at how the life drains from their eyes while their blood drips into my hands.

I guess when you've experienced the things I have, you learn quickly that immortality is only granted through people's memories.

Ru leans forward, resting his cigar in the ornate ashtray on the corner of his desk. "Then pay attention. We have someone who's interested in being a new *partner.*" Ru grins. "Wants to expand our distribution. Run our pixie to new corners of the universe."

"Fascinating." I dust a piece of lint off my suit jacket. "Who is it?" I ask, purely to appease him. I have zero interest in bringing on someone new. We've been using our current drug runner for the past three years, and I vetted him personally. Watched him sweat through his clothes while he watched our pixie dust get loaded on the plane, hidden inside crates of lobster. Sat next to him in the cockpit through the entire flight, twirling my hook blade through my fingers as he pissed himself from the nerves.

If you want to ensure someone's loyalty, you have to make sure they understand *why* you deserve it. And I've made sure that people understand the end of a blade hurts worse when the person wielding it enjoys causing pain.

Ru wipes his hand over his mouth. "You've heard of NevAirLand planes?"

I freeze in place, the blood in my veins icing over. I'm quite sure I've never mentioned that name to anyone, especially Ru.

"Can't say that I have." My jaw quivers.

"Well, you must be the only one." Ru laughs. "The owner, Peter Michaels, just moved here."

My heart slams against my ribs. *How could I have missed this?* "Oh?"

Ru nods. "He's looking for a new *adventure*." He smiles, his slightly crooked teeth gleaming. "It's only fair for us to welcome him in properly, let him know how things around here work."

My hands twitch with the rage that spikes inside me whenever I hear Peter Michaels's name. I reach out and pick up my tumbler, my grasp tight around the crystal as anticipation blooms in my chest.

How fortuitous that the man I long to kill is serving himself to me on a silver platter.

"Well, I think this sounds like a wonderful opportunity." I smile.

Ru picks up his cigar. "I wasn't asking your permission, kid, but I'm glad you're on board."

"So when do we meet with him?" I sip from my drink, trying to tame the quick beats of my heart.

"*I* meet with him tonight. *Alone.*" He narrows his eyes.

My gut clenches. "Let me go with you, Roofus. You shouldn't meet him alone."

Ru sighs, running a hand through his ridiculous bright red hair. "You're too intimidating, kid. I need this meeting to be friendly."

Can't argue with him there.

"At least take one of the boys." The thought of Ru alone with Peter Michaels sends a chill up my spine.

Ru blows a ring of smoke in the air.

I lean forward, knuckling the top of his desk. "Roofus. *Promise* me you won't go alone. Don't be foolish."

"And don't forget your place," he snaps. "*I* run this, not you. You answer to *me*. How about you show your gratitude and, for once, just do as you're fucking told?"

My teeth grind at his tone, and if he were anyone else, I would thank him for the reminder right before I cut out his tongue. But Ru gets away with a lot of things that no one else does.

I first saw Ru when I was thirteen—two years after I was shipped to America to live with my uncle. Reading in the library, I heard a commotion down the hall and went to investigate the noise. Peeking through a crack in the office door, I watched, mesmerized, as a large man with olive skin and dyed red hair loomed over my uncle's desk, threatening him within an inch of his life, a gun at his temple and menace bleeding through his thick Boston accent. It was awe-inspiring, truly. I had never seen my uncle cower before anyone. It was usually his favorite pastime to see others fall to their knees for *him*.

As a politician, it happened publicly often.

As a person filled with rage and perversion, it happened in private even more.

So I found this mystery man enthralling and took to following him when he left, desperate to emulate his power. I suppose you could call it obsession, but I had never known anyone like him. Had never seen someone command obedience from a man who ran the world.

I wanted to know how to do that too.

But at thirteen, I hadn't mastered the art of being undetected, and Ru knew I was stalking him all along. Took me in and taught me everything he knew. Introduced me to the streets of Bloomsburg and kept me sane through the nightmares that plagued my sleep.

So I'll defer to what he wants, because there isn't a single soul on this planet who has taken care of me the way he has.

There was once, but that was long ago. Another lifetime, really.

"You're right," I say. "I trust your judgment. It's everyone else's I don't."

Ru laughs and opens his mouth to respond, but a knock on the door interrupts.

"Come in," Ru grunts.

Starkey, one of our younger recruits, pops his head in. "Sorry to interrupt, boss." His eyes slide to mine, widening as he quickly looks away. "There're a few girls trying to come in with fake IDs. Making a hell of a time for us downstairs."

"You come up here to bother us with this shit?" Ru snaps. "What the hell do we pay you for?"

I grin at Ru's temper and walk to the security cameras, looking at the one aimed over the front entrance. Just as Starkey says, there are three girls, one of whom is currently screaming in our bouncer's face. *Pathetic.* I continue my perusal, my eyes locking on the beauty standing off to the side.

My stomach tightens as my gaze trails along her body in a tight blue dress. Her arms are wrapped around her middle, her eyes darting back and forth between the bouncer and the cabs that line the street.

Annoyance snaps in my chest with the fact that I can't see her as clearly as I'd like. But I see her enough to know she looks uncomfortable. Innocent. Definitely doesn't belong in a place like this. And for some reason, that shoots a thrill straight to my cock, making it thicken and pulse as I imagine all the ways this place could defile her. There are not many people who inspire a reaction from me. A life of *not* reacting has bled into my skin, hardening into an impenetrable shield, nothing allowed in or out. Just an empty shell with a single purpose.

The fact that this girl has tweaked my interest even a modicum has my curiosity piqued.

"Let them in," I interrupt, my eyes still on the brunette beauty.

Starkey stops rambling, his eyes shooting to me before landing back on Ru. "Are you sure? I—"

"Did I stutter?" I ask, turning to face him. "Or maybe it's the accent that gets in the way of you understanding?"

"N-no, it's just—"

"It's *just*," I interrupt. "Clearly, you're in need of some guidance on how to handle the situation. Or have I misunderstood your reasoning for bringing this trivial issue to our attention?"

Ru smirks, leaning back in his chair.

"No, Hook. You didn't misunderstand."

"Hmm. Then it's a problem, to be sure." I nod. "Tell me, would you agree that we need to fire whoever is working the door?"

"Um, I don't—" Starkey starts.

"After all, if he lacks the ability to control a group of females, how can we be sure he'll handle anyone else?" I cock my head.

Starkey swallows, his Adam's apple bobbing. "I... They're—"

"You see," I continue, slipping my hook blade from my pocket and flipping it open. "Subduing a woman is all about control." I walk toward him, twirling the stainless steel between my fingers, the intricate brown design of the handle sliding against my skin. "A delicate weaving of power. A give-and-take, if you will. Supplying them with the absolute *pleasure* of your dominance." Stopping in front of him, I pause the knife as I grasp it in my palm. "Clearly, our bouncer this evening possesses more of a submissive gene." My free hand reaches out, straightening his tie. "I understand how difficult it must be to recognize the same trait within yourself." I lean in close, allowing the tip of my blade to rest against his throat. "Be a good boy, Starkey, and let. Them. In."

"Yes, sir," he mumbles.

I pat him on the shoulder, and he spins and rushes out the door.

Ru points at me with his cigar, amusement lining his eyes. "And *that* is why you aren't coming to this meeting."

I smile, straightening the cuffs of my jacket. "That's fair. I'm off to the main floor anyway. I have a bouncer to make disappear and a sudden appetite for something *pretty*."

Ru chuckles. "Just make sure they're legal."

Grabbing the door handle, I pause. "Ru?"

He grunts.

"Make sure Peter knows I'm *so* looking forward to meeting him face-to-face."

Character Profiles

Evelina Westerly

Name: Evelina "Evie" Westerly

Age: 24

Place of birth: Kinland, Illinois

Current location: Kinland, Illinois

Nationality: Irish American

Education: High school with self-education beyond

Occupation: Member of the Westerly Irish Mob. Enforcer, assassin, producer of drugs

Income: Unknown; family is worth a fortune

Eye color: Dark brown

Hair style: Brown but dyed black.

Body build: Very petite

Preferred style of outfit: Knee-high black stiletto boots. Flowing black skirts and tight tops and/or band tees, hoodies (comfortable clothing) with Vans.

Glasses?: No

Any accessories they always have?: Rose-gold Desert Eagle

Level of grooming: Slightly messy but always clean. Black manicure

Health: Healthy

Handwriting style: Small and rushed scrawl

How do they walk?: Shoulders back, with a confident aura

How do they speak?: Harsh and to the point

Style of speech: Regular, some slang, educated but not pompous

Accent: Midwestern

Posture: Decent

Do they gesture?: Mainly with her facial expressions, not too much hand gesturing

Eye contact: Always

Preferred curse word: Fuck

Catchphrase: "Good boy."

Speech impediments?: No

What's laugh like?: Not many people hear it, but rich and melodic

What do they find funny?: Not much, she's a grump

Describe smile: Beautiful, quirky

How emotive?: When in control of her emotions, she isn't very emotive, but when she loses control, she has blasts of extreme expression.

Type of childhood: Neglected by parents, loved by her sister. Had to grow up fast. Was always the "weird" kid.

Involved in school?: She was an outcast in school but was extremely intelligent and loved to learn. Named most likely to become institutionalized in the yearbook

Jobs: Always worked for her family

Dream job as a child: Writer

Role models growing up: Her older sister Nessa

Greatest regret: Not going with Nessa on the boat the night she was killed

Hobbies growing up: Writing

Favorite place as a child: Somewhere quiet in the woods, and by herself where she could be with her journal and her thoughts

Earliest memory: Her mother leaving her during a tornado and going to comfort Dorothy instead, even though she was scared

Saddest memory: Losing Nessa and then losing Nicholas, realizing he betrayed her and wasn't who she thought he was

Happiest memory: When she met Nick again in Ireland and had a second chance

Any skeletons in the closet?: She airs her skeletons out in the open

If they could change one thing from their past, what would it be?: Keeping Nessa from being killed

Describe major turning points in their childhood: Her father going to prison. Dorothy being terrible to her. Her mother abandoning them. Nessa raising her and then being murdered by Dorothy.

Three adjectives to describe personality: grumpy, cynical, vicious

What advice would they give to their younger self?: Live for yourself

Criminal record?: Yes, ends up a fugitive on the run

Father:

- **Age:** Middle aged
- **Occupation:** Skip of the Irish Mob stronghold in Kinland, Illinois
- **What's their relationship with character like:** She was loyal to a fault and he manipulated that by using her brains to make him an empire.

Mother:

Age: Who cares

Occupation: Hopefully dead

What's their relationship with character like: Nonexistent

Any siblings?: Dead older sister Nessa and an older sister named Dorothy

Closest friends: Cody

Enemies: Dorothy and anyone else who gets in her way

How are they perceived by strangers?: Weird and intimidating

Any social media?: No

Role in group dynamic: Loner

Who do they depend on:

Practical advice: Ezekiel

Mentoring: Nobody after Nessa died

Wingman: Cody

Emotional support: Nobody

Moral support: Nobody

What do they do on rainy days?: Has a better day than usual because she loves the rain

Book-smart or street-smart?: Both, incredibly intelligent and street-smart

Optimist, pessimist, realist: Pessimist

Introvert or extrovert: Introvert

Favorite sound: Silence

What do they want most?: To kill Dorothy

Biggest flaw: Blind loyalty to family and placing people on pedestals without realizing everyone has their own agenda

Biggest strength: Her unpredictability and people underestimating her because she's a woman

Biggest accomplishment: Learning to live for herself

What's their idea of perfect happiness?: Living in Ireland, off the grid

Do they want to be remembered?: No

How do they approach:

> **Power:** Demands it only when necessary
>
> **Ambition:** Has it when she needs it but isn't something she is always harnessing
>
> **Love:** Longs for it
>
> **Change:** Doesn't like it

Possession they would rescue from burning home: Her sister's shoes

What makes them angry?: Annoying people. People who betray her or treat her like she's stupid

How is their moral compass and what would it take to break it?: Nonexistent

Pet Peeves: People treating her like she's dumb, people underestimating her because she's a woman, and people bothering her when she's trying to work

What would they have written on their tombstone?: Here lies Evelina Westerly. Leave her alone.

Their story goal: Evelina starts the story out by being drowned in her grief and loneliness. She aches for love and for family although she will never admit it out loud. She has a blind loyalty to her family name and takes the responsibility on for her family even when she shouldn't. Her goal is to overcome her demons, allow herself to work through her grief, and realize that everyone is flawed, we all deserve love, and blood isn't always thicker than water. By the end of the story, she will have learned that she needs to figure out who she truly is and to live for herself instead of people pleasing with blind loyalty. When she does that, she'll be able to open herself up to the kind of love that she deserves and has longed for since the beginning.

Nicholas "Brayden" Woodsworth

Name: Nicholas Tennyson Woodsworth
Age: 32
Place of birth: Chicago
Current location: Chicago, Illinois
Nationality: American
Education: College
Occupation: DEA Agent
Income: $40-60K/year
Eye color: Green
Hair style: Short and dark
Body build: Tall and built but not bulky
Distinguishing features: Sharp jawline and dimples
Preferred style of outfit: White T-shirt, blue jeans, and a leather jacket
Glasses?: No
Any accessories they always have?: No
Level of grooming: Moderate
Health: Healthy
Handwriting style: Messy

How do they walk?: Laid-back and easygoing, confident

How do they speak?: Witty, smart-ass

Style of speech: Normal

Accent: Midwest American

Posture: Good

Do they gesture?: Yes

Eye contact: Almost always

Preferred curse word: Doesn't have one

Catchphrase: Doesn't have one but calls Evelina pretty girl

Speech impediments?: No

What's laugh like?: Deep and raspy

What do they find funny?: Likes to antagonize people and see them get upset, finds it humorous

Describe smile: Dimples, full smile with almost perfect teeth

How emotive: Not very

Type of childhood: Surrounded by drug addicts. Neglectful drug-addicted mother who abandoned them to her family who also struggled with addiction

Involved in school?: Not overly involved. Played sports. Named most likely to become a cop in the yearbook

Jobs: Worked at a fast-food restaurant as a kid and then as a waiter while he was in school

Dream job as a child: Always wanted to work in law enforcement to help the war on drugs

Role models growing up: Nobody

Greatest regret: Not being enough to keep his older sister clean

Hobbies growing up: Loved to read poetry because it reminded him of when he had a "loving" mother

Favorite place as a child: At school where he wasn't reminded of his home life

Earliest memory: His mother reading to him in bed

Saddest memory: Finding his sister drugged out on the streets

Happiest memory: Evelina saying she loved him

Any skeletons in the closet?: Yes, but only that he's a federal agent sent undercover

If they could change one thing from their past, what would it be?: He takes on responsibility for everyone so he would want to change anything he could

Describe major turning points in their childhood: Mother abandoning them. Sister becoming addicted to drugs

Three adjectives to describe personality: Charming, coldhearted, playboy

What advice would they give to their younger self?: Other people's choices aren't your responsibility

Criminal record?: None beyond what's needed to happen while he's undercover

Father:

Age: N/A

Occupation: N/A

What's their relationship with character like?: Never knew his father

Mother:

Age: Gone, probably dead

Occupation: He never knew what she did

What's their relationship with character like?: Nonexistent.

Any siblings?: Yes, one older sister named Rose.

Closest friends: Seth

Enemies: Probably several, most of them in prison or dead

How are they perceived by strangers?: Attractive, smooth talker, and lacking depth of real emotion

Any social media? Yes but very basic due to his job

Role in group dynamic: Leader

Who do they depend on:

- **Practical advice:** His sister
- **Mentoring:** His boss
- **Wingman:** Seth
- **Emotional support:** His sister
- **Moral support:** Seth, his sister

What do they do on rainy days?: Read

Book-smart or street-smart?: Both, mainly street-smart

Optimist, pessimist, realist: Realist trending toward slight optimism

Introvert or extrovert: Extrovert

Favorite sound: Evelina's laugh

What do they want most?: To feel like what he did mattered

Biggest flaw: He doesn't believe in love due to everyone he's loved disappointing him in his life

Biggest strength: His loyalty

Biggest accomplishment: Never having done a drug in his life

What's their idea of perfect happiness?: He has no clue what happiness looks like to even imagine it

Do they want to be remembered?: Yes

How do they approach:

- **Power:** Commands it
- **Ambition:** Seeks it

Love: Rejects it

Change: Isn't bothered by it

Possession they would rescue from burning home: The old book of poems his mother used to read to him

What makes them angry?: Evelina and people who create the drug problem

How is their moral compass and what would it take to break it?: Fairly strong; it would take his entire outlook on life and what matters in it to break his morals.

Pet peeves: None that bother him enough to care

What would they have written on their tombstone?: Nicholas Woodsworth. The calm in the chaos.

Their story goal: Nicholas starts off as an emotionally unattached, charming, quick-witted guy whose life centers around his career. His own family and upbringing were not stable due to drugs that ran rampant in the streets of Chicago, and that and his penchant for taking on responsibility when it isn't really his to hold made him want to do nothing more than rid the streets of the very thing that cost him a stable childhood. His story goal is to open himself up to love and realize that not everything is his fault, and he can't change the past. That good and evil aren't always as simple as black and white, and love is so overpowering and all-consuming that it can make even the coldest of hearts beat out a different rhythm. His character arc will actually evolve from him being someone who is so stringently against anything "morally gray" into him breaking his morals and shifting them because he has finally found the ability to let himself feel the love that he's been running from for years.

LITTLE LOVE SPELLS

"Ode on Melancholy" by John Keats
"My Life had stood—a Loaded Gun" by Emily Dickinson
"Sonnet 151" by Shakespeare
"Bright Star" by John Keats
"To a Stranger" by Walt Whitman

THANK YOU FOR READING!

Enjoy *Wretched*? Please consider taking a second to leave a review!

Come chat about what you read! Join the McIncult Facebook group: facebook.com/groups/mcincult

JOIN THE MCINCULT!

EmilyMcIntire.com

The McIncult (Facebook Group):

facebook.com/groups/mcincult

Where you can chat all things Emily. First looks, exclusive giveaways, and the best place to connect with me!

TikTok: tiktok.com/@authoremilymcintire

Instagram: instagram.com/itsemilymcintire/

Facebook: facebook.com/authoremilymcintire

Pinterest: pinterest.com/itsemilymcintire/

Goodreads: goodreads.com/author/show/20245445.Emily_McIntire

BookBub: bookbub.com/profile/emily-mcintire

Want text alerts? Text MCINCULT to 833-942-4409 to stay up to date on new releases!

Acknowledgments

To my husband, Mike: Thank you for all you do. I love you.

To my best friend, Sav R. Miller: Here's to the smokies. Love you and wouldn't want to do this without you.

To my team: My PA Nicki, cover designer Cat, my editor Christa, and the rest of the Bloom fam. Thank you for keeping my life in order, making my work pretty, and pushing me to constantly grow.

To the McIncult: Thank you for being my biggest supporters and loving the words I write. All this is possible because of you.

To *all* my readers, new and the OGs: Thank you for taking a chance and picking up my books.

And last but certainly not least, to my daughter, Melody. You are now and always will be the reason for everything.

About the Author

Emily McIntire is an Amazon Top 15 bestselling author of painful, messy, beautiful romance. She doesn't like to box herself into one subgenre, but at the core of all her stories is soul-deep love.

A longtime songwriter and an avid reader, Emily has always had a passion for the written word, and when she's not writing, you can find her waiting on her long-lost Hogwarts letter, chasing her crazy toddler, or lost between the pages of a good book.

ALSO BY EMILY MCINTIRE

Be Still My Heart: A Romantic Suspense

The Sugarlake Series

Beneath the Stars

Beneath the Stands

Beneath the Hood

Beneath the Surface

The Never After Series

Hooked: A Dark, Contemporary Romance

Scarred: A Dark, Royal Romance

Wretched: A Dark Contemporary Romance